e for the
Professor Prather Mystery Series

"Debut author Angela introduces a charming amateur sleuth, fun and well read. She so lovingly describes the town of Copper Bluff that readers can feel the breeze and smell the autumn leaves. Cozy enthusiasts who like Joanne Dobson and Sarah R. Shaber will dive into this new series."
—Library Journal

"Emmeline's shrewd questioning of students and professors uncovers hidden motives and secrets in this clever academic mystery."
—*Publishers Weekly*

4 Stars: "Em is a force all her own and bodes well for this new series."
—RT Reviews

"Each of the characters was realistic and engaging [....] A real joy to read."
—*Readers' Favorite Book Reviews*

"Em is a terrific character—outspoken, funny and fearless except in the affairs of the heart. I hope to read more of Mary Angela's Professor Prather books."
—Map Your Mystery blog

"[A] delightfully quirky, fiercely intelligent and immensely likable protagonist."
—Lee Ann Roripaugh, SD State Poet Laureate

A Very Merry Murder

A Professor Prather Mystery

MARY ANGELA

CAMEL PRESS

Kenmore, WA

CAMEL PRESS

For more information go to: www.camelpress.com
www.maryangelabooks.com

Cover design by Aubrey Anderson

A Very Merry Murder
Copyright © 2018 by Mary Angela

ISBN: 978-1-60381-655-7 (Trade Paper)
ISBN: 978-1-60381-656-4 (eBook)

Library of Congress Control Number: 2018944706

Printed in the United States of America

For Quintin, with love

Acknowledgments

To my mom, thank you for your unwavering enthusiasm for Professor Prather. Sometimes I think you know her better than she knows herself. She and I are lucky to have you in our corners.

To my husband, Quintin, who never complains about my early alarm, even on the weekends. Thanks for always understanding.

To my daughters, Madeline and Maisie, thank you for telling me everything is great even when it's not. I think you're pretty great, too.

To early readers of this book Sharon Engberg, Samantha Engberg, and Elena Hartwell. Thank you for not running the other way when I asked for a favor.

To family, friends, and fellow bookworms. Thank you for purchasing or borrowing this book. I know it's in good hands.

To my professors at the University of South Dakota, who so many years ago inspired this wonderful world I get to live in, thank you. A hundred times thank you.

To the faculty at the University of Sioux Falls, especially Kevin Cole and David DeHoogh-Kliewer, and also Steven

Matzner at Augustana University. I'm always amazed by teachers' willingness to answer bad questions without batting an eye. Thank you.

To Catherine Treadgold, thank you for editing my work. I learn something new every time I read your corrections (okay, fifty things).

A special thank you to Camel Press for publishing this series and to Jennifer McCord, Aubrey Anderson, and Phil Garrett for your considerable knowledge, advice, and dedication. I appreciate all that you do.

Chapter One

Up and down Oxford Street, Christmas decorations were beginning to twinkle, lighting up the snow in globes of red, green, and gold. In my little bungalow, nestled in the middle of the block, I was decking the halls (or porch, rather) with tiny white lights. I danced delicately between tacking up strands and shooing away my cat, Dickinson. It was late Thursday afternoon, and with Dean Martin crooning in the background and my first batch of sugar cookies in the oven, the holiday spirit was upon me. The Grinch himself couldn't have stolen it away.

December is a magical time in Copper Bluff, South Dakota, and to say so isn't hyperbole. This I discovered my first Christmas on campus when a group of carolers stopped to sing at my front door. At first I was stunned; I'd never seen a caroler in Detroit, my hometown. When they finished, I hardly knew what to say. But eventually I remembered my manners and grabbed a package of Oreos out of the cupboard. This year, I would be armed with homemade treats. I had candy, sprinkles, and sugar in every color. When the carolers arrived, I would be ready.

As I fastened the lights to the windows of my screened-in porch, I noticed Mrs. Gunderson, my neighbor, approaching. Cloaked from neck to ankles in faux fur, she looked festive in her red pill hat and matching scarf. Her hands were clutching a plastic-wrapped plate. My goodies! I jumped off the stool, landing on my feet with a thud. Dickinson, my tabby cat, claimed the space, her spotted orange paws dangling off the miniature ladder.

I rushed to open the door. "Hello, Mrs. Gunderson."

"My goodness, what beautiful lights," she said, slowly making her way up the front path. When she reached the porch, she carefully wiped her feet on my Ho! Ho! Ho! mat and handed me the covered plate. "Merry Christmas, dear."

"Oh thank you, Mrs. Gunderson. You're too kind." I glanced at all the different confections on the plate. "Did you make those little—"

"Thumbprints?" She smiled patiently. "I know they're your favorite."

"And I have something for you," I said. "Come in."

When I entered the house, I sensed the timer had beeped already, for the smell of burnt sugar tinged the air. I rushed to the kitchen, checking the digital clock on the stove; it read END. I stomped my foot. *Damn Dean Martin.* "Have a seat, Mrs. Gunderson," I called from the kitchen, hastily grabbing the cookies from the oven. "I'll be right there."

"Anywhere in particular?"

"You choose," I said. "Would you like coffee?"

"I'm just going to stack these folders ... here. Yes, coffee please. With cream."

I brewed a K-Cup and slid the sugar-sprinkled snowmen, which looked more like wrinkled Michelin men, onto the decorative tray I'd purchased at Winkles Pharmacy. When the coffee finished, I searched the fridge for cream, and finding none, put in a little Coffee-mate. Maybe Mrs. Gunderson wouldn't notice the difference.

"Well, they're not as pretty as yours are, but hopefully they taste good." I placed the tray of warm cookies and coffee on the table. Then I went back to the kitchen to get my cup. When I returned, she was studying the cookies.

"Thank you, Emmeline. These are cute …."

"Snowmen," I said, taking the seat across from her.

"Of course. Snowmen." She took one, dusting off the excess sugar sprinkles. "Did you refrigerate the dough?"

I shook my head, unwrapping the plate of treats she had given me. It was jam-packed with peanut butter kisses, cherry bars, frosted sugar cookies, thumbprints, fudge, and peanut brittle. It had taken me an hour to make one bad batch of sugar cookies; it must have taken her days to prepare all these treats. "I didn't. I didn't have time. I wanted to make sure I had some on hand in case the carolers came."

"You have to refrigerate the dough, dear, if you want it to keep its … shape."

"I'll remember that for the next batch." I took a bite of fudge. It was a heavenly marshmallow nut masterpiece. Even if she critiqued my baking skills for the next thirty minutes, the fudge alone would be worth it. "This is amazing."

She took a sip of coffee to wash down the not-so-soft sugar cookie. "That's my mother's recipe. It's said to have captured at least one man's heart, my father's. He loved it so much that he bought all four pounds at the church bazaar. Of course she made it every year afterwards." She looked out the window. "I always think of that when I make it. Isn't that silly?"

"Not at all," I said, wiping my fingers with a napkin. "It's terribly romantic."

She smiled, showing off perfectly straight dentures. "I'm making some for the Winter Festival next weekend. First Lutheran will have a table downtown. Maybe you'll stop by with your sweetheart."

"What sweetheart?" I said, but I knew very well to whom she was referring. Despite her grandmotherly appearance, she was as smart as any professor on campus. She made it her business to know the town and all its residents, including me.

She pushed aside her half-full coffee cup. Maybe she detected the artificial creamer. "You know. That big fellow with the blond hair? He comes around quite a bit."

"Lenny? Oh, he's not my sweetheart." Not that we hadn't considered the idea. We had, but lately, life had gotten in the way. He spent the summer in Concord, Massachusetts, teaching a workshop on Transcendentalism, and I spent most of the fall attending conferences and writing lesson plans for my first proposed course on campus: Crimes and Passion: Women Writers of the 21st Century. It was a class about mystery and romance authors, and I was knee-deep in research, which actually meant I was rereading many of my favorite novels. Jim Giles, the English chair, thought the class was an excellent idea and hoped it would quench my thirst for solving crimes. Here was a formal way to study it—and not get personally involved. It was a win-win, for the students and me. They got to study something besides the classics, and I got to teach something besides composition.

Mrs. Gunderson raised her eyebrows. "Well it's something to keep in mind. I had been married a decade by the time I was your age."

"I'm only twenty-nine!" I said.

"And thirty is knocking at your door." She stood and put on her coat. "Thank you for the cookies, Emmeline. It was very thoughtful of you."

I stood too. "You're welcome. And if you'd like me to hang up some lights for you, just let me know. I'm pretty good with a hammer."

"Lights do detract criminals, you know, and my front stoop is so dark." She considered the offer as she donned her red pill hat. "Yes, my front stoop. That wouldn't cause you too much trouble, would it?"

"No trouble at all," I said. "I'll need a way to work off all those goodies."

After she left, I took my cat, Dickinson, off the stool and placed her on the wide wooden windowsill. I had one more strand of lights to string and wanted to finish before tomorrow. Fridays I taught on campus and had promised Lenny I would meet up with him and a quartet from Minneapolis Friday night. The quartet, Jazz Underground, would be performing Saturday in the Holiday Music Series. Lenny knew one of the players and would be joining the quartet as a guest guitar player. The other acts in the month-long series were folk and classical, so I imagined the quartet's music would add a jazz and blues component. Whatever Lenny played would sound terrific. Though he was Jewish, he loved Christmas music because "Yeah, Neil Diamond." Besides, he wasn't going to turn down his first formal invitation from the university. Although he played many local venues, he'd never performed for a college event, unless you counted the English Department's holiday party, which was more a semester's end hootenanny.

After tacking up the last twisted cord, I walked outside to admire my handiwork. My house looked cute and cozy with the icicle lights highlighting my little spot on the block. On the corner, white clouds of smoke puffed from the chimney of my neighbor's square brick abode, which was decorated with gingerbread men, and all six windows of the two-story across the street were outlined in multicolored lights. To my right was Mrs. Gunderson, with her twinkling miniature tree framed by old-fashioned tieback drapes, and to my left was the pair of psychologists with no lights but a beautiful rope of greenery festooned to the front railing. Of course there were the students, about a block down on Oxford, who were less careful with their decorations. But some were graduate students and took time to put in a colored light bulb or count down the days until finals in fake snow on a window. It always gave me a chuckle when I passed because, really, I was counting down the days too. For an English professor, finals meant grading—and a lot of it. In the upcoming weeks, I had many portfolios, papers, and projects to read and tabulate. Before I could enjoy one day of winter break, I would have to mow through sundry comma splices, dangling modifiers, and sentence fragments.

The reminder was unwelcome, and I pushed it out of my mind, focusing instead on the quiet beauty of Copper Bluff.

It was as if the tiny town was sleeping, I decided. Not sleeping, exactly, but napping under a light blanket of snow. It had put away the busyness of fall harvest and rested under the peaceful promise of the holiday. People took time to volunteer at churches, visit the elderly, and write Christmas cards (yes, write!). Shopping was fun, not stressful, because it usually aided a local charity or family, and the whole town turned out, paying inflated prices for someone's benefit. The Winter Festival that Mrs. Gunderson mentioned was an all-day block party. The entire downtown came alive, and it was one of my favorite events of the year. I anticipated it like a child anticipates Christmas morning, waiting to unwrap the package that was Copper Bluff. As I picked up my box of holiday décor, Dickinson pawing the trail of gold garland, I decided there was no place I'd rather be.

Chapter Two

—

"What do you mean, come home?" It was early Friday morning, and my mother was on the phone. She spoke in a rush, having called me on her way to work at the high school, where she taught art. I half listened as I filled my coffee pot with water, my home phone balanced between my shoulder and ear.

"Your aunts aren't free on Christmas, so we're doing Christmas early. They're arriving next weekend, and I want you to come home."

"This weekend?" I said, still groggy with sleep.

She huffed a breath. "Goodness, Emmeline. It's nearly seven o'clock. Aren't you awake? I said *next* weekend. Your aunts are coming *next* weekend, and I want you to come home too. I took time off."

I hit the coffee machine ON button and sat down on a kitchen chair, wrapping my fuzzy yellow robe around my knees. Any time my aunts returned to Detroit, it was an event: dinners, drinks, and after enough drinks, dancing. When I was young, I eagerly awaited their arrival; my dad eagerly awaited their departure. I always knew something exciting would happen, something unexpected, when they were around. It made turning down my mother's invitation that much harder. Still, there was no way I could make a trip back these last few weeks of the semester.

I braced for her objections. "I'm sorry, Mom, but I just can't right now. We only have a couple more weeks of classes, and I have to stay here."

"But you didn't come home for Thanksgiving. I haven't seen you for … well … a long time."

"I'm going to be home over break. We'll see each other then. I'm staying all week, remember? We're going to take that cooking class?" Right now, my mom was into Thai cuisine. Next month it might be Chinese or Italian. I teased her that she had traveled the world over in her art and cooking classes, but the truth was she only dreamed of distant lands. It was one of the reasons she had named me after my great-great-grandma Emmeline. When she and my dad retired, she was finally going to see the world, one all-inclusive cruise at a time.

"It won't be the same. Your aunts—" There was a loud honk on the line and then a curse word. "I tell you, Em, these drivers are making me crazy. I need a vacation. A real one."

The beep of the coffee maker brought a thought to my head. I swear that machine has magical powers. "I have an idea. Why don't you come down here for a couple of days? Just you and me. We'll go shopping. Bake cookies. Exchange gifts. They have real carolers down here, Mom. I'm not even kidding."

"Carolers?" she said wistfully. "Like in the Lifetime movies?"

"Exactly like Lifetime movies."

"That would be wonderful." A muffled noise and then another honk. "I don't think obscene rap music blaring from a car window counts as Christmas carols, young man!"

A wave of sympathy washed over me. I didn't miss Detroit's morning traffic jams. They made even a blithesome worldview such as my mother's darker. For years, she'd taught drawing and painting classes at a public high school, tangling with some of the toughest teenagers in town. But she believed in art and its transformative powers; she wasn't one to give up easily. A few years ago, she'd assumed a new role as a mentor to at-risk students, teaching art therapy. Although she was no longer in the classroom, she visited several schools on a daily basis, saving today's troubled youth one masterpiece at a time.

"Mom?"

"I'll think about it," she said. "The thought of getting out of here for a few days is right up there with winning the lottery."

After we said our goodbyes and hung up, I thought about our conversation. She must be really distressed to consider leaving Detroit and her students behind, even for a few days. Although spontaneous and unconventional, she was incredibly committed to her job and rarely took time off. It sounded as if she could use a vacation right now, and I hoped she would come to Copper Bluff, if only for a few days. It would be just what she needed before the holidays.

An hour later, I was on campus, bundled up in my knee-length parka, my boots crunching softly on the snow. In the quadrangle, the white powder lay like a newly tucked sheet over the dead winter grass and dusted the rooftops of Stanton, Winsor, and Harriman Hall like confectioner's sugar. With each step I took, the world's troubles grew farther and farther away, and as I approached Harriman Hall, and my office, the blaring noise of Detroit's traffic and the conversation with my mother were temporarily forgotten.

Harriman Hall was old, and not old in a distinguished way like Stanton or Winsor. They had their rose quartzite stones and ornate turrets, respectively. Harriman had its plainness and anonymity. *That brick building next to Winsor*, I often heard students describe it. What it did offer, though, were two beautiful maple trees, their bare branches lined with snow, and the English Department, the site of most of the goings-on in my world.

Barb, our secretary, had done a nice job decorating our

floor—and Jim Giles's office door. Despite that Giles, the chair of the department, was married to one of the most gracious women I knew, Barb had an obvious crush on him. She not only decked his door, she copied his syllabi and tabulated his evaluations faster than you could say "joy to the world"—gifts at the top of the rest of the faculty's wish lists.

Around the department were other nods to the holidays, such as a small tree placed on the table outside Barb's office. Someone had taken the time to wrap the old books in brown paper, tying colorful ribbons around each one. Across from Barb's office was Lenny's, and he'd taped a paper menorah to his door. On my door were jingle bells that chimed noisily as I turned the key. The faint smell of pine cleaner greeted me as I entered the tiny room.

Although small, my office contained my most beloved possessions: old books and papers and a black push-button phone dating back to the 1970s. I don't know when I'd become so nostalgic, before the move to Copper Bluff or after. My degree, French literature, inclined me toward historical texts and papers. Despite my attachment to the past, a new laptop computer sat on my wooden desk, looking silver and futuristic among all the brown and antique. I'd purchased it last spring and loved its mobility and efficiency too. It took up half the space of my old desktop and was small enough to fit into my satchel.

I unwrapped my scarf and hung it on the hook by my door along with my coat. Our faculty meeting wasn't for twenty minutes, so I had time to check my inbox. The last month of the year brought a digital deluge with it. Students who had been lackadaisical about their grades for fourteen weeks suddenly turned into diligent scholars. They finally cared about points, participation, and all the things I'd tried to hammer into their heads from the first day of fall. Extra credit was their last hope, and they wondered what events they could attend and where. There was no venue or task they wouldn't consider if it meant ten extra points. I huffed as I scanned twelve new emails. If only they had shown such enthusiasm weeks ago.

"Em, you're here," came a voice from the doorway.

I turned to see Claudia Swift, a creative writing professor and very dear friend. She wore a green blouse, gold scarf, and boots with four-inch heels.

"I have something for you." She pulled out a package from her sheer, billowing sleeves.

"Claudia! It's so early. I don't have yours wrapped." The truth was I didn't even have it purchased.

She took a seat across from me in the alcove chair. "It's not early for me. It's late. I've been carrying it since Italy, and I decided the minute December arrived, I would give it to you. Open it."

Claudia and her husband, Gene, had gone on a couples' cruise to Italy last spring to rekindle their on-again/off-again relationship while their two children stayed behind with grandparents. A tenured professor, she was able to get away with a semester-long sabbatical, which had been a success on many levels. One, she and her husband renewed their marriage vows in romantic Venice, and two, she had written fifteen poems, some of which were accepted for publication. It would be years before I would feel as secure as she did in her position. Yet during my pre-tenure review in the fall, Giles assured me I was on track for associate professor in three years and accepted my first proposed course, which was heavily enrolled. All around, it had been a good semester.

Untying the black ribbon and unwrapping the tissue paper, I realized the gift was Italian leather and very expensive. I would need to rethink my gift-giving budget. "A clutch! It's beautiful, Claudia. Thank you."

She waved away my thanks. "You're always carrying around all that change for the vending machine. I figured you might as well have some place to put it."

I turned over the tan leather purse in my hands. It was soft and supple and one of the most gorgeous accessories I'd ever owned. "It's perfect. I'll use it tonight. I'm meeting up with

Lenny and Jazz Underground. They're in town for the concert. He asked if you wanted to come."

She twisted her brown hair into a bun and secured it with one of my pencils. "Lenny. How is that going?"

"How is what going?"

"You know, Em. Your relationship."

I laughed but could feel my face grow warm. "We don't have a *relationship*. We're just friends. You know that."

She grabbed another pencil and now looked a little bit like a geisha with two sticks coming out of her hair. "What about *the kiss*?"

Lenny and I had stolen a kiss in the library some months ago, but things had never progressed from there. The summer and fall had torn us in different directions, and both of us were fairly new to campus and therefore focused on our careers. "The kiss? Well, the kiss was wonderful, but I have more important things going on in my life right now. Like the faculty meeting in a few minutes."

"There's nothing more important than love. Make time for it, Em, or it won't make time for you."

Was she quoting a poem, writing her own, or simply being Claudia? It was hard to tell.

She stood to leave. "Where and what time? I can see you're going to need my assistance."

As if she were a wise counselor and an expert on love, I thought. Her husband had been living in the basement for the last year and a half. He'd just moved back upstairs. "Seven o'clock at the bed and breakfast on the bluff."

"The Candlelight Inn. How lovely."

"I've never been there, but I thought it was a curious choice for lodging. Wouldn't the quartet want to stay in town, where they could practice?"

She shook her head. "Not at all. The owners are locals and give discounts to university faculty. I know because I've had to book rooms a time or two for our visiting writers. They adore it. And who wouldn't? It's the perfect place to write—or play. If

I remember correctly, it has a nice grand piano."

"I can't wait to see it," I said, packing up my satchel. "I could pick you up."

"Yes, do," she said, following me out the door. "It'll be a girls' night out."

"Emmeline, faculty meeting," Giles said loudly from his next-door office.

Claudia and I exchanged a smile.

"I remembered," I called back, locking the door behind me. "On my way now."

Office doors opened and closed as faculty members joined us in our walk toward the lounge, where the last meeting of the year was being held. At the beginning of the semester, we met in a larger classroom so that teaching assistants could join in. But this meeting was for faculty only—and Barb. She was positioned in the corner near the coffee maker with a steno pad. She'd be taking notes and charging for this morning's libations.

The most diligent professors were already seated, including Jane Lemort, our medieval scholar, Thomas Cook, our hip new rhetorician, and Reed Williams, our Shakespearean god. To be honest, I dreaded talking to Reed and knew he would be addressing the faculty. It was as if he lived in the sixteenth century. One never knew when a quote from a sonnet or allusion would drop from his lips, and this listener was afraid of appearing clueless.

A tall man with a thin face and large nose, Reed would update us on the events surrounding the exhibition of Shakespeare's first folio. He'd discussed it many times since last spring, when he'd secured its arrival for the following year. Dressed in an Oxford shirt buttoned to the neck, he was seated at the front of the room, looking over his notes. His shirtsleeves didn't reach his wrists, probably because his arms were so long. I took a chair near the back of the room, expecting Claudia to take the empty seat next to me, but she selected an empty chair near Reed. Perhaps she, too, had an update to give. As luck would have it, Lenny raced in at the last minute, took the available chair, and shrugged off his coat. He smelled like the cold winter snow. I smiled at his red cheeks. They were a nice contrast to his spiky blond hair and dark eyebrows.

"Good morning. This won't take long. I know some of you have class," said Giles, who stood at the front of the room. Although he was the model of calm before the storm, he detected the anxiety in the room. It was the time of year when even thirty minutes were hard to spare. "We have a few updates and a reminder, and then you'll be on your way."

His brown eyes slowly surveyed the room. I tapped my toe. What was he doing? Taking attendance? Lenny sensed my impatience and passed me a Lifesaver. He knew if anything could calm my nerves, it was candy.

Giles continued, reminding us about final grades and due dates. He also mentioned the Visiting Scholar lecture series and the need for volunteers next year. Then he gave the floor to Reed, who took his place at the front of the room. Standing well over six feet tall, Reed stooped as he inserted a flash drive into the computer.

"I know we discussed planning for Shakespeare's Garden last year, so I won't repeat those details. I will tell you, however, the progress in the conservatory has been outstanding, and we're on schedule for planting this spring. The garden will be one of the venues for events surrounding the first folio's arrival."

Reed discussed Shakespeare's first folio, showing us pictures of the book on the overhead screen, and as he did, his bland face lit up and his nose turned red. The book, dating from 1623, held thirty-six plays. Eighteen, including *Macbeth* and *The Tempest*, would have been lost without its publication. When it arrived on campus, student actors would perform a scene from *The Tempest* in the renovated garden, and scholars would come together for an all-day symposium. The department would offer films, music, and cake. It would be a month-long celebration, he said. He hoped everyone was looking forward to it as much as he was. I found it hard to imagine anyone enjoying it more than he.

Claudia stood to assure him we were all very excited. She announced that the Creative Writing Department would be hosting a Shakespearean sonnet contest during a write-in. If professors knew of creative writers in their classes, they should refer them to Claudia or Allen Dunsbar, the other creative writing professor. She scanned the room, but Dunsbar wasn't present. Famously uninterested in anything except his own novels, Dunsbar hadn't bothered to attend.

When the meeting concluded, Lenny and I stood to leave. I referenced Dunsbar's absence. "How does he get away with never attending? I leave early once, and I'm called out at the next meeting."

Lenny shrugged. "You know what they say. Tenure is the ticket to easy street."

Easy street, I thought as I tucked my scarf into my coat. That was the road less traveled by me. If only there were signs, it might not be so hard to locate.

Chapter Three

After a full day's teaching, I looked forward to leaving campus for the weekend. As the semester drew to a close, my students grew needier, taking up every office hour with problems they thought only I could solve. So I was walking more quickly than I should have been when a patch of ice caught me unaware, and I slipped, landing on my bum in the snow. A few students looked in my direction and attempted to look concerned. One boy even called out, "Hey, Ms. Prather, are you okay?"

"Perfectly, thank you," I said, attempting a little too quickly to right myself. My satchel fell off my shoulder, and its contents were scattered on the path. In my haste to leave, I'd forgotten to close it. I grabbed the pencils and pens, which I knew could cause another accident. As I reached for one of my notebooks, I saw André Duman fast approaching, a knight in shining armor in any modern sense of the description.

"Oh, Emmeline. You have had a fall. Let me help you," he said, gathering up a far-flung notebook.

I tried nonchalance, but it was difficult. First of all, I was on my knees in the snow. Second, he was so handsome he made even happily married women quiver. "I'm good."

He put the notebook into my satchel and zipped it closed. Then he held out his hand. "You are not good. You are hurt?"

I took his hand. "Only my pride. That's the second time this year. And in the middle of the quad both times."

"You are too much in a hurry. You are so busy. All the time."

He was right. I was always frantic to get one thing done or another. He, on the other hand, was never frantic, only passionate. How well I knew the difference.

I dusted off my rear. Along with his dark eyes and wavy black hair, André was the quintessential Frenchman: the accent, the style, the scarf. I'd been obsessed with all things French since I was a young girl, when I found out about my namesake, great-great-*grandmère* Emmeline. So when I looked at André, it was hard not to recall how I'd once imagined my future: fabulous, French, and oh-so-romantic.

"Are you on your way somewhere?" He handed me my satchel.

"Just home," I said. "I guess I'm a little anxious for the weekend to begin."

"Ah. I know what you mean. I am on needles and pins waiting for the semester to end. The distance learning class has been a great waste of time."

We walked on the path toward the cross street. "How *is* that class? Did the technology get any easier?" André had been arguing for a French major on campus ever since he came to Copper Bluff, a few years before I was hired. But when last spring's excursion to France was thwarted by murder and fall enrollment didn't increase, he was stuck teaching introductory courses as well as two new distance courses conducted via computer. From what he'd said, I'd gathered the technology was too high of a hurdle to clear in a foreign language course.

"It gets no easier. It gets worse. They have final presentations next week, and I don't know how I will grade them with the delay in speech." He threw up his hands. "I hear three words out of ten!"

"How frustrating," I commiserated. "With all the advancements in technology, you would think distance learning would be better. In a rural state like South Dakota, making it more effective should be a top priority."

"*Allez.* The priority is farm subsidies. You know the story."

Of course he was right. The state was a major producer of corn and soybeans. Beyond the campus were dozens of farms, the land now covered in thick blankets of snow, the late nights of harvest a distant memory. As one drove across the state, the landscape changed. Across the Missouri River, the countryside became drier, hillier, and grassier. Badlands National Park, in fact, boasted 244,000 acres of mixed prairie grass. No more farms, just cattle ranches, attesting to the very different economies of the state.

"I know the story," I said. "I just wish I could help." André had gone through a lot last spring and deserved a break from campus drama.

We faced each other as we approached the cross street. "I know you do, but you are not so good with the technology, if I remember right. Lenny says it is your Achilles heel."

I rolled my eyes. "Lenny says a lot of things. Are you going to the concert Saturday?"

"I wouldn't miss it," he said, tucking his maroon scarf deep into his coat. "I will see you there?"

I nodded. "I'll look for you."

I turned and walked down Oxford Street, noting the number marking the days until winter break in the frosted window at the end of the block.

That night, I took extra care with my dress. Most days, I threw together outfits with little forethought. I never had the time to coordinate a "look," though I was a sucker for crimson. The crimson Scarlett O'Hara wore in *Gone with the Wind* when she had to confront Melanie Wilkes and everyone at Ashley's birthday party? That crimson I would buy every time. Tonight was important. I was meeting the members of Jazz Underground, the quartet playing in Copper Bluff on Saturday, and Lenny knew one of them personally. If I remembered correctly, it was the piano player, Isabelle. They'd grown up together in Minneapolis and still kept in contact. She was a professor in Minneapolis, and some of the others in the quartet had ties to the college, too. That's why they'd booked the concert here.

After ransacking my closet, I decided on a gold and black sweater with black leggings. Black was a safe choice. It went with everything—at least that's what I'd heard. I rarely wore it myself, but the outfit looked elegant lying on my bed. It was dressy but not too dressy. Plus I had a pair of boots that were ankle-length with a nice heel. When I finished dressing, I checked myself out in the bathroom mirror. My hair was wind-blown and needed a few squirts of shine serum. I smoothed the product over my curls, and the frizz disappeared.

Dickinson watched me from the edge of the bathtub as I dabbed on red lip gloss.

"Oh, I know what you're thinking," I said. "I never wear lipstick, and you're right. I don't. But it's the holidays, and what's a holiday outfit without a touch of red?"

She feigned interest.

"It'll match these red earrings, see?" I said, revealing the dangling earbobs hidden beneath my hair.

Now she was interested.

"Sorry, Dickinson, no time to play. I have to go," I said, switching off the light and grabbing my leather coat. Although less protection against the cold, it was dressier than my parka and went well with my outfit. Sure, I would shiver until I reached Claudia's house on Princeton Street, but getting the look right was worth it.

If Claudia was as concerned about her appearance as I was, it didn't show. She emerged from her house in an oversized cream-colored wrap, skintight pants, and the same high-heeled boots she'd worn earlier. Although sweeping and dramatic, it was her usual look. Her brown hair curled about her shoulders, but by the end of the night, it would be in a twist or bun. She rearranged it constantly.

"You. In this hotrod. Gorgeous," she said as she slammed the door. "What man could resist you?"

I laughed. I loved my red '69 Mustang convertible. "Claudia, you always know the right thing to say. I guess that's why you're a poet."

She batted her long lashes at me. "The right word. The right time. It's my thing." She checked her hair in the rearview mirror. "But I'm not kidding about the outfit. Total rock star."

Her compliment eased my mind. I hated worrying about my appearance, and I found I was doing a good deal of that tonight. I turned onto Main Street. "You look terrific, as always. I guess Gene decided to stay home with the kids?"

"He did. It's important for him to have one-on-one time with the children. Besides, you and I have hardly gotten together this semester. We've both been so busy."

"True. It's good to have a girls' night."

"Girls' night plus one very important guy." She gave me a wink.

"Where is this place again?" I asked, ignoring her inference to Lenny. We approached the downtown area, which was five blocks long and packed with cars. There were three bars in Copper Bluff, and they were all on Main Street. If students were looking for their friends on a weekend, they would find them here.

"A couple miles from this last stoplight. Keep going, and you'll run right into it."

As we eased out of town, the tiny shops and restaurants disappeared. Before us lay the winter prairie, barely visible under the night sky. I focused on the white line of the curvy road, as there was nothing else to guide me. Darkness covered the landscape like spilled ink, and only a sliver of moon offered dim details of the countryside. After navigating the blackness for many minutes, I noticed a light to my left and guessed it was the Candlelight Inn. It was the only light for miles around.

"This is it," Claudia confirmed.

I turned down the long gravel road. At its end stood an elegant two-story Victorian house with a candle in each window. It was yellow, the color of my own house, with white scrolled trim and a sprawling wraparound porch. The surrounding trees sparkled with white fairy lights. In a word, breathtaking.

I parked next to Lenny's Ford Taurus, one of three cars parked in front of the carriage house. Once out of the car, I realized the house sat on the bluff for which Copper Bluff was named. It was a surprise, as always, to find this orange-colored cliff in the middle of the flat prairie. Below was a winding river and bottomland. Though the river didn't look like much, it was deceptively powerful, as the town's history attested. Once built near the river, Copper Bluff was forced to move atop the cliff when the river flooded. But South Dakota pioneers had staying power; they'd had to in order to survive life on the barren prairie.

Approaching the house, I noticed a cobblestone path that led to the wraparound porch. It must have been popular in the summer months. Who wouldn't want to savor a glass of wine or iced-tea as they lounged on the comfortable wicker furniture? I made a note to myself to return when the weather was warmer so I could spend some time walking the grounds. From the trellis, I imagined they had a beautiful garden, and the trees seemed to form a small orchard.

"Should I ring the bell?" I asked Claudia.

"I don't see why. The door's ajar. And look." She pointed to the front window. It displayed nine beautiful candles. "It must be happy hour."

Inside, I could see people talking, laughing, and drinking. Right away I noticed Lenny's spiky blond hair and broad shoulders. At just over six feet, he wasn't the tallest in the group, but his presence was the most imposing.

As I opened the screen door, a bell jingled. The gathering of people grew quiet.

"Em, Claudia, you made it," said Lenny, coming over to greet us. In a blue button-down shirt and dressy jeans, Lenny looked more student than professor. His dark eyebrows gave him a devil-may-care look, but his dimple betrayed his sweetness. The latter showed as he gave us a warm smile.

"Hey, Lenny," I said, "this place is amazing."

A woman in her forties met us also. She was tall and thin and well put together. "Hello, Claudia. It's good to see you again." She turned to me. "Welcome to the Candlelight Inn. I'm Alyssa Anderson."

Claudia nodded and took her hand. "Alyssa, how lovely. I thought your inn was beautiful in the fall, but I think Christmas is my new favorite season. I have to find a reason to get some more writers down here, and soon!"

Alyssa smiled. With a graceful gesture, she swept her blonde hair back with her fingers. Full of élan, she was well suited to her inn.

"The decorations are bad-ass," said Lenny, taking my coat and handing it to Alyssa.

And they were. The ivory banister that led upstairs was roped with swooping boughs of greenery. "Juniper," Alyssa explained when Claudia inquired. The fireplace in the library was adorned with it, too, and as much as I wanted to investigate the towering bookshelves, complete with rolling ladder, I followed Lenny to the dining room, where Jazz Underground waited to meet us.

"This is Em—Emmeline—and Claudia, from English. This is the quartet I'll be joining on stage tomorrow. It's been a blast getting to know them."

One of the men was tall, with long, muscular arms. The other was small, especially standing next to Lenny, but quite dapper in a black, fine-knit cardigan. His dark hair was cropped close to his scalp, about the same length as his beard, and his gaze was magnetic, making it hard not to stare.

"This is Miles Jamison. He's a professor at the U and plays bass," said Lenny.

"*Enchanté*," Miles said, taking my hand and kissing it.

"I told him you knew French. And this is Josh Arrends," said Lenny, indicating to the tall man. "He plays drums and gives lessons at the studio he and Miles own in Minneapolis."

"Hi," said Josh, keeping his hands in his pockets. His voice was quiet, but kind, and he seemed reserved if not altogether shy.

"And this is Belle—Isabelle Carr. I've known you since, what, sixth grade?" said Lenny. "She's the one who came up with the idea to throw us all together on stage."

"I can't even remember a time I *didn't* know you," she said, smiling. "And *nobody* calls me Isabelle."

If I responded, I wasn't sure how. I was too busy guessing how tall she was. Even in my boots, I didn't reach her shoulders. She was probably six feet with the kind of sumptuous and wavy golden-blonde hair I'd only seen on Barbie.

Claudia took her hand. "I know what you mean. We feel like we've known Lenny forever."

"Belle is a piano professor, and Kim is a grad student. She plays the trumpet," said Lenny.

Kim Young was petite, with dark skin and hair. "I'll graduate this spring with my Master of Music degree."

I shook her hand. "You must be very talented to already be playing professionally."

"She's incredibly gifted," said Miles before Kim could answer. His voice was deep and full of admiration. "I have the privilege of being her advisor, so I pleaded with her to join Jazz Underground when our trumpet player left."

Miles was obviously passionate about Kim's talent, and Kim was thrilled by the attention. She hung on his every word, reveling in the praise. "He's exaggerating. I was honored when Professor Jamison asked me to play."

"What Miles says is no exaggeration," Belle said. "I'm going to hate to see her graduate in the spring. I might just have to convince her to stay and get her DMA or PhD."

"The better, *less expensive* option," said Miles, his warm

gaze still on Kim, "would be to join me and Josh, giving lessons at the studio."

Josh's cheeks flushed. Did he relish the thought of working beside the cute Kim, or was he really that shy? I didn't have time to draw any conclusions. Alyssa took Claudia's drink order and mine and then disappeared. Her employee, a young woman with an edgy haircut and a dragon neck tattoo, pushed in a cart of cheese, crackers, nuts, and grapes. Then she scurried away to answer the door.

Alyssa returned with our wine, educating us on the types of cheeses and which paired better with white or red wine. All organic, the artisan goat cheese was her favorite. She ordered it from Sonoma Valley in California, and if that wasn't enough to convince us to try it, she said it was lower in fat, calories, and cholesterol than cow's milk products. That was enough to persuade me. I was still feeling guilty over yesterday's cookie binge. After Mrs. Gunderson left, I'd finished off the thumbprints and washed them down with a tall glass of milk. Any lower-calorie option was welcome this time of year.

The employee with the neck tattoo tugged at Alyssa's sleeve. "We've got a problem," she said.

Alyssa blinked. "What is it?"

"A student. I think she's been drinking. She wants to come in."

"Excuse me," said Alyssa. She and her employee saw to the disturbance, and the quartet continued conversing. Still, I could hear some of the discussion. Alyssa stated firmly that the event was for faculty members only. The door shut, and she returned. The employee was gone.

Alyssa provided an explanation as she passed out appetizer plates. "A student looking for a party. That's all. I had Pen take her home. That girl is a godsend."

It didn't surprise me that a student had wandered in looking for a party, but it did surprise me that the student had wandered so far. We were miles from Copper Bluff and the nearest frat house. What had driven her all the way out here?

A man entered holding a martini.

"Thank you, darling," said Alyssa. "This is my husband, Eric, one of the best bartenders in the county."

Eric handed Miles a fresh drink and retrieved a spent glass. His movements were measured, and though I guessed he was a considerate host, his good manners were not as natural as his wife's.

Lenny held up his glass of amber liquid. "He's got the best bourbon, for sure."

"Only the best for our guests," Eric said, putting his arm around his wife. They looked like a team in love. "Alyssa insists on the finest foods, so I insist on the finest liquor. People come here to relax. We think they deserve it."

"Enjoy," said Alyssa, "and please don't hesitate to ask if you need anything at all." They left us to our drinks and appetizers.

I took a sip of red wine.

"It's that time of year again, Em," said Lenny, nudging my arm. "Friends, wine … music? How about a song? I've got my guitar."

The first party I attended with Lenny, he and I started on a conversation about Transcendentalism that progressed through several glasses of wine and ended with a duet. Despite it being two years ago, I couldn't live it down.

"Oh, you sing?" asked Belle. "Lenny didn't tell me."

Her speaking voice was as beautiful as she was, and I suspected she could sing as well as play piano. "No, no," I protested. "Not much."

Claudia waved off my reply. "She's a terrific singer, amazing really."

"I teach English," I said.

"Oh right," Belle said. "I knew that. I hated English. It was my worst subject."

"Yeah, we get that a lot," said Lenny. "I never know how to respond. I'm sorry?"

Belle laughed, and her hair bounced around her shoulders. "You're so funny, Len."

I narrowed my eyes. *Len?* That just sounded wrong. I turned toward the elaborately set table and loaded my tiny plate with cheese and crackers.

"Hungry?" said Claudia, getting in line behind me.

"Not really," I said.

"Me neither," she said, cutting several hunks of gouda. "But after that lesson on artisanal cheeses, who can resist?"

"Alyssa knows a lot about food," I said, scooping up a few olives.

"She's a dietitian. She's taught some workshops on campus. That's how I met her."

"Fascinating."

Claudia reached for my arm. "Hey, don't let that leggy blonde get to you."

"Why would she get to me?" I whispered. "I could care less how long her legs are or how blonde her hair is."

"Because she's gorgeous," she whispered back. "And she seems very close to Lenny."

"Not that close," I said.

"*Len?*" she said with a dramatic question mark.

"Fine." We made our way back to the group. "They're close. You know what I'm close to? Getting my book finished. In fact, that's where I should be right now. Home. Writing."

Claudia couldn't respond. We had rejoined the group.

"Did you see they had a library?" Lenny said to Claudia and me. "Let's take our drinks in there." He glanced at my plate. "It looks like you got enough food for both of us."

We fell in line behind him, Josh, and Miles. Belle and Kim were gathering appetizers for themselves.

Located across the hall from the front parlor, the enormous library held six built-in mahogany bookshelves (four on one wall and one on each side of the fireplace) and a shiny baby grand piano. No wonder the quartet was staying at the Candlelight. With an entire corner reserved for music, the members could rehearse right here. Music stands and even a guitar were at their disposal, and I wondered if the Andersons themselves played. The sheet music collection was almost as impressive as the book collection.

Two long, leather sofas were positioned in an L, with a heavy-looking walnut coffee table placed in front of them. Claudia, Lenny, and I put our drinks here, sitting next to each other on the tufted couch. Miles sank into the sofa next to us, as did Josh. They talked about an upcoming event at the studio.

Lenny plucked a piece of Brie off my plate. "You look nice," he said, pointing at me with his empty toothpick. "You get a new ... shirt?"

I shook my head, and he took another piece of cheese.

"Something looks different," he said.

Claudia considered my outfit. "She's wearing black. She never wears black."

"That's all I wear: black ... and gray," said Belle, sliding into one of the facing wingback chairs across from the coffee table. "My closet could supply the wardrobe for a funeral procession. I need a new outfit for the holidays."

"No, that's not it," said Lenny. "I think it's the lipstick."

Desperate not to debate style with the fashion plate across from me, I turned to Miles. He and Josh had finished talking about the studio, and Josh had updated him on all the business particulars. "So, what classes do you teach?"

"This semester? History of Western Music and Analysis of Tonal Music. Not my cup of tea. But I also give private guitar instruction. It's a great way to discover new talent and keep up with the music scene. Otherwise, I'd go crazy teaching all day."

"Oh, face it, Miles," said Belle. "You'll be a hoary old professor someday just like the rest of us."

"God, I don't want to be a hoary old anything," said Lenny.

I watched Miles take a sip of his martini. Everyone did. His movements were mesmerizing, and the attention of the room fell naturally on him. In his early fifties, he had piercing brown eyes that glittered in the low light of the room. When they landed on you, it felt as if he knew you intimately, even if you'd only just met.

"You can't help it," he said. "The ivy tower takes it out of you, my friend. I'm telling you. By the time I hit sixty, I'll be looking for a sweater vest and a cane."

"Well, lucky for me we don't have any towers, and our buildings are made of quartzite—mixed with a little asbestos," said Lenny.

Claudia and I shared a chuckle. He was right. While guys like Miles raged against the machine of higher education, we could only laugh. We couldn't relate to the pressures at larger, more elite colleges.

"I'm serious. For artists like us, there's no better place to kill your soul," said Miles.

Alyssa, who carried two wine bottles, paused at the door. "More?" she asked as she refilled Belle's glass of white. Then she walked over to Claudia and me with the bottle of red.

"Don't get him started on *that* subject again. We heard about it all the way here," Belle said, tucking her feet beneath her.

Miles considered Belle's interjection. They were clearly comfortable sparring. The entire group, in fact, seemed to have a private language. It was almost like they were family. They could say things to each other they wouldn't say to anybody else.

"I know you don't like hearing it, Belle. But it's true. Some musicians don't belong at the university. They belong out there." He pointed toward the window. "Playing. Doing what they love."

"*You're* doing what you love. *Plus* teaching at the university," Belle said. She was not only attractive but sharp. She wouldn't allow Miles to dismiss academics without a challenge. Josh, on the other hand, was content watching from the sidelines. It wasn't that he lacked intelligence; he didn't. You could tell he had a lot of know-how about the studio and music. But he wasn't an academic. I guessed he was street smart and largely self-taught. A natural.

"You should quit," said Kim, plopping into the open seat

beside Miles. "You have the quartet; you have the studio. Why waste your time at the university?"

"The university does a lot for the quartet and vice versa. That's why." Belle spoke to Miles, not Kim, and Miles held her gaze for a moment. They were both natural leaders: authoritative, smart, and magnetic. But could two people lead one band? I had to wonder.

Kim touched Miles's leg, and he leaned back, avoiding her attention. "It's too late for me," he said. "I've got the studio to pay for. But you've got your whole life ahead of you, and you're popular now. That won't last forever. My advice is get out there—play your music. Don't let *someone* talk you into a DMA or PhD."

From her earlier comment, we all knew he meant Belle.

"That's not sound advice," said Belle, "especially coming from a music professor whose job depends on student enrollment." She took a sip of her wine and smiled. "If our retention rates drop any further, the studio is the first place I'm coming for a job."

Miles laughed, acknowledging the playfulness of Belle's tone, but I had taught long enough to know that retention rates were a serious matter on college campuses everywhere. Although they didn't apply as much to graduate students, who were already committed to higher education, they certainly applied to undergraduates, many of whom were undecided about the future. If Miles was encouraging students to pursue their dreams elsewhere, I could see how it could affect a department like Music, which isn't as heavily enrolled as other departments.

"I have to agree with Belle," said Lenny. "And not just because of job security. It's really hard for a musician to make it out there. It's like being drafted for a pro-football team. It just doesn't happen very often."

"What about Josh?" said Miles. "He made a full-time go of it."

I looked at Josh, who wore a flannel shirt, black jeans, and now a grin. Beyond the grin, his face betrayed irritation with Miles, which he suppressed before answering. He spoke with the same mild tone I'd heard earlier.

"I work full-time at the studio. I don't think that's what Lenny is talking about. Playing music and running a business are two different things."

"Oh, come on, Josh," said Miles. "I'm there every week, too."

"Once a week isn't six days, last time I checked," said Josh, downing the rest of his beer.

Kim laughed. "He's got you there, Miles. You didn't even know about the basement flooding last spring."

Josh smiled at Kim, and Belle smiled in appreciation of the joke.

"You guys can give me a hard time all you want," said Miles, "but you also have to give me a little credit. If it wasn't for the studio and my recording contacts, Jazz Underground wouldn't have a CD selling nationwide."

The group stopped chuckling.

"I'll give you that," said Josh.

"Me, too," said Belle. She held up her glass. "Here's to our fearless leader."

We raised our glasses, and the mood lightened. Still, I wondered about Miles. His personality was as big as his ego, and no matter the conversation, he made himself the center of it. Maybe it was just part of being a musician; maybe he attracted attention wherever he went. Or maybe it was his debonair looks or attitude. Regardless, the spotlight shone brightest on him, and in a room full of performers, I wondered if that was a problem.

Chapter Four

———

L ater that evening, others from campus joined us, mostly faculty members from the Department of Music, including the chair, Tad Iverson. He and Miles were both Minnesota alums and greeted each other warmly. With the festive conversation and decorations, it felt like a holiday party. Claudia, always comfortable performing, recited a little Beat poetry to Lenny's acoustic guitar. I kept my karaoke urges in check, despite Lenny's begging. Although I loved music, loved just being around it, I didn't want to embarrass myself in a room full of real musicians. There were enough performers here already; they didn't need one more. Instead, Belle accompanied him on the piano with a folksy rendition of "God Rest Ye Merry Gentlemen." It was a beautiful duet, and if tonight's performance was any indication, tomorrow's concert was going to be a must-see.

As it neared eleven o'clock, Claudia and I ducked out of the library and into the entryway. It was starting to snow, and my Mustang didn't do well on slippery roads. Alyssa retrieved our coats, insisting that Claudia and I return tomorrow for brunch. Claudia said she would love to, but her kids had a dance rehearsal for *The Nutcracker* in the morning. I admitted I would like another look around the library, and Alyssa implored me to check out anything I liked. We were chatting about my favorite books and this semester's classes when Lenny joined us.

"Hey, where are you guys going?" asked Lenny. "The night's young, and so are we."

I nodded toward the window. "It's starting to snow."

"I'll walk you out," he said, taking my coat from Alyssa. She was deep in conversation with Claudia about *The Nutcracker*.

"Are you spending the night?" I asked, as he helped me shrug into my leather jacket.

"No, I'm taking off in a bit. I don't want to be tired for the concert, and these guys could go all night." He glanced in the library. "Besides, they've rented all the rooms."

"I bet it's nice to spend time with your friend Belle." Although I meant it, the statement came out emotionally flat.

"It's nice to spend time with *you*," he said. "It feels like it's been one thing after another this semester."

"I know."

Claudia joined us at the door.

"We'd better get going. It's really coming down now," I said.

As we thanked Alyssa for the food and drinks, Lenny opened the door to a new sheet of falling snow. It fell to the ground, like a snow globe that had just been shaken.

"Beautiful!" said Claudia, stretching out her arms. "It's going to be a white Christmas after all."

Lenny gave her a grin. "It was pretty white already."

She ran her glove across the top of the stair railing, brushing off a layer of snow. "Yes, but my kids will be ecstatic in the morning. There's nothing better than waking up to snow."

I agreed. Fresh snow made everything look new again.

We were walking toward the carriage house but stopped when we heard a noise. At first, I thought the sound was our boots crunching the snow; then I realized it was voices on the back porch.

"Sounds like someone else is excited," said Lenny.

After I listened to the conversation for a moment, "excited" wasn't the word I'd use. "Tense" was more apt. The voices were male; that much was certain. And one was probably Miles's. His was the only deep voice in the group, besides Lenny's, and Lenny was right beside me.

Claudia thought so too. "That's Miles. He's fighting with someone."

"I wonder," said Lenny. "It sounds like him."

He started walking again toward my car, and I grabbed his elbow. "Wait."

"Em Prather," he said, giving my shoulders a squeeze, "the consummate eavesdropper."

"Shhh," I hushed.

Despite our silence, it was hard to make out the words. The snow was like insulation, padding the countryside in fluffy white cotton. Yet I did hear the man tell Miles this was his last chance at something; at what, I didn't know. Whatever it was didn't worry Miles. He let out a nasty laugh and the person went inside, the door slamming behind him.

I looked at Lenny for an explanation.

"You know musicians. They're passionate types." He shrugged. "It's nothing."

I continued walking toward my car. "Do you know who Miles was talking to?"

"Probably Tad Iverson, from the Music Department. He's the only guy I know who would know Miles. He's the one who extended the invitation to play at Copper Bluff."

I asked Lenny how they knew each other, since one taught here and the other in Minnesota.

"Belle said they've played together at university events, festivals. They both play jazz. And Iverson is a Minnesota alum, so he gets back to Minneapolis a lot." He shoved his hands into his pockets. "I'm just glad they invited me to play. They're all professionals in the business."

"You're really good, Lenny," I said. "As good as any

professional."

"I agree," Claudia said, opening the car door.

"You guys are nice, but I'm nowhere near their level. In their eyes I'm just an untenured English professor."

"Well, that's not the worst thing in the world, is it?" I said.

"It's right up there," said Claudia and shut the car door.

Lenny and I stood alone by the side of the car, and I smiled in Claudia's direction. It was good to have her back from Italy.

"So, come to brunch with me tomorrow," Lenny said. "Alyssa invited you, and I want you here, too. I'll pick you up at ten."

I hesitated. The invitation was genuine, but I didn't want to intrude. "Are you sure? If it's group members only, I understand completely."

"I'm positive. Besides, how many French things have you dragged me to? And you know my grasp of French begins and ends with *bon* and *jour*."

"Uh, one … or two, if you're counting Foreign Films Night on campus, which was a complete disaster. You laughed during the entire movie."

"It was funny," he protested.

"It was *Port of Shadows*!"

He seemed to be recalling the film and smiled.

"But if you really *want* me to go …" I said.

"Of course he does, Em. Now get in the car. I'm freezing," Claudia hollered through my door, which was ajar.

"All right," I said with a laugh. "I'll be ready at ten."

I started my car and turned it toward the long gravel road that led to the highway. Framed in the rearview mirror, the house looked like something out of a children's picture book. The smoke from the chimney, the snow on the rooftop, the lights in the windows—it couldn't have been lovelier. And recalling the gourmet food and fine wine, I welcomed the chance to come back tomorrow.

"So that went well," said Claudia as I turned onto the highway.

I gave her a side-long glance. She was clearly being sarcastic. "It wasn't so bad, was it?"

"No, not at all, if you don't count the leggy beauty with the blonde hair and sexy voice. Then it was great. You had a *great* conversation with a *married* man about the wonderful collection of books in the library." She was redoing the twist in her fine brown hair.

"It *was* a wonderful collection, and what do I care if he's married? His wife was right there. She's an avid reader herself, a very likeable woman."

She quit fiddling with her hair. "Do you like Lenny or not?"

"Of course I do. You know that. But I'm not going to force anything. You have to let fate do its job. If it's meant to be, then it's meant to be."

She threw up her hands. "Fate! Ha! Relationships are work. If my marriage to Gene has taught me anything, it's that. If you want a relationship with Lenny, you need to work at it."

She made the thought unpleasant.

"Oh, I know what you're thinking. But this isn't a Jane Austen novel. Lenny isn't going to emerge from the fog one day. If you want a relationship, you need to go get it."

"And that means what?" I said, approaching downtown Copper Bluff. "Slighting his good friend Belle, who happens to be gorgeous and talented and extroverted?" I shook my head. "I don't think so."

"That's not what I'm saying. I'm saying be open to possibilities. Like brunch. If it weren't for me, you would have closed the door on an opportunity."

I turned on Princeton Street and then into her driveway. "I thought he probably wanted to spend some time with his musician friends. Like you spend time with your poetry friends, or I spend time with my—"

"Books," Claudia finished.

"Hey, that's not fair. Mrs. Gunderson came over just last night. We shared a cup of coffee, not to mention a plate of Christmas cookies I baked *myself*."

"And what's Mrs. Gunderson's first name?" she asked, gathering her purse.

I opened my mouth and shut it. I had no idea.

"Think about it, Em," she said as she opened her door. The house was dark. Only the Christmas decorations lighted the way. "But don't think too long. Lenny will be back in the morning."

Chapter Five

Late into the night, I thought about what Claudia had said. Part of me thought she had a point. I couldn't expect Lenny to recognize my feelings through osmosis. But another part of me wasn't in a hurry to declare my love for anyone. My work as a professor was important and took up a good deal of time. And Claudia was right about my books. They hadn't let me down yet. Besides, Lenny and I hadn't shared an intimate moment since last spring. Shouldn't fate have intervened by now?

The thoughts that plagued me Friday night fortunately disappeared by Saturday morning. It was a cloudless blue sky, and the newly fallen snow sparkled like sugar in the sunlight. I put on a bright-red sweater and a pair of dangling gold earrings and clipped my hair into a messy bun. Belle would no doubt be wearing something black and elegant, but I didn't care. I felt festive, and for me, that meant color.

Lenny knocked on the door as I was finishing my makeup.

"Coming!" I yelled from the bathroom.

Lenny was admiring the lights on the front porch. "Wow, did you do all this by yourself?"

"Yep," I said. "I'm doing Mrs. Gunderson's house next."

"I'm impressed. You can hang lights, speak French, and solve murders. Your talents are far-reaching." He leaned down to pet my cat. "Hey, Dickinson."

I rolled my eyes. Sometimes I thought Dickinson liked Lenny more than me. She went out of her way to swerve along his legs and jump on his lap when he sat down. Today she leaned hard into his hand to get the best scratches behind the ears.

"I just have to grab my coat." With no cloud cover, the air was crisp and cold, so I decided on my black parka with the fur around the hood. Everyone in town had at least one parka, if not a second one for snow blowing. With winter temperatures often dipping below zero, one needed a heavy coat, especially walking around campus.

I paused as I returned to the living room, taking in Lenny's attire. He was dressed up for the concert and looked devilishly handsome. He wore a black sport coat that accentuated his broad shoulders and a crisp white shirt. His hair, still damp, was spiked on top.

"You look great, by the way," I said. "I can't wait for the concert. It's at three, right?"

He nodded. "We practiced last night."

"How did everything else go after we left?" I said, shutting the front door and following him out to his car. "Any more *discussions* between Tad and Miles?"

"Nada," he said. "It was like it never happened. Maybe it was your imagination."

"Claudia heard it too."

"And that substantiates it how?"

We shared a laugh in the car, but both grew quiet as Lenny drove through town. My thoughts turned to Lenny, the concert, and his life as a performer.

"Do you ever think your music career might turn … professional?"

Lenny glanced at me. "What, like, quit teaching?"

"I don't know."

He considered the idea a few minutes before answering. "I've toyed with the notion a couple times. But playing music is fun right now. If I did it full time, it might become work. You know what I mean?"

I nodded.

"Besides, what would my students do without me?"

"Surely perish," I said with a smile. Although we joked, Lenny was a good teacher. He knew and cared about the material and was as passionate as any English professor I'd ever met. Yet his teaching philosophy was different, easygoing. If he failed someone, it was because they hadn't shown up. Almost any other reason was off the table. The students loved him for that, flocked to his classes, forgot their assignments, and left feeling good about themselves anyway.

My philosophy was pretty much the opposite. If my students returned, it was because they liked the challenge, liked earning an A, liked knowing it was the equivalent of a gold star. And we had fun. Despite the seriousness of the course work, I could be a little bit awkward, and no matter how hard I tried, it showed sometimes in my classes.

Lenny turned down the tree-lined lane to the bed and breakfast. The Candlelight Inn looked as stunning as it did at night, minus the lights and candles. In the daylight, I could see its proximity to the bluff. Behind the house was nothing but blue sky, a curtain behind a picture of a well-cared-for home.

"Do you smell that?" Lenny asked.

I nodded. "I thought I was imagining things again."

The smell of maple syrup and bacon welcomed us as we got out of the car and approached the door. Belle and Kim greeted Lenny as we stepped inside. Belle wore a black duster that would have dragged like a steam-punk wedding train on me. On her, though, it hung the way it would have on a mannequin, accentuating her tall frame. Kim wore a dark sweater and red-plaid mini-skirt. She *looked* jazzy—and young.

"Well, aren't you adorable," said Belle as I took off my coat.

"How did you get your hair to do that?"

I didn't know how to respond. "Thank you" didn't quite seem appropriate. "It's naturally curly. I just put it in a clip."

"I always wanted curly hair." She tossed her hair over her shoulders.

"Are you kidding?" said Kim. Her dark hair was cut in a bob with perfect, straight bangs. "Women would kill for hair like yours."

Lenny laughed. "Yeah, I couldn't see you in curly hair, Belle. That would just be wrong."

Wrong? The word was as annoying as *adorable*. But I chose not to let it bother me. I was eager for the afternoon concert, not to mention the morning's brunch. From the smells coming from the kitchen, I knew it would be delicious. "No Alyssa this morning?" I said, looking for a place to put my coat.

"I think she ran upstairs for something, but she's making a wicked breakfast. Super gourmet," said Kim.

"Nice," said Lenny, taking my coat. "I'll find a place for this."

"Do you know where the restroom is?" I asked.

"Someone's in the bathroom down here, but there's another one at the top of the stairs to the right," said Kim.

I thanked her and walked up the staircase, which was festooned in juniper and holly. The house was a towering two-story, and the stairs went on forever. On the landing was a table with lots of family pictures: parents, grandparents, in-laws, and a younger version of the fair-haired Alyssa or perhaps a sister, her eyes arrestingly beautiful. Above the table hung a gorgeous tapestry of Copper Bluff. It looked old, and I wondered if the land or the house itself had been passed down through generations. It wouldn't have surprised me. I'd heard many stories of families who had been here for years, the same names cropping up all over the countryside.

Down the hallway, to my right and left, were rooms with gold knobs, some with fringed keys. I turned to the right, finding the kind of pale-pink bathroom you'd expect to see in a classic Victorian house. It was replete with pictures of ladies in hats, all sizes and colors, and a claw-foot tub.

As I shut the door, I could hear voices in the room next door. Then I heard a giggle. I wondered who it could be, since the only girls I knew staying in the house were Kim and Belle, and they were downstairs. Maybe it was Alyssa. Kim said she was upstairs, and she hadn't greeted us at the door.

As I washed my hands, I glanced at my reflection in the mirror. *Adorable. That's something you'd call a two-year-old.* I was a sophisticated woman. I'd graduated summa cum laude. I spoke a second language. I …. A squeal interrupted my thoughts, and I quickly wiped my hands and opened the door.

As I dashed toward the room on my left, I realized too late that the squeal was one of delight. Miles, the bass player, was holding a woman very close and kissing her neck. I recognized at once it was the employee with the tattoo.

"Oh, I'm so sorry," I said. The couple separated.

Miles looked vaguely amused. "Don't be. I was just satisfying Pen's curiosity. She'd heard musicians make the best lovers."

"I think you're mistaken. I think it's poets," I said.

"Music is a kind of poetry, wouldn't you say?"

I shrugged. "Well, Bob Dylan did win the Nobel Prize for Literature."

Alyssa joined the group. She was visibly upset. "What's going on in here? Penelope, you're supposed to be downstairs, frosting the cinnamon rolls."

Her anger had no effect on Pen. She and Miles shared a secret smile. "Duty calls," she said and skipped down the stairs. Alyssa was quick on her heels.

I turned to leave and had descended only a few stairs when Miles caught up with me.

"Emmeline, right?" His voice was deep. It was the kind of voice you heard on the radio, the kind you remembered.

I nodded. I would have kept walking, but he stood on the step in front of me.

"That is a lovely name. I bet you hear that all the time. I bet you hear how lovely you are."

Normally I would have laughed it off. I was no good at flirting, and his come-on was over the top. But after the *adorable* comment, I just stood there, letting his words soak in. *Lovely.* Now there's a compliment any woman could appreciate.

"Damn, Miles, you got Em blocked in there. Move out of the way. She's hungry!" Lenny also had a deep voice, and it was all that was needed to break the split-second spell. His furrowed brow at the bottom of the steps didn't hurt either.

Miles did move, but not before flashing me a reckless smile. I could see why Pen had been giddy upstairs. He had rock-star appeal that probably made the ladies flock to him after a performance.

When I met Lenny at the bottom of the steps, he promptly took my hand and led me to the front parlor. Shocked by the gesture, I didn't say a word. Now didn't feel like the right time to make a joke, especially with Belle looking on.

Connected to the formal dining area, the room that had been stocked with crackers and cheeses last night was now brimming with brunch items. On the sideboard were Mason jars filled with fruit smoothies, labeled with our names in cursive handwriting. The straws were red and green striped and oh so festive. I took a long sip of my drink, contemplating the dynamics of the visiting quartet.

I decided Miles was the leader, despite Belle's strong presence. He had that *it* quality that was hard to describe but easily sensed. Maybe he didn't belong in the classroom. Last night I'd thought he just had a big ego, but today I saw him differently. The group deferred to him because of his talent, presence, or attitude—I wasn't sure which. Maybe all three. Even Belle, who was powerful in her own right, knew this. Her jests went only so far. Josh, who was the co-owner of the music studio, seemed more like Miles's employee. From what I'd overheard, I concluded that he conducted the daily operations and worked long hours. Both he and Miles revered Kim, the young virtuoso, and pitched the studio to her whenever they could. To have the talented Kim Young associated with the studio would be incredibly advantageous, a major selling point.

"You're thinking something," said Lenny. "What is it?"

I turned to him. "It's so interesting, isn't it? The different personalities that come together to play one thing, like a song? It must be nice to belong to a group like that."

"It's pretty cool. Kind of like having a second family."

I sipped my drink, nodding. "I was thinking that very same thing last night. Were you and Belle good friends? Or, I mean, *are you*?"

He set his empty glass on the mirrored tray. "That's okay. We're still friends, but she's definitely a bit more … polished than she used to be. Maybe that's just how it goes when you teach at a big university."

"Maybe," I said. I didn't want to say anything negative about his childhood friend, but she did come off as a little pretentious. She was certainly more self-involved than either of us.

"Whose ready for breakfast?" asked Alyssa, gliding into the front parlor.

"There's more?" said Tad Iverson, who must've arrived before we did. "The mini muffins and smoothie filled me up."

"Not me," said Belle. "I'm starving."

I glanced at her plate. It was littered with two muffin wrappers and a cantaloupe rind. She was probably one of those women who could eat whatever she wanted and not gain a pound. How fitting.

If the rest of the house was pretty, the dining room was gorgeous. The table, decorated with an elaborate winter centerpiece, went on forever. It seated twelve, and this morning the diners would be Lenny and me, Miles, Kim, Belle, Josh, Tad, Alyssa, and Eric. I took a chair next to Lenny, who poured me coffee. I sipped it gingerly, savoring the gourmet roast, while the others took their seats. Belle sat on the other side of Lenny, and Miles took the head of the table, to my right.

Pen, Miles's kissing partner, was helping to carry various dishes to the table. She must be working all weekend because she'd been here last night, too. She carried a large tray of smoked meats from the kitchen: sausage patties, chorizo, and bacon. Alyssa followed with silver trays of scrambled eggs and pancakes. When Pen stopped short, Alyssa bumped into her, knocking a pancake from the plate. Alyssa, perhaps still angry from the incident upstairs, glared at Pen.

"Please be more careful, Penelope."

"It's *Pen*," she shot back. "Only my dad calls me Penelope."

Alyssa smiled patiently. It was the same smile I gave students who showed up the last week of class after not attending all semester.

"These are so good," said Josh, who sat across from me. He took another bite of pancake. "What kind of syrup is this?"

Alyssa placed the salt and pepper shakers on the table. "It's real maple syrup. We're so used to the artificial kind, we don't even know what maple syrup tastes like."

"Everything is delicious," I agreed. "Thank you for inviting me."

"I knew you'd like another opportunity to peruse the library," she said with a wink.

Kim, chewing thoughtfully on a slice of bacon, said, "I wish I could say I was a reader. I'm not. I admit it." She shrugged her shoulders and took another slice from the tray. "Books always put me to sleep."

Miles let out a laugh. "This is why I like students. They speak the truth! I'm so tired of hearing academics gush over this book or that."

Kim giggled. She was pleased with his approval. But to the rest of us, his comment felt like a personal dig, and Lenny and I shared a look. Before either of us could respond, however, Tad beat us to it, his ruddy complexion turning blotchy. I had a feeling he was the easily agitated type but had learned to control his emotions because of his position as department chair.

"That's a heck of a statement for a man in your position to make," said Tad. He took a breath. "Books are the lifeblood of any university."

Miles set down his fork. "*My* position? I'm a guitar player and songwriter. What do I care about books?"

"You're also a college professor, a fact you often conveniently forget," said Belle.

Miles leaned back. "We can't all be academic conformists. Some of us are trying to create something authentic."

The table fell silent. The retort was meant for Belle, but all of us who taught at the university felt its sting. My blood grew hot; I could remain silent no longer.

"If that's the way you feel, Miles, you should quit," I said. "It's self-centered teachers like you who give academia a bad name. No one needs your attitude, least of all your students. Some of us are trying to influence the next generation in a positive way."

"Tell me, Emmeline, when did telling the truth become a negative thing?" asked Miles.

"When the narcissistic version of it fell from your mouth," I shot back.

Miles grinned. "Well, you are a little spitfire, aren't you? I had no idea."

"Here are the cinnamon rolls!" exclaimed Alyssa. She was happy for the interruption, which brought the argument to a halt.

Pen carried in a gilded platter of glazed goods, and Alyssa stood to help dish them out. "These are so hot. Let's start here." She heaped a gooey roll on Belle's plate.

"Don't just stop at one, sister," said Belle. "Let's have another."

I stabbed my sausage. I was really starting to dislike her.

MILES WAS THE FIRST TO finish breakfast. He'd eaten in a hurry, and I wondered if my comments had hit home. He'd acted unconcerned at the time, but now he looked out of sorts and slightly pale. His ornate chair squeaked against the hardwood floor, and he wiped his brow with the back of his hand. "Damn, that chorizo was spicy, wasn't it?"

I didn't think so, but then again I was a fan of spicy food.

"I need a glass of water," he said and headed to the sideboard table, which held a pitcher of ice water.

Lenny turned to me. "What an ass," he whispered. "I'm glad you said what you did."

"He made me so mad," I said. "I had to speak my mind."

"Are you guys talking about Miles?" said Belle, leaning over Lenny.

I nodded.

"He's not as bad as he seems. He likes to shake things up. It's just part of his … mystique." She stood. "The girls love him. He has his own following at our concerts."

I remained silent, unwilling to excuse his behavior simply because of his popularity.

"Come on, Em," said Lenny. "Let's go to the library. You can check out the books."

"I'll be there in a minute. I'm going to finish my coffee."

"You're an addict. You know that, don't you?" said Lenny.

I pointed to his empty cup. "So are you."

He and the others left the table, and I remained behind with Alyssa and Eric. I asked Alyssa if she needed help clearing the dishes, but she pointed to her husband and said that's what he was for. She also motioned to Pen, who entered the room.

I wandered through the connecting front parlor, deliberately stalling. I didn't want another run-in with Miles, and I knew he would be in the library. Today was too important to get into another argument. I could play nice, couldn't I? I hadn't spent so much time with my books that I didn't recognize the value of keeping the peace.

I was looking out the lace-covered window in the front parlor when I heard a voice behind me.

"I'm sorry about what I said in there. You were right to call me out."

I turned around. Miles was standing close. "It was nothing," I said, letting the curtain drop.

"I was a jerk. Forgive me."

I bet those lines had worked on countless numbers of fans. "Nothing to forgive," I said. "I can get a little passionate about teaching."

"I can see that. But not all teachers are like you." He squinted and turned away from the window. I felt my brow crease in question.

"Migraines. They've plagued me for years. I feel one coming on."

"Let's sit down," I said, moving toward the small settee. Instead of taking a chair, he joined me on the settee. He wasn't a large man, so there was room for us both. Still, he sat close enough that I felt uncomfortable. I wedged into the crook of the seat. "Maybe you should go lie down before the concert. It might help your headache."

He nodded toward the stairs. "You want to come upstairs and join me?"

I knew he was joking, but the look in his eye was so odd that the suggestion frightened me. I wondered if he was on something. I had heard Lenny talk about musicians who thought drugs enhanced their performance. Even some poets and writers thought so. Maybe that was the case here.

My answer was a forced laugh. I didn't want to be the cause of any more disagreements. I stood and moved toward one of the oil paintings on the wall, but he followed me. He reached for me, and his hand caught my hair. He undid my clip, and my curls fell down. I jerked away.

"You ... you are my Aphrodite. You entrance me with your beauty."

Aphrodite was the goddess of love and beauty in Greek mythology. She was an inspiration to poets, writers, musicians, and artists—and apparently Miles. Although I enjoyed art, music, and literature, I couldn't see the resemblance.

He hooked my waist with his hand and tried pulling me

close. I could feel his heavy breath on my face. Though small, he was surprisingly strong. My reaction was quick, and I gave him a push. "Get away from me," I yelled.

He stumbled into a table, knocking down several glass figurines, which shattered on the hardwood floor. He followed after, landing flat on his back.

"Em! What happened?" Lenny and the others stood at the doorway.

"This jerk thought he could get handsy with me." I was still shaking with anger.

Lenny came to my side and put an arm around my shoulder. I was trembling. "God, I'm sorry. I thought you were finishing your coffee."

Kim bent down next to Miles on the floor. She shook his shoulders. "Miles. Miles!" She spoke to the group, still in the doorway. "He's not waking up."

Tad assessed the situation with a quick glance. He took out his cellphone and dialed 911.

Only then did I move toward Miles. I started chest compressions and mouth-to-mouth, a first-aid class coming back to me all at once. I frantically pumped the chest and blew air into the mouth of the man who, minutes ago, had almost assaulted me. But it was no use. I dropped onto the floor beside him.

Kim looked at me in disbelief. "I think you killed him."

Chapter Six

—

Kim was right: the reluctant professor was dead. But I couldn't have killed him. Although I had reacted swiftly, I was a petite woman. I wasn't strong enough to kill Miles, and he hadn't hit his head on anything but the floor. How could have I exerted enough force to kill him?

I stood. I needed to get away from the body.

"Em didn't do anything. All she did was defend herself," said Lenny.

"Lenny's right. He grabbed for me a couple of times. All I did was give him a shove." I heard myself saying these words with conviction, but suddenly I felt dizzy and didn't trust my feet. The next thing I knew, Lenny's arm was supporting me, leading me to the couch.

"Are you okay?" he said.

It was as if his voice was coming from the end of a tunnel, and I tried to focus hard to hear what he was saying. I nodded.

"Maybe a glass of water?"

While Lenny went to get me a drink, the room whirred with action, but I felt detached. Belle or Josh must have fetched the innkeepers, because Alyssa and her husband, Eric, rushed in the room. They had been washing dishes in the kitchen and hadn't heard the commotion.

"Oh my god! What happened? What's he doing on the floor?" asked Alyssa. Then she looked at me. "And what's she doing on the couch?"

"I've called an ambulance," Tad Iverson said. "Miles isn't breathing."

Kim sat beside his lifeless body, crying. Belle joined her on the floor and held her hand.

Lenny brought in a glass of water, and I thanked him and took a long drink. I tried to shake off the fog that had enveloped my head.

"Emmeline," said Alyssa, "what happened?"

"Miles made a pass at me," I explained. "I gave him a push, and he fell. I don't know why he's not breathing. I didn't hit him that hard."

"He can't be gone … he can't be!" said Kim. Emotion overcame her all at once, her shoulders shaking with sobs. "How did this happen?" She turned to me with a look of confusion. "How could you?"

"For the last time," Lenny said, "Em didn't do anything. Look at her. She doesn't have the strength."

I wanted to say that my strength had surprised me, that I didn't realize I had it in me, but now wasn't the time. The police would be arriving any minute, and Lenny was seething with anger. The implication that I was a murderer seemed to be more offensive to him than me, or maybe he felt compelled to defend me against the accusation. Either way, the tone of his voice put a stop to further finger pointing.

"Should I try?" asked Eric. Kim nodded, and Eric kneeled beside Miles to check his pulse. No sooner had he touched his wrist than a loud knock sounded at the front door. It opened, and Officer Beamer from the Copper Bluff Police appeared in the doorway along with my former student Sophie Barnes.

"Stand back please, sir," said Officer Beamer. "We'll take it from here." The EMTs rushed in behind him, surrounding

Miles. Minutes passed as they worked to revive him. Although they scrambled to administer injections and hook up a defibrillator, it was no use. One of the medics looked at Beamer and shook his head.

Officer Beamer was a solid man with straight shoulders that belied his age, which was nearing seventy. Only the gray streaks of hair above his ears and wrinkles near his eyes revealed his years.

"We need somebody over here, too," said Lenny to a passing paramedic.

Officer Beamer stared in my direction with real concern.

"Somebody assist Ms. Prather. Now," he said. The paramedic flew to my side.

"Professor Prather! Are you okay?" asked Sophie Barnes. A detective on the police force, she'd graduated from the university with a degree in criminal justice and had been one of my best literature students.

"Absolutely fine, Sophie," I said, trying to sit up. The paramedic held out her hand to stop me.

"We have evidence of shock over here. Her pupils are dilated, Lieutenant." Another EMT with a medical bag joined the medic examining me. They took my blood pressure and felt my pulse before asking more questions.

"Really, I'm fine," I said. "I just felt a little dizzy and had to sit down."

"I thought she was going to faint," added Lenny.

"Good god, I wasn't going to faint." I was incensed by the accusation. I had just flattened a man who tried to grope me—and given him CPR. Obviously I was above fainting under duress.

"I caught her," Lenny said, ignoring me.

The EMTs continued their examination. "Slightly elevated heart rate. Blood pressure ... slightly elevated. Temperature, normal. Do you want us to take her in?"

"Please, I'm okay," I said, sitting up. "I was just shocked ... by the death."

"I have a hard time believing you're okay, Ms. Prather, but fine," said Beamer. "If you say you don't need to go to the hospital, then you don't need to go to the hospital. You can stay here, for questioning."

"She's the first one I'd question, Officer," Kim said. Her sadness had quickly turned to suspicion.

"Emmeline was the only one in the room with Miles when he died," Belle explained. "He was on the floor like this when we came in."

"Em didn't do anything wrong," said Lenny. "The guy was all over her. I saw him try to block her in on the stairs earlier."

Officer Beamer was known for his investigative acumen. I trusted him to come to the right conclusions. "Are you the owners of the inn?" he asked Eric and Alyssa. They both nodded. "Is there a place we might go to take statements?"

"Of course," said Alyssa, moving back into her role as hostess. "The library is just across the hall."

"We'll let the medics finish their work here. Officer Barnes, you're in charge."

Sophie gave him a professional nod, looking a lot less like the student from literature class and more like a seasoned professional. She directed the investigators as Alyssa led the group into the library.

Painted with streaky sunlight, the library was brighter than it had been Friday evening. The fire still crackled and snapped, but the heavy brocade curtains were open, revealing floor-to-ceiling windows and French doors that opened to the wraparound porch. Now the room looked even larger than I guessed, and I wished for such a library someday. But with my meager salary, I would need a library card if I wanted access to a collection this posh.

I tripped over the rug as I approached one of the couches, and everyone looked in my direction. I waved off their concern but still felt a bit woozy. I wondered why. It wasn't like me to lose my cool. If anything, I became more alert under pressure, not less. Yet I could be a little clumsy, especially with a room full of people watching.

Officer Beamer asked some general questions about what we were doing here and the events leading up to the breakfast. Tad Iverson answered most of them, as he was the one orchestrating the holiday series on campus. Plus he was chair of the Music Department, a position of authority. Belle spoke for the quartet, assuming the new role as leader. When it came time for me to explain the moment before Miles's death, Beamer asked everyone to leave, saying that he was ready for individual statements. Lenny was reluctant to go, but I gave him a smile expressing a confidence I didn't really feel, letting him know I would be okay.

"Can I bring you anything, Officer, before I go?" Alyssa asked.

"No, I'm fine, thank you."

Beamer waited until she shut the door before he spoke. "Ms. Prather, trouble seems to find you wherever you go. Even at Christmas."

He sat in one of the wing-back chairs across from me, the light from the sun shining on his face. Although it was only midday, his face gleamed with perspiration, and the heavy crease between his eyes showed.

"It seems that way, I know," I said. "But I have nothing to do with this group of individuals. Well, except Lenny. You know he teaches in the English Department. As Belle explained, he was invited to play with the quartet."

"So, you didn't know the victim. You just met him this morning," Beamer stated.

"I met him last night. Alyssa and Eric hosted an open house for music faculty and the quartet."

He was ready with his notebook. "And who was here last night?"

I rattled off the names of the people I remembered as he wrote them down. I also told him about Miles's interactions with Kim and Pen. "Miles was Kim's academic advisor, and Pen had some sort of relationship with him, but I'm not sure what. I saw them kissing upstairs. Maybe she had something to do with his death."

Instead of writing the possibility in his notebook, he shut it.

"You were in the room with him when he died. How upset were you with him?"

I let out a breath. "Obviously I was upset, but I wasn't *murderous*, if that's what you mean. *I* was the one who gave him CPR."

He tapped his pen on his notebook a couple of times. "You were shaking when I arrived. Your friend said you felt faint."

"Lenny exaggerated. He's overly concerned about me because, well, we're good friends."

He rubbed his chin.

"We kissed once in the library. That's all." I don't know why I felt compelled to explain my love life to Officer Beamer. It had nothing to do with my current predicament.

"The paramedics. They say you showed evidence of shock. Maybe you realized what you had done."

"You and I both *know* I didn't kill him. I shoved him; that's all. He shouldn't have even fallen. You know what I think? I think he was on something. I think my pushing him had nothing to do with his death."

"I won't know anything, Ms. Prather, until I've conducted a thorough investigation. And involuntary manslaughter is a serious crime."

I opened my mouth but couldn't get any words to come out. Our budding friendship meant nothing in this context.

"As far as being on 'something,' do you mean drugs?"

I nodded. "Some kind of drug, yes. He was sensitive to sunlight, which he said was because of an oncoming migraine, but I wonder now if it wasn't an effect of a drug. He didn't look at all well."

"Well, drugs will show up on the initial tox screen. If he was on something, we'll know." He leaned in closer, studying my face. "Are you sure you're feeling all right? If you are, I'm finished with my questions."

"One hundred percent," I said, standing to leave. "Never felt better."

He quirked an eyebrow.

"I mean, except for Miles being dead. I would feel even better, of course, if he were alive." Cringing at my own words, I walked toward the door before I could say anything else to incriminate myself.

Chapter Seven

While Lenny finished his interview, I waited with the others in the family room. The most informal room in the inn, it was located in the back of the house. Its furnishings were more functional than decorative: a curved sectional, recliners, and a flat-screen TV. Although I tried to peek into the parlor to see what was happening with the crime scene, the guard at the door blocked most of my view. Still, I could see people coming in and out of the room, and I knew that my old student, Sophie Barnes, would tell me what was going on if I prodded her. Maybe later, I thought, when the other officers weren't around. I didn't want to get her in trouble.

I slouched into a recliner with one of the books from the Candlelight's collection. I wasn't really in the mood for reading, but with the quartet—now trio—huddled in the corner and Lenny being interviewed, I needed some distraction.

It could have been my imagination, but I felt as if Belle and Kim were talking about me. I thought I heard my name and looked up from my book. I put it down on the dark wooden table beside me. I needed to address the elephant in the room. "I just want you to know how sorry I am that Miles is gone and that I had nothing to do with his death."

Kim started to speak, but Belle grabbed her hand and gave it a squeeze. "We know you didn't, Emmeline. If Lenny says you didn't, then you didn't."

"As women, I'm sure you can appreciate my actions. I couldn't let him paw me like that without doing something," I said.

Kim crossed her arms. "You liked flirting with him earlier, on the steps."

I didn't realize she'd seen us. It probably had looked as if I was enjoying his attention. "He gave me a compliment; that's all. I promise you he was a much different man this morning. He pursued me quite aggressively."

"Miles didn't have an aggressive bone in his body," she said. "Maybe you overreacted so Lenny would come rushing to the rescue. His attention has obviously been elsewhere." She looked at Belle.

"I can assure you I'm perfectly capable of defending myself." Despite my attempt to remain calm, my words came out harsher than I intended. Belle noticed and went into professor mode.

"Hey," she said, standing. Her long vest fell perfectly into place. No one would have guessed the ordeal she had just been through. "Let's go get a cup of coffee, Kim. I need caffeine and could use the company."

I silently watched them leave. So did Tad and Josh, who were also in the living room.

Tad glanced in my direction. "Don't worry about Kim. She's a young grad student who's just lost her mentor. Miles was a cad when it came to women, even back when we went to school together. It's unfortunate, really, that the last impression we have of him proved just that."

I'd forgotten that Tad was a Minnesotan alum. "What will happen with the concert?" I asked.

"Oh, I canceled it. That was the second call I made," he said.

"Any chance it will be rescheduled?" asked Josh. His

question was quiet but concerned.

"I'll try my best. We have another concert scheduled Saturday that we can't push back. We need to get it in before winter break. But we might be able to figure out something for Friday. Losing your guitarist means you'll have to either adjust your arrangements or find a replacement who's a really quick study."

What bad timing. Lenny had been looking forward to this event for a month. Perhaps he could cover Miles's parts? That was up to him or the group, I supposed. There was still the faculty holiday party, but that was impromptu and subject to the whims of the creative writers. If the mood struck them right, music would be preempted by poetry, or intellectual debate. I was reminded of Tad's argument with Miles. Lenny said he thought it was their voices coming from the veranda.

"Last night when we left, we heard Miles arguing with someone outside. Was it you?" I asked Tad.

His brow furrowed. "I don't recall arguing with him. I mean, in a general way, we had our arguments, yes. He was the consummate artist, thinking he should devote more time to his work. I understood that. I really did. Juggling family and work hasn't been easy for me. But I thought it was wrong of him to downplay the university. The quartet wouldn't have half the gigs it does without university connections."

"Hmm. So it must have been someone else with him on the veranda," I said. I glanced in Josh's direction.

"Hey, don't look at me," he said. "I was inside all night. Ask anyone. Ask Kim."

The way Josh said her name told me he liked her as more than just a friend. He said it intimately, as if she knew his comings and goings, maybe even his secrets. How he felt about Kim's adoration of Miles, I couldn't say. I've known students who have hung on their professor's every word. Perhaps that was the case here.

Lenny appeared in the doorway. "Hey, Em. I'm done. Let's get you home."

I stood.

"How'd it go?" Tad asked Lenny.

"Fine. I know Beamer from before. He asked me a few questions about Miles. You guys knew Miles better, so your interviews will probably be longer."

"Not much better," said Tad. "He changed quite a bit in the last couple of years. He seemed … bitter. More hostile toward the university. But I suppose that's life, right? People changing on you."

"Yeah, maybe," said Lenny.

"I'm going to try to reschedule the concert for next weekend," said Tad, looking over at Josh. "If the group is up to it. Lenny, could you cover Miles's parts?"

"Sure," Lenny said.

"Josh, you okay with that?"

Josh nodded. "You bet."

"We'll talk on Monday," said Lenny, helping me shrug into my coat. "Right now I have to get Em home. See you, Josh."

We walked past the sitting room on our way out. Most of the crime scene investigators had left. Sophie and two others remained. I caught her eye as I walked by, and she gave me a nod. I wanted to call her over, and she would have come, but I couldn't do it with her colleagues looking on. I understood how that would look for her professionally, so I kept walking—straight into Belle.

"Are you guys taking off?" Belle asked Lenny.

He nodded. "I gave my statement to Beamer. He said I could go. How about you?"

"Kim's in there now. I suppose I'll be after her." She put her hands in her pockets. "I just can't believe it. Miles is dead."

"I'm sorry, Belle," Lenny said, giving her arm a quick squeeze. She closed her eyes, and a big fat tear rolled down her cheek. "I know you knew him a lot better than I did."

I wanted to offer my condolences, too, but didn't want to sound insincere. I hardly knew Belle or anyone else in the quartet, and Kim's reaction made it clear that she blamed me for Miles's death. Perhaps the rest of the group did as well.

Lenny and I continued toward the door. Lenny was careful to hold my arm all the way to the car, and I wondered if he thought I might still faint. If anything, though, the blast of cold December air revived my senses, and for the first time in a few hours, I felt normal again. My brain felt as clear as the sky, leaving me to wonder about the circumstances surrounding Miles's death.

When we were on the highway, the Candlelight Inn safely in the distance, Lenny began to talk. "I'm sorry I wasn't there. I had no idea that creep would try anything like that."

"Don't be. It wasn't that big of a deal."

He gave me a look.

"I mean, I know it turned into a big deal when he died, but up until then, I had things under control."

His hands tightened on the wheel. "Still, it pisses me off."

"Well, I wouldn't be too angry. Obviously he got what was coming to him."

"God, Prather. Don't say things like that out loud."

I shrugged. "It's only us. Granted, Miles was self-centered and arrogant, more than a little caddish with women, but that doesn't mean I thought he deserved to die. Someone thought so, though. Someone decided to give him what they saw as his comeuppance. I just wonder who."

"I'm going to pretend I didn't just hear you say that."

"What? You think he just died suddenly at the ripe old age of fifty-something? Obviously, this is murder."

"Come on, Em. It's Christmas."

I looked out the window at the white snow covering the fields. "A very merry murder, then."

TEN MINUTES LATER, LENNY WALKED me into my house and insisted on grabbing me a pillow and a glass of water before he left. After I shooed him off, Mrs. Gunderson, who was on her front porch, kept him another minute.

"Hey Mrs. G," Lenny called out.

"Hello, Leonard," she answered.

Lenny glanced back over his shoulder. "Seriously?"

"She knew it was short for something. I couldn't lie."

"Leonard, I'm making some fudge for the Winter Festival next weekend," she continued. "I hope you can come. Emmeline could use the company." More quietly, she added, "She's shuttered in that house day and night."

Lenny let out a laugh. "I think that's just Em's style. She's kind of a loner."

"Not by choice, dear. Not by choice."

Lenny was still laughing as he let go of my screen door and walked down the steps. But I heard him say, "You can count on me, Mrs. G. I'll be her chaperone."

I leaned back into the pillow, closing my eyes. As if Claudia's efforts weren't sufficient, Mrs. Gunderson was getting in on the matchmaking game. That was all I needed. Mrs. Gunderson was nosy enough without butting into my personal life. She had all sorts of ideas on the way my house should be kept. I'd heard plenty of advice on how to cut my grass and hedges, when to clean my windows and with what, and how many lights to install and when to keep them on. (Her answer was, "All the time.") If she started giving me dating advice, I would have to draw the line. Taking dating suggestions from a seventy-something widow was really just too much. Everyone had a last straw, and that was mine.

Lying on the couch, I let my mind drift from dating to the morning's events. It seemed impossible that a few hours before, a man had died right before my eyes. I knew my shoving him hadn't killed him ... or had it? My stomach did a flip-flop at the possibility. No. There was something wrong with him, something making him act more aggressive than usual. Kim said he didn't have an aggressive bone in his body, and I believed her. Before, his flirting had been hardly serious and even playful, but in that room, alone with him, I'd felt fear.

I sat up and folded the throw, placing it over the edge of the couch. Maybe it wasn't murder; maybe it was drugs.

The preliminary toxicology screen might show he was on something. I could ask Sophie to let me know after the initial results came back. That would clear me of any wrongdoing, not to mention ease the guilt that nettled my mind. She and Beamer would see that he had overdosed on some drug and that I had nothing to do with his death. I nodded. Of course they would.

The thing was, he hadn't acted like a person who had overdosed. He wasn't falling down (well, except when I pushed him), and he wasn't shaking. He appeared in control of his senses. But for some reason, the idea of an overdose stuck in my head. It was the look in his eyes. I shook off the haunting recollection. There was nothing to do now but wait—and grade papers. Glancing at the stack of sixty folders on my coffee table, I realized I didn't feel like doing either one.

Chapter Eight

———

Sundays in Copper Bluff were usually peaceful. However, during the Christmas season, most stores opened early and bustled with activity. Today, all along Main Street, the old-fashioned lampposts glittered with holiday garlands, and store windows popped with colorful lights. The Book Barn, Copper Bluff's downtown bookstore, offered a terrific display of Christmas titles, including *A Christmas Carol*, *Cricket on the Hearth*, and *The Night Before Christmas*, not to mention a stunning assortment of holiday cards with gold-foil envelopes. I stopped and gazed in the window for several minutes before forcing myself to continue toward Café Joe, where Claudia was meeting me. We had agreed to have coffee (or tea, in Claudia's case) at one o'clock.

Café Joe hosted many of the events put on by the English Department, so it was my and Claudia's go-to meeting spot. Located on the corner, Café Joe boasted a great location and an even better atmosphere. Round tables could be arranged just about anywhere for an event, and near the register local goods were displayed, such as pottery, chapbooks, and artwork. Behind the register was a chalkboard featuring the day's specials written in bubble letters with colorful chalk. Even if the college kids who worked there couldn't make the drinks correctly, they still looked appealing.

Claudia was waiting at a table by the front window when I walked in. In a multicolored scarf that went on forever, she looked spectacular. Despite having two young kids at home and an active professional life, she always looked very put together. She glanced up from her chai latte as I approached.

"Hey, Claudia. I'm going to order lunch. Do you want anything?"

She shook her head. "Gene made a huge breakfast this morning. I couldn't eat a thing."

After considering the specials, I decided on the chicken salad croissant and chips. Carrying an oversized mug of black coffee, I returned to the table, where Claudia grilled me about the death of Miles. When I told her I was in the room when he died, she demanded every detail. By the time I'd recounted my story, lunch arrived, and I took a big bite of my croissant, a piece of chicken falling out of my sandwich and onto my plate. Claudia stared at me in surprise.

"It's a wonder you can eat at a time like this," she said.

I dabbed my lips with my napkin. "A time like what?"

"Like this," she said, spreading her arms to indicate the enormity of the situation. "You were the last person to see Miles alive. You flung him to the floor, and now you're a suspect in his death. I know these things, remember. Gene's a lawyer."

I couldn't forget. She wrote about her husband, Gene, and his wandering eye in her poetry. "You aren't suggesting that I was wrong to push him away, are you?" I asked.

She shook her head. "Of course not. If there's anything I know about, it's womanizers, and that womanizer had it coming. What I'm saying is that the police will consider you a person of interest. My advice to you is stay away from the Candlelight Inn."

I considered her words. "How did you say you knew Alyssa, again? Was it from the university?"

"Did you hear a word of what I just said?"

I took a drink of my coffee before answering. "Of course I did, and I completely agree. I was just asking about Alyssa in case I need to … host an event or secure a reservation for a traveling lecturer."

She twisted her hair off her neck and dug in her purse for a pencil. "Uh-huh. Because you organize so many events on campus."

She was right. As a faculty member in my third year, I barely made it to events, skipping as many as possible without showing up on Giles's radar. I was too busy making lesson plans, grading papers, writing proposals, and generally advancing toward tenure to do much else. I admired faculty who juggled much busier schedules than mine. Either they were more committed, or I was less so. I was still deciding on which when Belle and Lenny strolled up to the door.

"Well, if that doesn't just figure," said Claudia, pushing a pencil through her bun.

Despite the dip in my stomach, I aimed for a positive tone. "I really like Belle. She's nice."

She nodded toward the window. "It looks like Lenny does too."

I didn't have time to respond before Lenny and Belle were at the table.

"Hey Claudia. Em, I tried to call you this morning. How are you feeling?" asked Lenny.

Claudia narrowed her eyes. I hadn't told her that I'd felt faint after Miles's death. I didn't want her to assume I couldn't handle the situation. I most certainly could and had. "I feel fine. Perfectly fine."

"I thought you'd be halfway to Minneapolis by now," Claudia said to Belle.

I bit my lip to avoid a smile. Claudia could get away with saying things that the rest of us couldn't.

"They're leaving tonight," said Lenny. "Tad Iverson is trying to hook us up later in the week. Friday, probably. Belle and the rest of the group will be back next weekend."

"Alyssa said we could stay for free. Wasn't that sweet of her?" said Belle.

"Incredibly," said Claudia.

"Mind if we join you?" Lenny asked. He was already grabbing two chairs from a nearby table. "That sandwich looks good."

I cut it in half and put it on a napkin. Sooner or later he would want a taste. "Where's Kim?"

Belle scooted her chair next to mine. "She's pretty shaken up. She's been crying on and off all morning."

"And yet you're here, with Lenny," said Claudia. She smiled so kindly after her observation, it was hard to take it any other way than concerned.

"Josh stuck around in case she needed something," Lenny said.

"I know Miles was Kim's advisor, but was there something more to their relationship?" I asked Belle. "Is that why his death has upset her so much?"

Belle hesitated. "Kim was infatuated with Miles. Sometimes I think she mistook his high regard for her talent as high regard for her charms. I can't say I blame her. She's young and impressionable, and the quartet travels everywhere together. Late nights … you know the story." She looked over the featured coffee drinks on the laminated card propped up in the middle of the table. "And he certainly wasn't the type to dissuade her."

"What do you mean?" I asked.

She put down the card and pulled her long braid over one shoulder. "Miles loved his admirers, and he had plenty. I mean, you just can't change musicians like him. They do what they do for the applause. They feed off it."

"I've known guys like that," said Lenny. He took a bite of the sandwich I had given him. "They get more of a rush from that than the music itself."

"I was waiting for Kim to move on, especially with

graduation drawing near. I guess now she'll have to. You want a latte?" she asked Lenny.

"Nah. Coffee. Black."

She left the table to place their order.

"What about Josh?" I asked. "Do you think he has feelings for Kim?"

"Why would you think that?" Lenny asked. "He seems pretty quiet to me, the type to keep his head down, nose to the grindstone."

Claudia nodded her head. "I saw that, too. The little looks Josh kept giving Kim all night. There's something to that."

"I thought so," I said. "And yesterday morning, when you were giving your statement, he said something that made me think he liked Kim as more than a friend."

Lenny took a chip. "What'd he say?"

I waved away the question. "It wasn't what he said. It was *how* he said it. I could tell he cared for her."

Lenny looked from me to Claudia. "So what if he does like her? What's wrong with that? Josh is only, what, five years older than Kim? Maybe I'm missing the picture here, but I don't see the problem."

I leaned in close to Lenny. "What's wrong is that he might have killed Miles out of jealousy. To get him out of her head for good. There is no better motive for murder."

"I think you mean *worse*," he shot back. "And there's no way Josh murdered Miles. I can't imagine a guy like that killing anyone, especially a friend. Besides, you were with Miles when he died. No one else was in the room."

I leaned back in my chair. "I know."

"If I were you, I'd think about that before I expressed my theories in public. The cops might start pointing fingers at you."

"I told her exactly the same thing," said Claudia.

"Oh, oh? Are we in public now?" I could feel my face getting hot. "I thought I was among friends."

"The café is a public place last time I checked," said Lenny, lifting his eyebrows.

I glared back at him.

"You two," said Claudia, taking her last sip of chai, "have a troubling communication problem. I know, because Gene and I have had one for years. But I have no time to convince you— too much Christmas shopping—and frankly, I'm not in the mood. I'll see you Monday." And with that, she stood and left.

Lenny and I watched her walk out the door.

"That was odd," said Lenny.

I agreed.

"She just loves making a dramatic exit," said Lenny, taking another one of my chips.

"True," I said. If Claudia weren't a poet, she could have been an actress. She had the style and the charisma for the job. "So, could you ask Belle about Kim and Josh?"

He glanced over at the cash register, where Belle was taking the drinks from the barista, and let out a breath. "Fine."

"But be discreet." I imagined him pulling Belle aside in a dark corner, asking her questions about love and relationships. "I mean, not in a discreet place, but in a discreet way. You know what? Just let me ask her."

Belle handed Lenny his coffee before she sat down with hers. "Sorry that took so long. I guess they weren't sure how to make a double soy Frappuccino. What happened to your friend?"

This was why Lenny and I ordered plain coffee. Café Joe had a revolving door of student workers. You couldn't get a decent cappuccino until mid-spring, when the students had been working about a year.

"She had to go," I said.

"Abruptly and without saying goodbye," Lenny added.

We exchanged a smile.

I tried to think of a casual way to bring up Kim and Josh. "I was going to ask you something." I looked out the window at a group of boys walking by, pretending to remember. One of the boys waved, and I turned back toward Belle. "I was wondering about Josh. He's so quiet. Do you know if he's interested in anyone?"

"What do you mean, like dating?" She took a sip of her drink and looked surprised. Obviously she wasn't used to her Frappuccino being concocted quite this way.

I nodded. "Right. Is he dating anyone?"

She glanced between Lenny and me. He had a lopsided grin on his face, and I wondered why.

"I don't think so," she said. "I can ask him for you, though. I'm sure he'd love to go out. You have a certain *je ne sais quoi* that he'd appreciate."

Lenny couldn't wipe the smile off his face. Belle thought I was asking about Josh because I was interested in him romantically. Well, that was okay with me. We were close enough in age; it was a good enough explanation. Maybe it would give me an excuse for hanging around to find out more information. Lenny knew the real reason I wanted to talk to Josh, and that was all that mattered.

"You know, maybe I'll just tag along when Lenny drops you off at the Candlelight. I would like to say goodbye to Josh and Kim anyway."

"Good idea, Prather," said Lenny. Belle nodded, but he was being sarcastic. He didn't want me getting involved in this case, and I understood why. It was the busiest time of the year for us, and our lives didn't need more turmoil. However, ignoring the crime wouldn't make it go away. We understood that better than most people. I needed to know what happened that morning, if not to satisfy my curiosity then to prove my innocence. Although Miles's death hadn't been classified a homicide, I'd bet my Christmas cookies it would be. Someone would be charged with Miles's murder, and it wasn't going to be me. Although the holidays often required compromises, I wasn't willing to spend winter break in a jail cell.

Chapter Nine

———

Despite the macabre circumstances, the drive out to the B&B was incredibly serene. The view from the backseat was uninterrupted blue sky. Far from the packed stores and holiday clamor, it stretched for miles, in all directions without obstruction. Just after moving from Detroit, I'd found the prairie desolate, but not anymore. Three years later, I craved drives like these into the countryside. I wished the circumstances were more favorable, of course. A talented musician had lost his life, which was depressing. The world needed more art and beauty, not less. It was all we could cling to in uncertain times, the songs and stories that would go on playing long after we were gone.

When we approached the Candlelight Inn, the house appeared much as it had the first time I saw it, despite being the scene of a tragedy. The wraparound porch, the intricate peaks of the roof, the gingerbread trim—all the details of the Victorian mansion—had been impeccably restored. Belle and Lenny hurried inside to gather the group's belongings, but I lingered outdoors, mesmerized by the size of the place. I wandered around the perimeter, taking in the view of the bluff. It was staggering from this angle, the house perched upon what had to be the bluff's highest point. Far below was the river, feeding the bottomlands like a never-ending source. It was amazing, really, that a place like this could exist in the middle of South Dakota's flat landscape. I was awed by the elevation and wondered at the danger of living so close to the edge.

When I grew chilly, I walked in and was greeted by Alyssa. Although her face appeared drawn with fatigue, she was the consummate hostess. She wore a trendy sweater that revealed toned shoulders, and her hair shone under the lighted entry chandelier. She took my coat, telling me that Lenny and Belle had gone upstairs to retrieve Jazz Underground's suitcases. I gravitated toward the front parlor. It was hard not to stare at the spot where Miles had lain on the floor. I shivered, and Alyssa asked me if I wanted my coat back.

"Sure," I said. "And you know what? Maybe I'll wait in the library by the fireplace. I'd love to take another look at your collection."

"Come on," she said. "I just put on a fresh log." Her sweater flared behind her as she led the way.

The most noteworthy room in the house, the library was certainly regal. There was no other word for it. Filled with leather-bound books as well as classic paperbacks, it invited guests to sit down and relax. If you preferred to make music, you could try your hand at the lovely baby grand piano or the guitar leaning in the corner. And if you didn't like either of those options, you could play one of the card or board games displayed on a separate shelf.

"You must be an avid reader. This is quite a room," I said, motioning toward the bookshelves.

Alyssa chuckled. "I read some, true, but with the college in town, most of my guests are academics. The library's more for their benefit than mine. I purchase some at the campus bookstore, and most of those are downright cheap. Just don't tell my guests. They think they're rare. I do have a lovely gardening section, though, that I'm proud of." She pointed to three shelves in the middle of a bookcase.

I moved closer to inspect the books she indicated: guides to flowers, herbs, and healthy eating. Growing things was in the blood of these Midwesterners. I couldn't grow a single tomato plant; it was as if fruits and vegetables detected my sweet tooth and saw it as a betrayal. Now Mrs. Gunderson, she was a natural. Her backyard was a cornucopia of vegetables, flowers, and foliage. Her food garden encompassed half her backyard.

"I have to check on my cake. I'll be right back," said Alyssa.

"No rush. I could entertain myself for days in here." And I could, especially with no one to hurry me along. Gilded in gold, the hardcover books were exquisite. I wondered if anybody had read them; they were in that good of shape. Reaching for a less expensive paperback, I heard a noise. I peeked around the bookshelf to see who or what had caused the disturbance. Lenny and Belle stood at the bottom of the staircase, Belle's arms around his neck. Paralyzed by something like fear, I watched them embrace. Belle's voice was muffled. Perhaps she was saying goodbye or that she would miss him. I didn't stick around long enough to hear. My need to get away was surprisingly intense. I drifted toward the French doors, looking for a crack in the atmosphere to swallow me whole.

Alyssa told Eric to bring the luggage to the group's van. Then she walked into the library and glanced toward the bookshelves. "Emmeline?"

With the mention of my name, Lenny and Belle entered, too.

"Yes?" I said. My voice emerged as a squeak. I cleared my throat.

"What are you doing back there?" asked Lenny.

He moved toward me, but I advanced before he could come any closer. Having no desire to let on that their embrace had bothered me, I recovered quickly. "I was admiring the view of the bluff. It's breathtaking from here." I refocused on my reason for coming, trying to put the encounter I'd witnessed between Belle and Lenny out of mind. "Where's Josh?"

"He's on his way down," said Belle.

"And Kim?" I said. "Is she doing any better?"

"Somewhat. At least she has her things packed," said Belle.

"Hey," said Josh, entering the room in two long strides. Although he was older than Lenny or me, he looked young. Maybe it was his grungy clothing or lean build. He was tall but not lanky, with muscular arms—perhaps from drumming or manual labor. His straight hair was combed forward and covered his forehead.

"Hi, Josh," I said. "I'm glad I got a chance to say goodbye before you left." I hadn't talked to Josh much, probably because of his reticence. He stuck to himself and didn't really speak unless spoken to, which made it hard to approach him. I seized the first idea that popped into my head.

"I love Poison," I said, pointing at his shirt. "Very cool band."

"Yeah?" said Josh. He had a kind smile. "They're not the most popular group. But I like the oldies."

I didn't know if the songs of a 1980s hair band counted as the oldies, but I didn't argue. At least I knew who they were. "Oh, I listen to everything," I said. "Even Poison."

Lenny let out a snort. "Name one song."

"I didn't know there was going to be a test," I said, stalling until something came into my head. "There are so many. Well, I have to go with the ever popular 'Nothin' but a Good Time.' You can't go wrong with that classic."

"You're funny, you know that?" said Josh. "You remind me of my English teacher from high school."

"I get that a lot," I said. Josh was easier to talk to than I'd imagined. Despite his quiet demeanor, he was friendly and down-to-earth.

Belle motioned toward the entryway. "I think Eric needs help with the luggage, Lenny. I'll help, too."

Belle thought I wanted to be alone with Josh, to inquire

about his dating status, which was fine by me. It gave me more time to figure out his relationship with Kim. It also gave me a reason for hanging around asking questions.

"So, the concert will be rescheduled," I said after they'd left.

He nodded. "It's going to be different without Miles, but the college gave us an honorarium. We need to fulfill it—whatever that takes. And we're thinking Lenny can fill in for Miles."

Unlike the rest of the group, he didn't have the university to fall back on. He depended on the studio and its success. No wonder Miles chose him for a partner. Not only was he an excellent drummer, he was also a dedicated manager and hard worker. He was probably much better suited to the business aspect of the studio than Miles or some other artist who might struggle to balance art and industry.

"It wouldn't be smart to offend Tad Iverson or the university by ditching out on our obligation," he continued. "We play a lot of college events."

It was time to work in one of my transitions. "You know who also seems smart? Kim. She's a grad student, right?"

"She's twenty-six," he said a little too quickly. "But yeah, she's very smart. She's in grad school for music performance."

His answers told me he cared for her, but I wondered how much. Obviously a group like Jazz Underground would be close. They played events together all the time and practiced late into the evenings. But had their friendship turned into something more serious? That's what I wanted to find out. "You and Kim are friends?"

He shrugged. "We run in the same circles. We have some of the same friends."

I glanced toward the foyer, where Lenny was back from hauling luggage. I needed to try another angle. "Tad said he might reschedule the concert for Friday. Do you think Kim will be up for it?"

"I hope so. I hope we can talk her into coming back. She might not want to, especially to this B&B, you know? But Alyssa is comping us a weekend, so we can't afford to pick another place to stay."

I nodded. "I understand her reluctance to return. She and Miles seemed very close."

"Honestly, it's better for her that he's gone. Relationship-wise. I don't want to diss him, because he was a fantastic musician, but he wasn't the type to get involved with. Women, fans ... Miles flirted with everyone." He gestured toward me. "Obviously."

"I observed that firsthand," I said.

"Kim did, too. But she still thought the guy hung the moon." He shook his head. "I didn't get why she was interested in someone like that and not a regular guy."

It didn't take much imagination to see Josh was the regular guy he meant. "Maybe with Miles gone, she'll be able to move on to someone more ... suitable."

He nodded. "Yeah, maybe. She probably won't be dating anyone for a while, though."

For a while. With those words, Josh revealed his hope to date Kim in the future. He wouldn't admit it, but his feelings were as clear as the hurt on his face. He might not have Miles's star power or good looks, but he was a solid drummer and a nice guy. What Josh didn't understand, and I did, was that students are easily impressed—and influenced. To have a guy like Miles say you had talent was the best compliment of all. It was no mystery to me how she'd become infatuated with him.

Lenny indicated he was ready to leave, and I prepared for more hugging. Thankfully there was none. We simply said our goodbyes to the group and got into Lenny's car. Lenny mentioned Kim and her swollen eyes. Could I believe how bad she looked? She must've cried all night long. I nodded in agreement but was having a hard time talking. It was silly, really, that I should be so put out by one little hug. He and Belle were childhood friends; they were close. But we were close, too.

When we reached Main Street, a couple of blocks from my house, Lenny cleared his throat. I realized then we'd been driving in silence. "Em, what's wrong? You haven't said two words since we left. Was it something Josh did? Did he say something?" He sounded worried.

"No," I said, grabbing my purse. "Nothing like that. I talked to him about Kim. He definitely has a crush on her, whether he admits it or not. He talked a little about the studio. I think he pretty much runs the place."

"So, that's good. You found out what you wanted to know." He pulled up alongside my house and put the car in park. I had no choice but to meet his eyes. They were so dark they were almost navy and awaited my response. But I couldn't admit the embrace bothered me. Instead I put on a mitten.

He reached for the other mitten and held it hostage. "*I* haven't done something, have I?"

"It's nothing," I said. "It doesn't matter."

"It must be something, or I wouldn't have to play twenty questions. It's not like you to hold back."

He was right. I was never shy about saying what was on my mind. "I saw you and Belle embrace at the bottom of the stairs."

He returned my mitten. "Is that what this is about? I guessed as much earlier, but then after seeing you and Josh in the library, I wasn't so sure. You seemed fine."

"That's because I *am* fine," I said.

"I'm going to level with you," Lenny said, facing me. "I don't know why Belle hugged me back at the inn. We haven't been close for years. I assume she's more broken up about Miles's death than she lets on. She's trying to be strong, I guess, for the group."

"*Embraced.*"

"Semantics, really?" Lenny said.

I crossed my arms.

"Prather, I—"

A knock on the window startled us both. It was Mrs. Gunderson.

"I'm sorry, Mrs. Gunderson," I said as I rolled down my

window. "I didn't see you there."

"Of course you didn't, Emmeline. You were too busy arguing."

"Oh, we weren't arguing, Mrs. G," said Lenny. "We were just debating the definition of the word 'embrace.' Em clearly doesn't understand that an embrace requires reciprocation."

"Oh, there was reciprocation, all right. A big healthy dose of it," I said.

"I'm sure you're overreacting, dear," said Mrs. Gunderson. "Leonard is a good boy, and you're so dramatic. However, that's not why I came over." She pulled her muslin scarf down around her ears. "After you're finished, I'm ready for you to hang my lights. It gets dark quickly, and I go to bed early. But take your time."

"Take your time" wasn't a phrase in Mrs. Gunderson's vocabulary. I understood it to mean, "Do it right now." Lenny laughed, and I cracked a smile as I watched her totter away. "I'd better go. She can be quite adamant when she wants something done."

"I could stay and help. I'm pretty good with outdoor illumination."

"Thanks, but I'll be fine."

He touched my arm before I opened the door. "You know it didn't mean anything, right? I've known Belle all my life."

I searched his eyes. He wasn't lying, so why did I still feel unsure?

"I know," I said, trying to convey more conviction than I felt. It must have worked because after a moment, he gestured toward my lap.

"Don't forget your ear muffs," he said with a smile. "You'll get frostbite."

I put them on. "See you Monday."

I walked to Mrs. Gunderson's house, which, like mine, was a tiny bungalow with a front porch. Only a shared pathway divided our lots. All the houses on Oxford had alley access, so if residents had garages, they were out back. My garage was an old carriage house with cedar shingles, but Mrs. Gunderson's was new with two stalls. Tucked inside was a brand-new Cadillac that she never drove. How Mrs. Gunderson had money for such a car I couldn't say. Perhaps her husband had been wealthy or maybe her parents. I knew her family owned land in the vicinity and had farmed the area for a hundred years.

Greeting me with two strands of colored lights, Mrs. Gunderson directed their placement. She wanted them to go around the two front pillars at the top of the steps, which sounded easy enough until she handed me a box of tacks and told me to make sure each light faced outward. Every few inches, I would have to tack the strand in place, making sure not to hit the wire, as I went around and around the frozen column. Mrs. Gunderson peered at me from her cozy living room, tapping on the window with her long, manicured finger if something looked wrong or wasn't spaced correctly. Her dog, Darling, barked. All I could do was smile and grit my teeth.

Afterwards, she invited me inside for cookies and hot cocoa, a drink like none other. It was rich and creamy with whipped cream on top and shaved chocolate, too.

"This is the best," I said, wiping my mouth on a holiday napkin. Her table was dressed with a lacy cloth and her mugs painted with holly berries. At her feet was Darling, the fuzzy white friend that followed her everywhere. "I bet your kids love to come home."

She folded her hands neatly in front of her. "You know I have two sons, and I couldn't ask for better boys. But their wives ...." She tsked in disapproval. "They don't like to visit, even on holidays."

Sipping the hot liquid, I imagined she could be the mother-in-law every wife dreaded. Her thoughts were outdated, offensively so, and she didn't have the good sense to keep them to herself. But she was starting to grow on me anyway. Maybe it was her baking, or maybe Claudia was right: maybe it was sheer loneliness. No matter the reason, the holidays had brought us together more times than usual this year.

"Well, they must be crazy," I said, holding up what was left of my cookie. "I'd travel to Fiji to get one of these."

Mrs. Gunderson smiled. "Relationships can be hard. Sometimes you have to compromise."

I took the last bite. I had a feeling we weren't talking about her sons anymore.

She handed me another sweet, a perfect tree with green sprinkles. I tried in vain to resist. Besides, it was practically miniature. She called it a spritz cookie.

"Oh, I know what you're thinking. I'm just an old lady with old-fashioned ideas. But I know what I'm talking about. I was married to Bill for forty years, and I was just as pigheaded as you are. Thankfully, not as dramatic."

I started to say that I was not pigheaded, but she hushed me. "The important thing to know is that sometimes compromise is worth it. Not every time and not with everyone. But with that one special person? Think about it."

I decided not to respond. Discussing my love life with Mrs. Gunderson was one place I wasn't willing to go—yet.

After washing down the cookie with hot cocoa, I stood to leave before she could press another on me. I had a terrible sweet tooth, and everybody knew it, Mrs. Gunderson most of all.

Darling met me at the door. The white mop was happy to see me leave. He must have remembered I was Dickinson's owner.

I grabbed my coat off the ornate hall tree. *Now I know what the phrase "neat as a pin" means*, I thought as I shrugged it on. Everything was in its place; everything looked orderly. Each doily had a figurine placed perfectly in the center. Dust didn't have a chance here. There wasn't a book or magazine to distract her from her housework.

Turning to leave, I remembered the question I'd wanted to ask her. "You know, Mrs. Gunderson, somebody asked me your first name the other day, and I was embarrassed to admit

I didn't know it."

"That's on purpose, dear. And being an old lady, I'm able to get away with it." She gave me a sly smile, and the powdered skin around her lips creased.

I returned her smile but waited patiently. I wasn't leaving until she told me.

Her narrow, bony shoulders became less rigid as she moved them up and down. "It's Gertrude. A horrible name, but a family one, and so it gets passed down."

"Hey, mine is a family name, too. And Gertrude's not a horrible name. Think of Gertrude Stein. How cool is that?"

She opened the door. "I'm sure I don't know who that is, but unless she's one of your writerly types, she probably dislikes it as much as I do. Those kinds go in for all sorts of odd names. You know what I mean. What do they call them?"

"Pseudonyms."

"That's right. Pseudonyms. Don't slip on the ice there."

"Goodnight, Mrs. Gunderson," I said with a wave, realizing that no matter what her first name, she would always be Mrs. Gunderson to me.

Chapter Ten

Two things went awry early Monday morning: my alarm clock and my plan. Another major disaster had hit the town of Copper Bluff—a snowstorm. It had taken out the electricity sometime in the night, and I awoke to a blinking nonsensical time on my clock. I shook off my sleepiness and padded to the window. The screen was stuffed with snow, making it impossible to assess the severity of the storm from my bedroom window. I walked to the front porch in my pajamas and opened the door to get a better look. A lot of fresh snow had fallen; it was hard to tell how much because the wind had blown through the street, making snow banks appear sharper and deeper than they probably were.

Moving toward the kitchen, I looked at my coffee-cup-shaped wall clock. I had plenty of time before my first class. The problem was I'd planned on waking up early to finish the feedback on my students' drafts of final essays. But I often had difficulty sleeping, especially when something was on my mind, and try as I might, last night I couldn't get Miles's death out of my head.

When I did fall asleep, I had terrible dreams, nightmares,

really. I tortured myself with the idea that I had really killed him. I kept replaying his last moments in my head. Had his head struck something? Was the floor slippery? Had I pushed him *that* hard?

Miles was on the small side of average. He was thin but compact, maybe five feet eight and probably one hundred and sixty pounds. Yet he was still a man, and I should have had a harder time pushing him than I did. Unless I was really that angry, which I wasn't. No, he'd been on some substance that made him an easy target. I was sure of it.

I reset the time on my coffee maker, hit the "on" button, and showered while the coffee brewed. This was a day for function, not fashion, so after toweling off, I layered a long-sleeved shirt with an oversized chenille sweater. With the wind still gusting outside, wool leggings and snow boots would keep me warm. Filling my travel mug, I grabbed my satchel and keys and walked out the door.

The nice thing about living only a few blocks from campus was that I didn't have to worry about shoveling a driveway or starting my car. One quick swipe of the sidewalk, and I was good to go. No matter the snowfall, the university didn't cancel classes, because students lived on campus, in the dorms. There was no excuse not to attend class. The problem was students didn't always understand the rationale behind the rule and skipped classes anyway. Under the circumstances, I kind of hoped some of my students wouldn't show up. I hated seeing their disappointed faces when I didn't have papers to return.

I stomped my boots just before entering Harriman Hall, the snow coming off in white chunks. Despite the storm, the electrical outage, and the incomplete drafts, I was feeling upbeat. There were only a few weeks left of the semester, and I was on the downside of the mountain of work still left to be done. Besides, the Winter Festival was coming up, and I couldn't imagine anything more beautiful than the downtown decorations after several inches of snow.

My positive attitude faded, however, the minute I stepped

into the second-floor hallway. Near my office stood not only Jim Giles but also Officer Beamer. Why couldn't Beamer have reached me at home? Why would he come to my office to seek me out? He knew where I lived. He had even come over once. He must have a reason for being on campus, but what that was, I didn't know.

"Emmeline," Barb, our secretary, called out, "the campus phones are out. Just so you know."

"Thanks, Barb," I said as I ambled down the hall. When I reached my office door, Giles greeted me with a half smile. His eyes blinked rapidly.

"Good morning, Emmeline," he said.

"Ms. Prather," said Beamer, touching the tip of his wool hat. His graying hair peeked out from the sides of it.

"Good morning," I said. "What a surprise, Officer Beamer. Are you here to see Lenny?" I began to unlock my door.

"No, but now that you mention it …."

I turned to Giles to explain. "The guitar player of Jazz Underground passed away over the weekend. A terrible thing. But I didn't know him at all. Not a bit."

"She was just in the room with him when he died," said Beamer.

A passing student stopped and stared in my direction. Giles shook his head. "I find nothing surprises me anymore. I suppose that's the wonder of getting old—or working with the young." With that, he turned and walked into his office.

I led Officer Beamer into my office and turned on the light. "I have to say I'm surprised you came to my office. You must have news that merits upsetting my department chair."

Beamer took off his hat and smoothed his thick, wavy hair. "I thought I'd catch you between classes. You didn't answer your cellphone."

I patted my coat pockets, back pockets, and finally my purse pockets before I found my phone. Although it did have a charge, it was turned to silent. I'd missed three calls: one from my mom, one from Lenny, and one from Officer Beamer.

"I didn't mean to get you in any trouble," he continued.

I motioned toward the seat across from me. "It's okay. Giles just thinks …." I leaned in to whisper. A door connected our offices, and I didn't want him to overhear. "He worries about my preoccupation with solving mysteries. He thinks it distracts me from my real work."

"And does it?"

I thought about that for a moment. "Not really. I mean, literally, the answer would have to be yes, because it keeps me from grading and whatnot, but *literally*? Not a chance. It's a great form of research and analysis."

Beamer studied me. His dark eyes, like onyx, were unwavering. "Ms. Prather, the reason I'm here is because you said you thought Miles was *on* something, like a drug."

I nodded. "That's right. I'm certain of it. Otherwise, why would he have fallen? It doesn't make sense. I'm strong, but not that strong."

"I agree. It doesn't make sense. The thing is, no evidence of drugs was found in the victim's urine or blood."

"You're kidding me," I said. "I'm shocked." Miles had to have been on something to make him act so aggressively. The man might have been a flirt, but he wasn't dangerous. Was he?

Beamer pulled a 3X5 notebook from his coat pocket. "Me too. That's why I'm here. I want to know what transpired in the minutes before the victim's death." He opened to a page full of notes. "Kim Young, the trumpeter? Is that what you call them? Sounds odd. Anyway, she and a couple others said you had an argument with Miles at breakfast. You told him to quit and called him," he scanned his notes, "a narcissist. Is that right?"

I nodded. "That's right. I said that. Students and parents pay hefty tuition prices, and he was obviously burned out. That's all I meant."

"Why didn't you tell me about your argument before?"

I blinked. "I didn't think to. It wasn't important. In fact, he apologized to me when he came into the sitting room."

"Did anyone hear him apologize?"

I shook my head. "We were in the room alone."

"He must've known you were angry if he apologized. How angry were you with Mr. Jamison?"

My pulse moved to my throat. I knew where this was headed. "Not angry, just irritated."

He flipped through pages penciled with notes. "But you said he made a pass at you. That he tried to grab you. Now, I don't know you that well, Ms. Prather, but I know you well enough to think that's something that'd make you pretty mad. Heck, it makes me mad."

I took a breath. "I was upset, sure. But he was a handsy sort of guy. Besides, like I said, I thought he was on something—or maybe he was sick. That's right! He had a headache. Did I tell you that?" I pointed to the notebook.

"Uh-huh. You said he mentioned migraines." He leaned over his knees. "Do you remember him hitting anything, like, I don't know, a table or a corner of something when he fell?"

"No. I've thought about it a lot. He fell flat on the floor."

"And why have you 'thought about it a lot'?"

Giles must have passed on his blinking to me because I couldn't get my contacts to quit sticking. "You know why, Officer Beamer. I didn't want … I wanted to make sure … I needed to know …." I took a drink of my coffee.

"That you didn't kill him?" Beamer said.

From beyond the connecting door, a book fell off the shelf.

I wanted to stay and see how Beamer's discussion with Lenny went, but I had class. My Crimes and Passion course was in Winsor, which was connected to Harriman by a rickety passageway. Despite its undesirable location, it was my favorite class and the most well attended. Although we studied female romance and mystery authors, the enrollees were as diverse as the writers we read. I had more male than female students, and not all were English majors. Many of them were taking the class as an elective, a course not required for graduation. For the first time, I had students who weren't forced to be there, and it made a huge difference in the way they approached the material—and me as well. Preparing lesson plans, I included questions they asked in class and answers they wondered about, digressing from a text more than I ever had. It was fast becoming my most rewarding teaching experience. I just hoped Giles would recognize its popularity and my enthusiasm and allow me to teach it again. The French Department hadn't materialized yet, and women's studies and women writers were closely related to my field of study. He admitted as much during my proposal and agreed it was a good idea. He thought it would be a way for me to study mysteries *professionally*. But with the death of Miles Jamison, he would be anxious about my personal life crossing paths with my professional life because of my involvement in a possible crime.

Most of the class was assembled by the time I hung my coat on the back of the chair, and by *most*, I meant the majority. These students were older and more mature; they wouldn't use the snow as an excuse not to attend. My afternoon class, composition, would be a different story. Despite being scheduled later in the day, students seized any excuse they could not to come. Most of them were freshmen, and the idea of skipping class was still novel. That wore off junior and senior years when students became more dedicated to their majors. Until then, I had to fight through the absences, chatter, and general disorder that a freshmen class brought.

"Good morning," I said. "I'm glad the snow didn't deter you."

"It could be way worse," said John Stanley, a large guy whose desk looked two sizes too small. The entire room felt small, probably because of the low dormer ceiling. Despite its large corner turret, Winsor had miniature rooms like this one that seated no more than twenty students. Even the podium was half the usual size and positioned on an old wooden table.

I laid my copy of *The Labours of Hercules: Hercule Poirot Investigates* by Agatha Christie on the stand. This short-story compilation worked great as a textbook for this class.

It contained twelve mysteries Hercule Poirot would solve before ending his career, and I could show how the mysteries correlated, however vaguely, to the mythical labors of the Greek god Hercules. They were short yet connected to many of Christie's larger works and themes and featured some of the same characters, like Inspector Japp. We were three quarters through the book, and I hoped we could get through all the stories before the end of the semester.

As I opened my text, Katelyn, or Kat as she liked to be called, asked me if I had heard about the death of the professor from Minnesota. I'd had her as a student last semester in the creative writing class I taught while Claudia Swift was on sabbatical. Kat was a fledgling writer, whether she realized it or not. I couldn't remember what she said her real major was, but I knew she would eventually come to the realization that her heart was in writing.

"I did hear about it. How did you?" I asked.

"I know a girl from Copper Bluff who goes to Minnesota. When I heard Dr. Iverson talking about him in the cafeteria, I recognized the name right away. What happened?"

The class waited for my response, but I wasn't sure how much to tell them. This, after all, was a class about crimes and passion. I felt it my duty not to dodge the subject. Yet I couldn't possibly explain how I was in the same room with Miles when he died, so I decided on a diplomatic response.

"I don't know how he died," I said, "but I do know he was in Copper Bluff to play for the music festival, which has been postponed. He was the guitar player for Jazz Underground."

"My guess is, the guy was younger, so probably a drug overdose," said John. "I mean, not to stereotype or anything, Professor Prather, 'cause I know you hate that, but what else could it be? He *was* a musician, and some of those guys get pretty tanked up before a show."

"He was also a professor, though," said Jackie, who was sitting next to John. "So I doubt he was on drugs."

John shrugged. "You never know."

"There's another explanation," said Kat, holding up her Agatha Christie book.

"Which is …?" said John.

She didn't have to say it out loud because half the students were already thinking it. But she did anyway. "He was murdered."

The class snickered, and we moved on. After the lesson, I pulled Kat aside. I wanted to know more about this friend who went to Minnesota. I could use some insight into Miles's personality, or at least his teaching style.

"I know two girls, actually. Carly was my next-door neighbor, so we're pretty close. Brittany I just went to high school with. Neither of them wanted to stick around Copper Bluff, so they enrolled at Minnesota. Carly's an actress, so obviously she didn't want to stay here."

"Obviously," I said. I knew artists had more opportunities in larger cities. Still, our Theater Department was top-notch.

"They were roommates. Brittany was the one who had the dead guy as a teacher. She played some instrument." Kat narrowed her green eyes. "Guitar. Anyway, she was crushing on him her first year. That's all she talked about. It drove Carly nuts."

Miles Jamison had been charismatic. I could see why a freshman would be enamored with his looks, not to mention his talent. "So, she liked him?"

"That's the understatement of the century. She worshiped him."

Maybe Miles was a better teacher than I thought. It sounded as if he'd inspired a couple of students. "So, what happened?"

Kat hoisted her backpack over her shoulders, and we walked toward the classroom door. "Carly got another roommate."

"But what about Brittany and Professor Jamison?" I shut off the light.

"Brittany joined some band and practiced all hours of the night. That's when Carly requested a different dorm room. I don't know if Brittany even goes to school anymore."

"If you remember, ask Carly next time you talk."

Kat stopped in the middle of the hallway. "Why? Is it important?"

"No, I'm just interested. That's all."

We shared a secret smile before parting ways. We were both too curious for our own good.

Chapter Eleven

———

When I left Winsor, I saw Lenny trudging through the snow, the collar of his wool coat turned up and his head down. I called out to him, and he stopped and waited for me on the half-shoveled path. Part of the problem was the wind; it kept blowing the snow into heaping piles on the walkway. The other part was the students, who crisscrossed the campus without concern for how much snow they brought with them. Some of them even made snow angels in the quad. But it was nearly finals, and I couldn't blame them for being lackadaisical. It was hard to care about anything other than the upcoming winter break.

"I wanted to talk to you before class, but I didn't have time. Did Beamer find you?" I asked Lenny.

"Yeah, he found me, and now I gotta grab something at the cafeteria. I teach at one."

"Me, too," I said. "I'll join you."

"What was Beamer doing on campus anyway?"

"He was here to see me," I said.

Lenny walked around a group of students huddled in a circle. "That doesn't sound good."

"I know, but I didn't have my cellphone on. He tried to call." I stopped on the path. "Beamer said Miles's blood came back negative for drugs. Can you believe it?"

"Yeah, I can." He pulled my arm, and we kept walking. "I never really thought Miles was a drug addict. I mean, he was a university professor, a business owner, and a pretty damn good musician. How could he manage all that with a drug habit?"

"Oh, it happens more often than you think. Not all drug addicts are poor street criminals. They're everywhere, even here," I said. "A lot of students struggle with addictions, prescription and otherwise. Adderall has become an epidemic on campuses everywhere."

A girl in front of the student union passing out flyers for the holiday parade gave us a second glance, and I took the sheet and smiled. Shaking his head, Lenny opened the door, and the smell of onion rings, tater tots, and just about everything else deep fried hit us.

One small buffet line was dedicated to salads and cold sandwiches, and we started there. Lenny waited for me as I made a chef salad, and I waited for him as he grabbed a few slices of pizza. We both snatched brownies at the dessert bar before paying. Then we walked to the crowded seating area.

It was lunchtime, which meant the room was packed and noisy, but not as packed and noisy as usual. Undoubtedly, some students were still in their dorm rooms, sleeping off the snowstorm. Lenny and I selected a table near the window, setting down our trays with a plunk.

"So, if Miles wasn't on drugs, which I still have a hard time believing, what happened that morning?" I said as I unfolded my napkin.

"That's what Beamer wanted to know. He wanted to know about your fight with Miles at breakfast. Someone mentioned it when he was taking statements. I said it wasn't a 'fight' and that you only said what the rest of us were thinking. He knows you're the kind of person who speaks her mind. I changed the subject by mentioning Tad Iverson. I said they had words at breakfast. I thought if I brought that up, it might save your ass."

I put down my fork full of lettuce. "Do you think it needs saving?"

Lenny's serious face broke into a smile. "I don't know, Em. That's what it sounded like to me. Beamer seems to think you killed him singlehandedly with your Herculean strength. That might constitute manslaughter."

Something niggled at the back of my mind, but I couldn't quite grasp it. "We both know that isn't true. So what happened? *Could* it have had something to do with Tad?"

He took a sip of soda. "Why does it have to be Tad? Or anyone? If nothing was in his system, it might have been something natural—like a heart attack. You hear about that happening, even to younger guys."

"I was in the room with him, Lenny. There was nothing natural about his death. I'm telling you. The guy was wild-eyed."

"Well, you have that effect on men. Or at least me," he said.

He was joking, but with the light falling just right on his handsome face, I couldn't contain a blush. I looked away. When did he start having this effect on me? We'd always teased each other, but now an unanswered question lingered between us. It colored all our conversations, even when the subject was murder.

Lenny grabbed my hand across the table, and I once again met his gaze.

"Em, the other day—"

"It must be true," interrupted Jane Lemort, the medieval scholar in our department. Her dirty-blonde hair was pulled into a severe bun, revealing dark roots, and a long string of gray pearls was doubled up around her neck. Usually she showed no interest in anything after the fifteenth century. I wondered why she wanted to talk to us today.

"I heard you were on Santa's naughty list, and here you are, being punished with cafeteria food," she continued. "The campus equivalent of a lump of coal."

Lenny let my hand drop. "Jeez, Jane, I didn't know you could make a joke. Christmas *has* come early."

She smiled and unbuttoned her black trench coat. She was pleased with her jest. "I heard you had a visit from the police this morning. Was it about the death of that music professor?"

"Officer Beamer … consulted me about the case." I decided this wasn't really lying, just careful word choice.

"Yeah, Em is teaching that Crimes and Passion course this semester. She's fast becoming an expert on both." Lenny winked at me.

She let out a small laugh. Like jokes, laughter was something we didn't hear from her very often. "I've heard of immersion courses, Emmeline, but this might be taking it just a little too far. Anyway, I'm sure there are experts on our campus more qualified as consultants, such as those in the Criminal Justice Department. I figured the visit was about your being with the quartet the day he died."

Enjoying our surprised faces, she continued, "Oh, you're not the only two with sources. Anyway, I don't care about that. I just want to know how he died. It didn't say in the paper."

"I have no idea," I said. "Nobody does."

"Oh." The disappointment showed on her face. "Well I guess we'll just have to wait to find out like everybody else. My guess is he was on drugs, meth maybe. It's huge in the Midwest."

This wasn't the first time I'd heard her say that. Whenever something happened that she couldn't explain, she blamed it on methamphetamines. But this time I didn't challenge her. "You're probably right, Jane. He was probably on meth."

With nothing else to discuss, she said goodbye and moved in the direction of the food line.

As Lenny and I finished our last bites, we talked about Jane and how she enjoyed controversy, as long as it didn't involve her precious reputation. She relished being number one in the department, which she kind of was. She was widely published, highly regarded, and deeply involved in campus happenings.

Sure, Lenny and I wanted all those things for ourselves; we wanted to leave our untenured days behind us as quickly as possible. Or at least I did. I longed for the day I would feel secure in my position, but I had to admit, there was something nice about staying on the fringes. I had pushed myself so hard and for so long in graduate school that I didn't realize the freedom that came with being the low man on the totem pole. It made me think twice about taking the upward climb.

As Lenny and I dumped our trays, I asked him how late he taught today.

"Four. Why?"

I put on my mittens as we approached the door. "Because I thought we could talk to Tad after class. Like you said, he did have words with Miles at the table. Maybe he knows something. And don't you need to talk to him about rescheduling the performance?"

"We talked this morning. It's scheduled for Friday night, but I know he'll be at Pender Auditorium this afternoon. Since the final concert in the series is on Saturday, we have to set up at another venue. He's hooking up the sound in there."

"Perfect. I'll meet you at Pender after your class." We braced for the cold as we left the student center, said goodbye, and walked off in different directions to our afternoon classes.

Stanton Hall was dotted with students darting in and out of classrooms, their wet shoes squeaking on the marble floor. Joining the clamor, I climbed the grand walnut staircase to my composition class, enjoying the pictures lining the walls of historic battles in gilded frames. The building housed a good deal of artwork, and on the first floor there was a small gallery open in the afternoons to the public. It was another reason why Stanton Hall was one of the most popular buildings on campus, and I was always happy when I was assigned a room like 208.

As I suspected, attendance was scant. Ten out of twenty-three students showed up, and it was hard not to be irritated when my lesson plan fell flat. The class lacked participation, and group work was hushed. Either the students hadn't read the material, or they felt reluctant to discuss it because of the change in classroom dynamics. When the class fell silent and I had run out of things to say, I dismissed it ten minutes early and meandered down the hallway, wondering if other teachers were having similar problems.

André Duman, the French professor, was definitely having problems. His room was empty, and he was talking to a blank screen. "I don't know if you can see me, students, but if you can hear me, please repeat, '*Il fait froid.*' Students? '*Il fait froid.*' Hello?" In white letters, the screen read, "Connection Lost."

"Hi, André," I said, poking my head in the door. "It looks like the snow is causing problems for you, too."

André was pressing keys on the computer. "I had it a minute ago, but now all is lost. No one can hear me."

I hid a smile. André pounded away at the keyboard as if he could make the computer reconnect by sheer force.

After a moment, he flung up his hands. "There is nothing more I can do. The computer is not responding."

I shrugged. "I had half my students and still had to let them out early. They were positively shy this afternoon."

He tucked his textbook and notebook into his satchel. "I tell you, Em, I do not know how much longer this will work. Final exams are in a couple of weeks, and they have yet to master the weather. We are moving that slow."

"It's an intro class?"

André nodded. "Beginning French for AP students."

AP stood for Advanced Placement, which meant these high-schoolers were bright enough to take introductory courses for college credit. The technology must have been a real obstacle for them to be struggling.

"They'll get it. Just be patient," I said. But if there was one thing André didn't possess, it was patience. His passion for French language and culture made him intolerant of technological delays.

He zipped his bag. "The story of my life here has been one

of great endurance, but what of your day? I heard a member of Jazz Underground died unexpectedly. Poor Lenny, dear fellow. Will the performance be rescheduled?"

I nodded. "It's been rescheduled for Friday night in Pender. Will you still go?"

"Certainly. It's the holidays, and I could use the Christmas cheer. I'm sure the band could use that as well. Was Lenny a good friend of the man who died?"

I shook my head. "No. He wasn't. Tad Iverson knew him, though. He's a Minnesota alum. I think he was the one who booked the performance."

"Well, the show must go on then," André said with a chuckle. "This show," he motioned to the screen behind him, "has just lost its top dog. Arf."

Behind him, the screen became a sea of high school faces. I didn't know what was funnier: the look on their faces or the look on André's when he realized that his classroom was online again. I backed out of the doorway before anyone could see me laughing.

Later that afternoon, I met Lenny in Pender Auditorium, one of the largest halls on campus. Built in 1925 but recently renovated, it seated over one thousand people. Massive gold organ pipes framed the proscenium stage, giving the entire space a regal look. The gold curtains on the balcony floor as well as the golden accents of the light fixtures were a nod to the hall's stately past. In my opinion, it was the perfect place for a holiday concert.

Lenny and I met at the rear entrance, which was accessible from the quad by two flights of outdoor steps. We both took a moment to catch our breath once we reached the lobby.

"I never remember the front entrance," said Lenny.

"Me neither," I said. "It must be my mind's way of tricking me into getting some exercise. So how'd Tad get the quartet rescheduled so quickly?"

He held open the auditorium door. "It was now or never. I'll be covering Miles's parts, so I've been practicing the material. Another band is scheduled to play on Saturday, and then it's finals. We're hoping it will be a strong finish to the series—like a double-header." He looked around the massive space. "I hope some people show up."

"Oh, they will," I assured him. "You've got quite a following in town. It's just a matter of getting the word out about the new date."

Lenny nodded. "Tad's already reached out to the city council and surrounding towns. He says that Miles's death has actually made people more supportive of the concert."

"Death can bring people together in a way other life events can't."

Lenny smirked. "Says the expert on all things macabre."

I shot him a look as we walked down the red-carpeted aisle.

The stage was dotted with musical equipment like drums, a keyboard, and microphones. Cords zigzagged across the stage toward speakers that were in various stages of assembly. In the middle of the mess stood Tad Iverson with his hands clenched at his sides.

"Hey, Lenny. Emmeline," he said as we approached the stage. "I thought you guys were maintenance. I've been waiting for them for over thirty minutes."

Lenny jumped on the stage. I took the stairs.

"It looks like you got all the equipment moved," said Lenny, glancing around. "I'm glad the band agreed to keep it here for the week. It'd be a hassle to set it up right before the concert. What's the problem?"

Tad's face was blotchy and stressed. "I can't seem to figure it out—how to get power to the amplifier."

Lenny shrugged off his coat. In an untucked flannel shirt and dark blue jeans, he looked more musician than professor. As he busied himself with the cords, I took the opportunity to talk to Tad about Miles. I told him the police hadn't found any drugs in his system and that they still didn't have the cause of death.

"I can't imagine what could have killed him if it wasn't drugs," said Tad. "He was a young guy, really. Maybe some heart condition in his family?"

"Perhaps," I said. It was the kind of comment people made when something went wrong. The heart was an easy organ to blame. "Tad, remember Friday night, during the open house? Do you know whom Miles talked to on the porch? You said it wasn't you."

"No," he said. "It wasn't me. It must have been Josh or Lenny. Those were the only other men, unless it was a woman." His lips turned up. "Unfortunately, Miles was a bit of a lady's man."

"It wasn't a woman," I said, "and Lenny was with me, so I guess that leaves Josh. I know they owned a studio together, but did Josh and Miles get along?"

"That's a good question. I just met Josh on Friday, so I really couldn't say. But from what I observed, Josh managed the studio. He probably did a lot of the legwork. I imagine Miles was better at playing the star than handling the business end," said Tad.

"Do you think that bothered Josh?" I asked.

"I'm sure. Wouldn't it bother you?"

I nodded. "So why let Miles get away with it?"

Tad let out a breath. "Miles got away with a lot because of his networking, his connections. You didn't want to make the guy mad. He could probably end your musical career if he wanted."

I was surprised. Miles might have been a jazz idol but he didn't seem like a jerk. "Would he have done that?"

He shrugged. "It's just the fact that he could."

"I found the problem," hollered Lenny from behind one of the speakers. "It's a fuse."

"Can you fix it?" asked Tad.

"Let me try something," said Lenny. I couldn't see his face.

"Did it carry over to academia? Did he have influence there?" I continued.

"I couldn't say. But I've met his type before. They like to rail against the byzantine politics, the bookish pedant, the hoary professor. They know nothing of education, really, and what it's like to educate and excite young minds."

Suddenly a guitar chord erupted out of the speaker. We looked in Lenny's direction. Guitar in hand, he smiled, showing the deep dimple in his cheek. Tad gave him a thumbs-up.

"So you didn't think he was a good teacher," I said, returning to Tad.

"Let me put it this way. I thought he was a better musician. He was a heck of a songwriter. He published well over a hundred songs."

Lenny joined us with something in his hand. "The amp is fine. It's the fuse. I swapped it with another, and it works. Just have maintenance replace it when they come."

"*If* they come," said Tad, frowning.

"This place is enormous," said Lenny, looking out on the empty red seats. "You think we can fill it?"

"I don't know about filling it, but I bet we'll fill the main floor," said Tad. "The last two concerts were very well attended—and they were classical. That's not everybody's cup of tea. I can tell you that."

"I'm giving extra credit to my classes if they come," said Lenny. "It might be self-serving, but I don't care. With all that's happened, it's the least I can do to thank the band for coming back down."

"Not self-serving at all," said Tad. "I'm doing the same and have encouraged other professors in Fine Arts to do likewise."

"And they're desperate for extra credit in the eleventh hour of the semester. At least my students are," I said.

Lenny picked up his coat. "I hope that's enough to fill this place."

Chapter Twelve

That night, Claudia and I went to the university's adaptation of *A Christmas Carol* by Charles Dickens with her children, Sylvia and Benjamin. They were twins, seven years of age, and despite their precociously mature attitudes, I worried about the content. *A Christmas Carol* could be scary. When I first saw the play in the theater at ten years old, I couldn't get over the size of the Ghost of Christmas Yet-to-Come. He was ten feet tall and gave me nightmares for weeks. Yet Claudia assured me the twins could handle it, and I believed her. The picture of well-behaved children, Benjamin sat to Claudia's left and Sylvia to my right, paging through the small programs they were handed by the ushers. If the forlorn house on the stage bothered them, they didn't say.

The effect of the frosty storefronts, dimly lit streetlamps, and cobblestone streets was spooky, and I found myself forgetting about Miles and his suspicious death and everything else. Literature had always done that for me, provided an escape to an alternate reality. As a teenager, unsure of where I belonged, I welcomed the alternative. As an adult, I still enjoyed a reprieve from my troubles.

Alexander Schwartz, the theater director, was a perfectionist in every way. But tonight's set was impressive, even by Alex's standards. Christmas and exams were no excuse for not putting in 110 percent. Dan Fox, his set designer, also had impeccable taste and was well traveled. His impressive research into other cultures and historical architecture always informed his designs. I imagined tonight's spectacle was an accurate depiction of nineteenth-century London and that Dickens himself would have approved.

Claudia, who had been talking to a colleague behind us as we waited for the play to begin, fidgeted in her seat. "Have you spoken with Lenny? Is the concert rescheduled?"

I had always admired Claudia's voice. Slightly breathless, it made the listener feel as if he or she was being told a great secret. Reading her poetry, she could mesmerize a crowd in a few minutes. I leaned in. "Yes, in Pender. Tad Iverson said the announcement will go out tomorrow."

"Belle will be back."

Glancing at her, I said nothing. Obviously Belle would be returning to Copper Bluff. The entire band would.

She studied me for a long moment, quizzing me with her eyes. "Something has happened. *Tell me.* Sylvia, don't bite your nails."

Sylvia's hand dropped into her lap.

"Nothing's happened," I said. "I don't know what you're talking about."

"Your reticence speaks volumes," she said, re-knotting her scarf. "Dish."

I let out a breath. "Well, there is this one thing. It's not a big deal though …."

"The show's about to start—don't make me wait for intermission," said Claudia. She turned to her daughter. "And Sylvia, don't bite your nails!"

I knew Claudia and her belief in her superior communication powers; she wouldn't be satisfied until I told her what was on my mind. "Sunday afternoon, after you left

Café Joe, we went back to the Candlelight Inn. I was waiting in the library, because you know Alyssa has that terrific collection, and when Belle came down the stairs with her luggage, she and Lenny … embraced."

Her brown eyes narrowed. "*Embraced*? Are you sure? Word choice is critical in this context."

Leave it to a poet to zero in on my language. "It was definitely an embrace. At least I think it was. I was trying to disappear into the curtains."

She tapped her fingertips together, considering my statement. "I'm pretty sure it was nothing. I know Lenny. And I know you. You're a lot more alike than you think. You save embraces for special occasions."

"Well, she must be pretty special then," I said, "because it was an embrace."

"Words tell no tales."

The house lights began to dim. "*Dead men* tell no tales," I countered but considered her opinion anyway. Maybe "embrace" was too strong of a word. When I thought about it, Belle *was* the instigator. Could Belle have seen me in the library? Could she have sought to make me jealous? If she had, it had worked, sort of. I felt more disappointed than jealous, but still, it was a reaction. Maybe there was another side to Belle that Lenny didn't know. He hadn't lived in Minneapolis for some time, and people changed more often than not. With the theater in total darkness now, I started to like the idea of a sinister Belle more and more. The words *ulterior motive* came to mind. But what could be her reason? She was a well-connected professor at a prestigious college with good looks to match. I certainly didn't pose a threat, did I?

Lights flooded the stage, and suddenly it was Christmas Eve. The problem of Lenny and Belle disappeared in a flurry of music and dialogue. Ebenezer Scrooge was cursing the holiday as carolers sang "God Rest Ye Merry Gentlemen." He was halfway up the steps of his crooked house before I remembered what was coming. I jumped as the doorknocker revealed Jacob Marley's face, illuminated in a dull light, eyes wide and spectacled, hair stirred as if by a "breath of hot air." The theater department had gotten it just right.

Sylvia grabbed my hand, and I gave hers a squeeze. Looking down at her composed little face, her brown hair drawn back in a high ponytail, I tried to comfort her fears with a reassuring smile. When Jacob Marley's ghost arrived, in a burst of smoke, lights, and heavy chains, she shielded her eyes with my arm, peeking out when she dared. I had to admit the scene was scary. First of all, it was just plain loud, and second, the content was really quite horrifying. The idea of a coworker coming back to haunt me was terrifying, and I instantly thought of Jane Lemort. She would relish the opportunity to tell me all the places I had gone wrong in my life and the number of links on my chain.

When intermission came, Sylvia was doing much better and ran up the aisle with her brother, Benjamin. Claudia told her she should hurry to beat the line in the women's restroom. When they were out of sight, Claudia turned her attention to me and picked up the thread of our earlier conversation. She wanted to know how I'd left things with Lenny.

"Fine. You know our theory about Josh and Kim?"

She nodded. "That he has feelings for her?"

"I think we were right. Josh was genuinely upset about Kim fawning over Miles. He said she deserved better, and by better, I think he meant himself."

"I have a feeling Josh is more complicated than we thought," Claudia said. "He seems shy, but you know what they say: still waters run deep."

I knew that aphorism was coming. "I'll find out just how deep on Friday, when he comes back to Copper Bluff."

"And Belle …?"

I shrugged. There was nothing I could do about her.

Claudia turned her head to one side. "One would think anyone with an ounce of sensitivity could see you and Lenny have feelings for each other. And Belle is so artistic. How could it escape her?"

"You're right. If our feelings for each other are obvious, why would Belle embrace Lenny at the bottom of the stairs? Is she impervious to our connection, or does she have an ... *ulterior motive*?" I was glad to say the words aloud. They hung in the air for a few minutes as we considered the possibility.

The lights flickered, and Claudia looked around for Sylvia and Benjamin. They were just returning to their seats.

"You have a point, Em, a very good point. If I were you, I would consider why she made a show of her affection just then. Was it to make you jealous, or was she trying to distract you from something or someone else?"

The children scooted into the row, the lights dimmed, and the show resumed, but I considered Claudia's words. It was possible that Belle was grieving for her band member or genuinely attracted to Lenny, but it was also possible that her affection was a ruse. After all the years she'd known him, which must have offered ample opportunities to become closer, why choose to pursue Lenny now? Did she really just discover her attraction to him—or was she trying to distract me from finding Miles's killer? I know which alternative I liked more—and I intended to look into it.

AFTER THE CURTAIN FELL, SYLVIA held my hand as we left the theater. "Ms. Prather, the Ghost of Christmas Yet-to-Come was pretty scary, wasn't he?" she said. "Do you think he was on stilts?"

"He was incredibly scary, and maybe he was on stilts. But my guess is the effect came from the costume design. They can do wonderful things with a bolt of fabric and some lifts."

"I didn't think he was scary at all," said Benjamin, who was walking in front of us with his mom. "I knew it was fake."

"Benjamin, it's perfectly acceptable to feel frightened," said Claudia. "The play was supposed to evoke pity and fear. There's no reason to deny your feelings."

Benjamin rolled his eyes at us, and I hid a smile, imagining what it must be like to have Claudia as a mother. I guessed life in their household could be very dramatic.

Outside the theater entrance, the Fine Arts Department had placed a table with sugar cookies and hot apple cider. Actors in Victorian costumes sang Christmas carols. I could've believed I was in nineteenth-century London had it not been for the flat plains, lack of row houses, and Tad Iverson, who drew my attention in the far corridor. With his jovial smile and copper beard, he might have passed for Mr. Fezziwig, though he didn't have the girth described in the book. He was shaking hands with a man I didn't recognize. Taking a cookie, I excused myself from Claudia and the children and walked toward Tad. I wanted to congratulate the Music Department on their outstanding singing—and find out what all the hand shaking was about.

"Emmeline, have you met Charles Hammer, the pianist for the famous Baxter Piano Trio?"

"Well, I don't know about *famous*," Charles said, taking my hand.

Expensively clad, Charles was thin with dark skin. If he had a wrinkle anywhere on his jacket or pants, I couldn't see it. He was the epitome of a sharp-dressed man.

"I agree with Tad. The trio is widely popular right now," I said. The previous summer, the group had played for English royalty and garnered nationwide press. I'd read about it in *USA Today*.

"You're too kind," said Charles. With his modest manners and smooth baritone voice, it was easy to see how he had the power to charm audiences. "Tad will be the famous one soon. I was just congratulating *him*."

I faked comprehension, nodding and smiling, but I didn't have a clue what he meant. The news was probably buried in some newsletter or email I'd failed to open, and I chided myself for not keeping up with my inbox now that I had a new laptop.

"Don't worry," said Tad with a laugh. "The university hasn't announced anything. It's just known to some people in the

Music Department. A composition I wrote was published."

"Congratulations," I said. "That's terrific news. I know little about the music-publishing business, but my writer friends tell me it's incredibly hard to get published." I worked as an assistant editor at the *Copper Bluff Review*, and even getting an article accepted in a small quarterly literary magazine was difficult.

Charles nodded. "It is hard. Like writing, it's about knowing the right people. If you co-write a song with someone who's already published, you have a better shot. Otherwise, it's almost impossible."

"And how do you get to 'know the right people' when you live in a rural state like South Dakota?" I shook my head. "That must make it extra difficult."

"It does," Tad agreed.

The group of carolers stopped near us and sang a quick "We Wish You a Merry Christmas." As they did, I admired their formal wear. Cookies, costumes, songs—the effect was festive.

"Miles was a master at it, and he lived in Minnesota—not exactly California," Charles said after the carolers left. "He knew everybody, and he promoted a lot of his students. I'm going to miss that guy."

My attention snapped back to the conversation. I knew Miles encouraged his students to pursue their dreams, but I didn't know he'd helped them get there. "I didn't realize you knew Miles. I'm sorry."

"Thanks," said Charles. "I appreciate that. Miles knew everyone. We played together a few times in Minneapolis. The guy was a genius on the guitar."

"Did he know anyone famous?" I asked out of curiosity. I attended concerts and performances whenever possible because I loved live music. Unfortunately most of them were at least an hour's drive away, if not more.

Charles shrugged. "He got one of his students a gig with Beyoncé."

"Beyoncé," I said. "That's impressive." I was beginning to understand Miles's attitude. If he thought he could connect students with stars like Beyoncé, I could see why he would encourage them to seize an opportunity if it arose. Why pursue a degree in music to get a job as a musician if a student could join a band right now? The music industry thrived on youth. One only had to look around at local venues to see that. Once singers hit middle age, it was out to casinos and state fairs for them, and that was only if they had impressive careers behind them.

Tad stuck his hands in his jacket pockets. "But not all students get so lucky. Plenty of careers end at nightclubs or with needles. As a father, I can tell you I wouldn't want my son or daughter getting caught up in a bad crowd. Some jazz musicians emulate guys like 'Bird,' Charlie Parker, who was a heroin addict."

"For sure," Charles agreed. "There's a lot of that in the music industry. Drugs. Booze. Sex. Not a place for impressionable young adults."

Claudia signaled to me, and I waved back. Sylvia was buttoning her red dress coat, trimmed in black fur, and Benjamin was pulling on his hat. They were ready to leave.

"Was Miles ever mixed up in any of that? Drugs?" I asked.

"It's possible, I suppose," Tad said, scratching his beard, "but you said the police didn't find any drugs in his system. He never used around me. What do you say, Charles? Did you ever know him to do drugs?"

Charles shook his head. "Not when we played. But he wasn't naïve. He knew it went on. You just have to ignore it. Especially if it's not affecting their performance."

I supposed it was what one had to do, but as a teacher, I'd have a hard time keeping my mouth shut, especially when it came to young people. We had a responsibility to students, even outside the classroom.

Sylvia and Benjamin started playing hide-and-seek behind the statues in the art gallery, and the look on Claudia's face said it was time to go. I congratulated Tad and his department one last time and shook hands with Charles Hammer. Then I was out in the frosty winter night, where the gleam of the moon on the snow chased away all thoughts of drugs, death, and murder.

Chapter Thirteen

———

The next day, Lenny said he would take me to Pete's Hardware to get a Christmas tree. There was no way my '69 Mustang would make it through all the new snow. Besides, his Taurus had a larger trunk than mine and a luggage rack. If we couldn't stuff the tree in the trunk, we could put it on the roof of his car.

I looked out the window. It was a lovely day for tree shopping. Monday's storm had passed, the clouds had cleared, and the sky was almost azure. Even the wind behaved itself, leaving the snow in the banks where it belonged. Yet it was chilly, just twenty degrees, and I would need my mittens. I had thrown the kitchen, the office, and the bedroom into disarray looking for them. When my cellphone began to ring, I dashed around the house following the sound. I found my phone—and my mittens—in my oversized backpack. I silently thanked the caller as I checked the ID.

"Hi, Mom," I said.

"And Dad," a male voice joined in.

"Your father's on the line, too," said Mom. "We're on lunch break." My parents liked to get on both ends of their landline and talk. I liked it too, except when they carried on their own side conversations. Then it could be annoying.

"Hi, Dad. I meant to call you back the other day, Mom, but my schedule's been so hectic. I'm sorry."

"No need to apologize," said Dad. "We understand. You're busy."

"Your father understands. I don't understand. It's a phone call, Em, not algebra."

Math was my Achilles' heel. I switched topics before she could say anything further on the subject. "Are you ready for your sisters' visit? What are you making?"

Dad let out a noise that sounded like a grumble. Mom's voice turned upbeat. "A standing rib roast, with apple dressing, and—get this—figgy pudding."

My mittens had snagged on a notebook in my backpack, and I carefully detached the yarn. "What is figgy pudding? Does it have figs in it?"

"Traditionally, maybe, but mine, no. It's full of raisins, currants, and brandy. I'm going to set it on fire."

"That sounds dangerous," I said, trying not to laugh.

"That's what I said. Her sisters plus alcohol? It's a dangerous combination," said Dad.

"You have it wrong, Michael," Mom argued. "The thirteen ingredients represent Christ and His twelve apostles, lighting the brandy represents the Passion, and the sprig of holly represents the crown of thorns. It's all very holy and appropriate."

Thirteen ingredients for one dessert? It was going to be a busy weekend. "I wish I could be there. Will Grace be bringing her dog?"

"Does she go anywhere without that damn thing?" said Dad.

My aunt Grace had a Lhasa apso that she took everywhere. My parents' cat, Chevy, hated the dog, and so did my dad.

"Of course she'll bring the dog," said Mom. "You can't expect that poor animal to sit in the kennel all weekend. And

I really don't see why you can't make it home for one day. You could drive back Sunday."

This was the only thing I didn't like about the holidays: people trying to talk you into events you couldn't or didn't want to attend.

"She can't take the Mustang. She'd have to fly, and there's no time to get a ticket. Be reasonable, Hope."

I tossed my backpack in the corner and looked out the window. Lenny was parking. "I really wish I could, but Dad's right. We've had a lot of snow down here, and the car couldn't make it. Lenny's here now. He's going to help me get a tree, so I have to go."

"What happened to that charming Frenchman, André? You never talk about him anymore," said Mom.

"Oh, he's still here. I talk to him all the time," I said, zipping up my coat.

"Doesn't his family own a winery?" she asked.

"Yes," I said.

She sighed. "I don't know why you don't expand your horizons, Emmeline. André has connections to France—and your ancestral roots. Lenny sounds like any boy you'd meet in Detroit. For all you know, he's from Detroit."

"What's wrong with Detroit?" said Dad.

"Nope, Minneapolis," I said at the same time.

"Minneapolis. It figures," said Mom.

"He sounds like a fine young man," said Dad. "He's helping her get a tree, isn't he?"

"Yeah, and he's Jewish," I said.

Dad let out a laugh before he hung up. Mom warned me to call her back this time.

I met Lenny on the curved pathway to my front door. He wore a bright-red winter parka and thick black gloves. Under the clear-blue sky, the air was ice cold. His car puffed little clouds of smoke into the frosty air.

He clapped his gloved hands. "I'm ready for anything you throw at me, Prather. Douglas fir, Fraser fir, pine—let's do this."

His excitement was contagious. "Let's!"

As he pulled away from my house, I said, "Can I ask you a stupid question?"

"Are you kidding? They're my specialty. I'm a professor," he said.

"Did your family get a tree when you were young?"

He shook his head. "No way. But it's not a dumb question. I knew a Jewish family that had a Hanukkah bush, which is, in truth, just a Christmas tree with different decorations—dreidels, Stars of David. And an interfaith family down the street had a tree and decorated it with their kids, who were raised Jewish. But my parents are pretty traditional, and Hanukkah wasn't that big of a holiday for us growing up."

"You don't mind going to get a tree with me, then?" I sneaked a glance in his direction.

"If you're asking if it bothers me, not in the least. I'm singing in a holiday concert, so yeah, no worries. If you want to know the truth, I'm kind of excited about it. Just don't tell my parents."

I laughed. "At least you don't get the guilt trip about coming home for the holidays. My mom's trying to talk me into joining them this weekend."

"Aren't you going home on break?" he asked.

"Yes, but my aunts won't be there. They'll be in Detroit this weekend."

He quirked an eyebrow. "Maybe they could come down here?"

"Nope, I asked. My mom's making figgy pudding—and setting it on fire."

"Is that what you're going to be doing when you get old? Setting things on fire? Mrs. G told me your cookies came close to burning the house down."

I felt my face scowl. "She said that? I thought she liked them."

"She's just worried about you," he said, patting my knee, "living all alone in that house."

I snorted. "*She* lives all alone in her house. It's my age. She thinks thirty's a spinster. I have one good year left, according to her."

"Come on, granny," he said. He pulled into a spot in the parking lot of Pete's Hardware. "Let's go find you a tree."

In the garden center, trees stood or leaned along the tall metal fence. Some were flocked with fake snow; others were wrapped in plastic mesh. A man was sawing a tree trunk while a father and his toddler looked on, and the smell of freshly cut fir and pine filled the air. I closed my eyes and inhaled. It really was the most wonderful time of the year.

"Wow, look at all these trees," Lenny said as he glanced around the perimeter. "I didn't know so many people still bought live trees."

"Really? We bought a real tree every year," I said. "It was *the event* of the season."

Lenny wasn't paying attention. He was walking toward a display of Fraser fir trees, his hiking boots making large grooves in the snow. "I like these." He stood one up, shaking it gently to free the branches. "What do you think?"

I examined it from afar. Nice shape, good top, straight trunk. "It's on the smallish side."

Lenny squinted. "It's seven feet."

There was no way I was going to pick the first tree I saw. "Let's keep looking."

We moved on to the display of Douglas firs. "Oh, this one is cute. Look how full it is," I said, pointing to a tree propped up next to the fence.

Lenny grabbed it with his thick glove and spun it around. "It's too full. You'd have a hard time keeping it from falling over."

"And its trunk is crooked," I said.

Next were the Scotch pines, the trees with the long needles. "Look at this. It's like a big soft porcupine," said Lenny. "I wonder if the needles will fall off."

"No," said the attendant, "and they're hard to kill. They're our best sellers."

"I don't know, Em. This might be the one for you. You're prone to killing things."

I stared at him. What was that supposed to mean?

"I mean plants, vegetables, flowers ..." said Lenny with a lopsided grin.

"Let's go back over here." I put my hood up. The cold was beginning to seep in.

As we walked toward the Frasier firs, his phone rang. "It's Belle," he said. "I'd better take it."

By all means, I thought as I inspected a tree, then scolded myself. I was acting like a jealous teenager, and I hated it. He could talk to whomever he wanted; I had no monopoly on his time.

"Congratulations," Lenny was saying. "That's good news."

I came out from behind the green boughs. What was good news?

"When do you leave?" he asked.

Maybe she'd found a new job in ... Antarctica.

"Nice," he said. "What did your chair say?"

I'm going to miss you? That would be an appropriate response to someone moving to the other side of the world.

"Definitely. It's a win-win." Lenny's eyes met mine, and he gave me a wink. I turned back toward the tree, embarrassed that he'd caught me eavesdropping.

After a few minutes of polite conversation, Lenny said goodbye and ended the call. He joined me at the tree, looking it up and down. "This is the first one we looked at."

It was, but I didn't acknowledge that fact. It was too cold to admit that I had been judging all the other trees against this one. "What's the good news? What did Belle say?"

Lenny pulled his cap out of his pocket and pulled it over his head and ears. "She's been chosen as a judge for the Cliburn. It's a prestigious piano competition. She's pretty pumped about it. She hasn't called me for years. We sometimes email, but that's about it."

"She's rather young to be a judge, isn't she?" The cold was beginning to seep through my jeans, into my legs, and I shuffled my feet to keep warm. "When I think of a judge, I picture someone middle-aged or older."

"She's more involved than we are. We could probably judge something if we bothered to go to more meetings on campus."

That was true. English faculty meetings were all we could handle.

The attendant asked if we needed help finding a tree.

"After searching the lot over," Lenny told him, "I believe we'll take this one."

I nodded, and the attendant picked up the tree and brought it over to a large machine that shook off the loose needles. He cut the price tag and asked us to pay inside. I couldn't wait to get indoors.

"Well, it's great news for her, but I still think it's extraordinary," I said as we approached Pete's.

We continued toward the register, where a little girl sitting at a folding table asked if we wanted a cookie and hot apple cider. They were one dollar. I said we'd take two, and she handed me the gingerbread men. I gave one to Lenny. Her mother poured the cider.

"You just don't like Belle," said Lenny, taking the cookie. "Admit it."

"What isn't to like?" I paid the girl.

"I don't know. She rubs you the wrong way for some reason."

The mom handed me a Styrofoam cup of cider. Then she poured Lenny's.

I was about to argue the point, but he continued, "She's changed—that's for sure. She's a lot more … I don't know … ambitious than she used to be. It kind of makes me glad I moved to Copper Bluff."

My heart did a little flip. The mom smiled at me as she handed Lenny his cider, and I wondered if she could read the relief on my face.

"Maybe I would be the same way if I hadn't left." He shrugged. "Who knows?"

I thanked the mom and daughter, paid for the tree, and walked back to the car with Lenny. The attendant was finished making the fresh cut and asked us which car was ours. Lenny pointed out his Taurus and helped the man fasten the tree to the roof with a cord he had in the trunk. We drove down the small city streets, the tree boughs gently scratching the roof, but the weather granted us safe passage all the way home.

Chapter Fourteen

———

As Lenny twisted the screws into the tree trunk, Dickinson kept him company. My attempts to keep her out of his way were futile. She didn't care what we were trying to accomplish; she only wanted to check out the new climbing post I had bought her. I just wished I'd kept my gloves on. The branches were sticky and sharp, and it was hard to hold the tree in one place.

Lenny got up from the floor. "You can let go."

We stood back and looked at the tree.

"It's crooked," I said.

He cocked his head to one side. "You moved."

"Or you did."

He crawled back under the tree. "Let's try this again."

He loosened the screws and stood back, telling me which way to move the tree. Left, right, forward, backward. He was trying my nerves. When the tree was straight, he ducked under the branches and tightened the screws. Just then my home phone rang. He stopped.

"I'm going to let the machine answer it," I said.

A few seconds later, a female voice came on the line. It was my ex-student with the Copper Bluff Police Force. "Professor Prather? Are you there? It's Sophie Barnes."

My hand moved. "It's Sophie from the police department."

"Anyway, I wanted to talk to you—but don't come down to the station." More quietly, Sophie added, "I don't want Beamer to know I talked to you."

"Hurry, Lenny!" I said.

"One more ... just a sec," he said.

Sophie went on, "Just call me when you get this message, will you?"

I ran to the phone just as Lenny finished twisting the last screw, but it was too late—for the call and the tree. Sophie hung up, and the tree leaned to the right.

"Next time *I* hold the tree and *you* fasten the screws," said Lenny.

I agreed. He was sprinkled with needles, and my hands were sticky with sap. Wiping my hands on a towel, I pushed the speaker button on my home phone and dialed the number. Lenny wanted to hear what Sophie had to say.

"Detective Barnes," she answered.

"Oh how lovely," I said. She had recently been promoted to detective and sounded very professional.

"I knew it was you, Professor. I just like saying it," said Sophie. I could hear the smile in her voice.

"And I like hearing it," I said. Lenny sat up. "So your call—it sounded important."

"I don't want to alarm you, but I need to give you a heads-up. Hair was found on Miles Jamison. It wasn't his."

"That's interesting," I said, leaning against the kitchen counter. Maybe this would give us a clue to his killer. "Do you know where?"

"In his hand."

My first thought was Pen, the employee from the Candlelight Inn. After all, I had caught them in a passionate kiss upstairs. I wondered if Kim had known about them. I made a mental note to go back to the inn. I needed to ask Pen how well she knew Miles. "This is good news. Maybe it will tell you something about his death."

"I'm not sure you understand," said Sophie. "You're going to be called down to the police station to provide a DNA sample."

"Me?"

Lenny stood and joined me in the kitchen.

The line became muffled, and I got the idea that Sophie was walking somewhere she couldn't be overheard. "Hair or skin under the fingernails are signs of a struggle. Beamer thinks you might have struggled with the victim before his death. Did you?"

My hair. Of course. He had pulled it down from the clip when he approached me. Was there a struggle? I wouldn't categorize it that way. But he got close enough for me to feel threatened, threatened enough to defend myself. For a second, I thought about my emergency stash of cigarettes. The new information was worrisome. Then I remembered I'd thrown them away last year.

"Professor?"

Lenny nudged me.

"No, we didn't struggle. He reached for my hair, though. He pulled it out of its clip."

The line was quiet for a moment.

"It might not be your hair," said Sophie.

I nodded silently. She was right. It could be Pen's. But one thing was certain: I was officially a suspect. Although the distrust bothered me, I was determined not to let it show. Sophie was just doing her job, and Lenny was growing more concerned by the minute. I felt obligated to remain strong for them.

"When Beamer calls, act surprised. Don't let on that you talked to me."

"I won't," I said. "Just please don't let him come to the campus to collect me. I can't imagine what my colleagues would say if they saw me leaving in a squad car."

"Don't worry. Beamer can be pretty cool when he wants

to be."

I agreed. He was cool-headed and considerate, not the type to jump to conclusions. I'd have to keep telling myself that.

After Sophie and I said our goodbyes, Lenny and I stood in the kitchen, half thinking about the phone call, half examining the tree from afar. Both were troublesome.

"So this is bad," said Lenny.

"The call or the tree?"

"I'm serious, Em." He turned from the tree and stared at me. "I don't know much about police procedures, but I'm pretty sure that when they link DNA to a crime scene, it's not good."

Worry etched his face, his furrowed brow making him look older than his thirty-one years. It was my turn to assuage his concerns as he had done so many times for me. "It's not as bad as you think. Did you meet Alyssa's employee, Pen?"

"I noticed her. She has a neck tattoo. I didn't meet her, though. Why?"

"I saw her lock lips with Miles upstairs the morning of the brunch. It could be her hair."

He shoved his hands in the pockets of his jeans. "The help, too? That guy was an ass."

"To be fair," I said, grabbing a piece of Mrs. Gunderson's peanut brittle, "the kiss was reciprocal. Pen seemed to be enjoying Miles's attention quite a bit." I offered the candy to Lenny and took another piece.

"Did he know her, or was he just *that* good looking?" He took a bite.

I munched quietly. I wasn't sure I wanted to answer the question.

"Really?" he said.

"Miles had good looks, a sexy voice, and stage presence." I shrugged. "I can see why girls flocked to him. But Pen? You're right. We need to find out if they knew each other, or if that was their first encounter."

"Oh no," he said, reaching for another piece of candy. "I

didn't say we needed to find out anything about anyone."

"Come on, Lenny. You've got a reason for going out to the inn. You could say one of your friends left something behind. Something musical."

He shook his head. "Musicians are pretty maniacal about their stuff. They don't just leave things behind. Besides, how do you know Pen will be there?"

"I don't. But Alyssa said they've been busy this December with Christmas travelers. Pen is probably working." I put a K-Cup in my Keurig. "Even if she isn't, we could still ask Alyssa. She might be able to tell us a little about her."

Lenny stared into the living room. "I think we have a more immediate problem."

"What could be more immediate than my impending DNA sample?" I said.

The tree chose that moment to topple over.

AFTER RIGHTING THE TREE, WE drove to the inn. Despite his initial protest, Lenny agreed to take a closer look at Pen's connection to Miles. It made sense to me that they knew each other, and I wanted to discern how. Pen was almost my age. She wasn't going to kiss a stranger, no matter how suave. That only happened in bars to twenty-one-year-olds, at least in Copper Bluff. So how did she know Miles and for how long? Could that relationship have figured into Miles's death? She'd certainly been physically close enough to kill him that morning. Then again, so had I.

I was pleasantly surprised to see two cars in the driveway as we approached the inn and hoped one of them was Pen's. It was Tuesday afternoon, and I'd worried no one would be around. From the puffs of smoke coming out of the chimney and the aroma of freshly baked goods, I knew at least one person was inside working.

"Man, that smells good," said Lenny as we walked up the pathway. "I don't know how Alyssa isn't three hundred pounds. I would be if I cooked all that amazing food."

"Agreed." I rapped on the door. "It's probably a good thing my baking skills aren't better."

"What a surprise!" said Alyssa. Even with her hair in a bun and flour on her apron, she looked great. "I didn't expect to see you two until Friday."

"I hope we're not intruding," I said.

"Not at all. Come in," she said, stepping aside. "I have a lunch tomorrow for the Copper Bluff Chamber of Commerce. They're expecting at least twenty local business owners. Pen and I have been baking since eight this morning."

Had I been baking several hours, for a group of twenty, no less, I would not have welcomed an intrusion. An unexpected visitor would have been met with downright hostility. But Alyssa was perfectly amiable and even happy to see us. I knew of only one host as gracious as that: Katherine Giles, Jim Giles's wife. She could host a large group of professors and graduate students without breaking a sweat.

"We'll be quick, so you can get back to it," said Lenny. "Kim misplaced her mouthpiece when she cleaned her trumpet, and she thinks she might have left it here. Do you think I could take a look around?"

"Of course you can," said Alyssa. "I know how important a musician's instrument is. My entire family plays. It would be terrible not to have it for the concert."

"I'm sure she has others, but you're right. Musicians get pretty nervous if we break our routine," said Lenny. "I'll just look in the library and maybe her room—if nobody is up there."

"Absolutely. I don't have any guests at the moment. I can quick show you which room was hers." Alyssa smiled. "Emmeline, if you'd like to take a peek in the kitchen, Pen might be able to spare a cookie. Tell her I sent you," she said with a wink.

While Alyssa and Lenny walked up the stairs, I made my way into the kitchen. Although the rest of the house was authentically Victorian, the kitchen was not. The white subway tiles and granite countertops were modern indulgences, not to mention the gourmet stainless-steel appliances. Pen was busy rolling dough on an enormous center island that housed a standup mixer, coffee grinder, juicer, and other state-of-the-art conveniences.

"Pen, right?" I said. Pen started. She had been so focused on the pastry she didn't see me come in.

"Sorry, I didn't hear you. Yeah, I'm Pen. You were here the other day, with the group of musicians."

I nodded. "One of them left something behind, so Alyssa is helping my friend Lenny look around. She said I could poke my head into the kitchen for a sweet."

Pen smirked, and her hazel eyes took on a reckless look I'd seen once before, upstairs with Miles. Her black hair was pushed off her forehead with a wide headband and secured in a miniature bun. I decided she was newly graduated.

"That sounds like Alyssa. You can have one of those éclairs if you'd like."

"Thank you," I said, taking the chocolate-covered confection. The cream melted in my mouth. "Wow. This is amazing. Where did you learn to cook like this?"

"I went to culinary school in Minneapolis."

A bell went off in my head. "Is that how you knew Miles?"

"The guitar player? No. I only met him last weekend." Her muscles flexed as she rolled the dough back and forth. Her bicep had a rose tattoo that bulged as she worked. When I didn't say anything, she looked up and laughed. "So why was I kissing him upstairs?"

I shook my head. "It's none of my business."

"That's okay. He and I met Friday afternoon when I was helping Alyssa prepare for the party. The group checked in early, and we were just talking. Alyssa scolded me for flirting with her guests, so I was paying her back. Miles was in on it. We thought you were her." She lifted the dough into a pie pan and began to flute the edges. "Poor guy. He was nice."

Miles must have relished his part in the façade. Not only

did he get to kiss a pretty girl, he also got to snub an authority figure. "I see. The kiss was about teaching Alyssa a lesson."

"Don't get me wrong," she said. She placed pie weights on the crust and slid it into the oven. After setting the timer, she turned back toward me. "I like Alyssa, but sometimes she treats me like a minimum-wage employee. I'm an accomplished pastry chef. I don't need that."

"I understand, but weren't you worried about losing your job?" I asked, taking a napkin and wiping the frosting off my hands.

"Are you kidding?" She turned toward the fridge and ducked her head inside. She checked the turtle clusters to see if they were set. "Where's she going to find a pastry chef of my caliber in Copper Bluff? She might not realize it now, but she will when I start my own business. Then she'll wish she'd shown me some respect."

Her confections would sell, no doubt, but I wasn't so sure about her attitude. Her inexperience showed, and while I respected that she wanted to be treated like a professional, I also realized that she needed to act like one, too. I hadn't made up my mind whether Alyssa was too demanding or Pen too careless when Alyssa breezed into the kitchen. The contrast between them was striking.

Everything about Alyssa said consummate professional: her home, her person, her manners. I could see how she might misconstrue a conversation between Pen and Miles if she feared it might harm her reputation. Instead of talking to Pen as an adult, she'd scolded her in front of Miles. Pen retaliated by acting the way she was treated: like a child. But how far would she go to teach Alyssa a lesson, and could one of her pranks have gone terribly wrong Saturday morning? I didn't have time to delve further.

Alyssa bent down and peered into the oven. "Wonderful! You got the piecrust finished. Did Pen tell you? She's a master at desserts."

I nodded. "The proof was in the éclair. It was delicious."

"I wish I were a better baker," Alyssa said. She was at the kitchen sink, washing her hands with lemon-scented soap. "But I studied dietetics—you know, nutrition. Too much time spent studying healthy eating habits, I guess," she added with a laugh.

"Your food is fantastic," I said.

"Cooking and baking are two different monsters," said Pen. "Lots of cooks can't bake."

"I can get by," said Alyssa. I had a feeling she wouldn't admit to not being able to perform any task in the kitchen. "But Pen's right: they require two different skill sets, I'm afraid."

It was quite possible I lacked both.

"That's why she needs me," said Pen. "I help her shine at these events."

Alyssa folded her used towel and placed it next to the sink. "Yes, you do. We make a good team."

They shared a smile. Pen was pleased with the verbal pat on the back.

Alyssa pulled out her cutting board and placed it on the shiny center island, glancing up at me. She obviously had work to do and didn't feel comfortable getting on with it while I was in her space.

"Lenny has to be about done," I said. "I'm going to let you get back to your work while I wait out there."

"Take your time," said Alyssa. "And yell if you need anything at all."

I thanked them both and walked out of the kitchen, briefly passing through the parlor. Although there was no white chalk outline, like in the movies, I could see exactly where Miles had fallen, where I had pushed him. It had all happened so fast; the only thing I could remember was the beating of my heart. It had echoed in my ears, messing up my head. But was it before or after I pushed him? I closed my eyes. I couldn't recall. The minutes were a jumbled mess. The only thing I knew for sure was the feeling of Lenny's arm around me, how secure I'd felt— and safe. Had I really been in danger from Miles? Had I acted out of self-preservation?

I walked into the library. I didn't have time to analyze my motivation, and maybe I was a little afraid of the answers I might find. I noted a large collection of Shakespeare's plays on the corner bookshelf; I must have been too enthralled with the mystery section days earlier to notice. I pulled out a copy of *Romeo and Juliet.*

"Em." Lenny strode into the library. "A rose by any other name would *never* smell as sweet."

I returned the book. "Did you find the mouthpiece?" I spoke loud enough that Alyssa or anyone else might hear.

"No, I didn't. Let's check in here," said Lenny.

We pretended to look in the couch cushions and on the floor, making noise to lend our search authenticity. When we knelt down behind the desk, Lenny spoke in a hushed tone. "How long do we have to crawl around on the floor to be convincing?"

"I talked to Pen," I said. "She didn't know Miles. I'll explain in the car. Did you find anything?"

He cocked a dark eyebrow. "You know I wasn't actually looking for anything, right?"

"I know, but you might have stumbled across something."

"Like ... a clue?"

I glared at him. We didn't have time for cleverness.

"I did find something interesting. An award for guitar—blue ribbon, first place. One of those you're supposed to hang around your neck but nobody ever does."

I dropped the corner of the rug I was looking under. "That *is* interesting. How do you know the award was for guitar?"

"It had a guitar on it," he said, leaning back into a seated position.

"Did it have anything else on it, like a name?"

"Afraid not. It was just one of those generic awards. 'Outstanding Performance for String Instrument,' etcetera, etcetera."

"Well, it had to have had a year on it," I said.

His look changed. "It probably did. But I don't remember."

"Do you think it was Miles's? He played guitar."

"Maybe," he said. "But why bring it with? That seems a little conceited, even for him. Besides, it had the South Dakota state seal on it."

"Let's go back … take another look," I said, scooting out from under the desk.

"No way."

I could tell he would need to be convinced. "Alyssa said we could take our time. That could mean a second sweep of the bedrooms."

"*Sweep*? Do you hear yourself, Prather? What do you think? You're FBI?"

"That reminds me, I wonder how much searching the Copper Bluff Police did. If the medal belonged to Miles, it should be in an evidence box somewhere."

"Lenny? Emmeline? Are you still here?"

"It's Alyssa!" I said, standing. My head hit the desk on the way up. Lenny put his hand on my arm and asked if I was okay, but he was suppressing a smile.

Alyssa peeked inside the library. "Is everything all right? I thought I heard something fall."

"Just Em's dignity," said Lenny. "She hit her head."

"Oh no. Can I get you an ice pack or something?"

"Not necessary," I said, admiring her embossed stationery. The gold letters AKA were centered on the linen paper. "It's only a bump." I gestured to the desk. "That's cute, AKA."

"I'm probably the only one in the world who still sends handwritten letters," Alyssa said with a laugh. "But I own a Victorian inn. Who can blame me?"

"Not me," I said, joining her at the door. "I applaud you for keeping up the art form."

"No mouthpiece?" she asked.

We shook our heads.

"I'll keep looking," she said. "If I find it, I'll let you know."

"Thank you," said Lenny as we followed her to the entryway.

"Kim would appreciate it."

We said our goodbyes and left. In the car, I told Lenny about Miles and Pen, how they were pulling a prank on Alyssa. As I recounted the tale, my mind lingered on the two-story house receding in the rearview mirror. One could almost forget a man had died there. The inn's charm made it easy. Of course the papers had mentioned it, but not even reporters with only soybean prices to report wanted to discourage the few visitors who came to Copper Bluff. Besides, Miles's death had been reported as an accident, not a homicide. Maybe the media was waiting for the autopsy to be completed before it pounced on a scandal. Or maybe it was hard to imagine anything as terrible as murder could occur at such a beautiful place.

Chapter Fifteen

When I got home, I charged my cellphone and turned the ringer on high. Sophie said Beamer would be summoning me to the station to give a DNA sample, and I wanted to be prepared. When he didn't call that evening, I expected he would contact me Wednesday morning before class, but he didn't, and I walked to campus worried that he might show up in person. *Jane Lemort would love watching me get my cheek swabbed*, I thought, as I walked down the snowy sidewalks of Oxford Street. *Open up, Emmeline. Say "ahh."*

I didn't know how the police collected DNA. I assumed I would have to go down to the station or to some other place where I would sit with people suspected of doing suspicious things. It was inconceivable, considering I was the one trying to find out what really happened to Miles. How it had come to this, I couldn't say. On the bright side, giving a DNA sample would allow me another opportunity to discuss the case with Officer Beamer, and I always learned something when I talked to him.

Climbing the steep stairs of Winsor, I glanced once more at my cellphone. Nothing. I silenced it, tucking it into the side pocket of my blazer, and entered my Crimes and Passion course. The wind blew hard against the windows, caked with snow, and the walls creaked and moaned. I decided to leave my coat on, at least for the time being. A look around the room told me that most of the students had made the same decision. *Whatever happened to the theory of warm air rising?* I thought as I took out my books. If that were true, this crooked third-floor dormer should have been the hottest spot in Winsor instead of the coldest. But as John Stanley, my football-playing student, said, "It could be way worse." I wasn't sure how, but I believed the adage all the same.

After writing the upcoming due dates on the board, I opened the text to the page where I had stuck a bright-yellow tab. We were on the seventh labor of Hercule Poirot, "The Cretan Bull." We would discuss the eighth and ninth labors Friday and finish the tenth, eleventh, and twelfth next week. Then the semester would be over, and we would break for the holidays. Although the stories connected to the original labors of Hercules only in the famous detective's mind, this story's resemblance to the myth was obvious. In the Greek tale, a bull was causing problems for the town of Crete, destroying crops and walls and generally wreaking havoc. So, too, was the case of a young man name Hugh, who is the metaphorical bull in the story. He leaves his room at night, sleep-walks, and while doing so presumably kills animals, including a sheep and a cat. But despite Hugh's behavior and belief in his own insanity, Poirot and Hugh's fiancé, Diana, are convinced he is sane. They believe he shouldn't be captured, like the mythical Cretan bull, and don't want him committed to an asylum. They are certain someone else killed the animals. His friends and family aren't so sure.

I started by asking what the students thought of the story and how it compared to the others. Right away they said they liked it, which was a good sign. If I had to wait a few minutes for a response, I knew it would be a long class period.

"I liked it a lot," said Kat. She was still wearing her coat and her hoodie. She sat bundled in the corner as if watching an outdoor sporting event. "I'm changing up my paper so I can include it. I think it fits better with the other ones I've picked."

I asked her to elaborate. "How do you decide which stories fit into which category? What patterns do you see emerging in Christie's writing?"

She didn't answer right away, so John Stanley added his thoughts to the discussion. "Honestly, before I took this class, I thought Christie was just some sheltered old lady, writing mysteries in an English country house. But some of these stories get pretty violent, when you think about it. I mean, the sheep and the blood. The cat and the knife? That's graphic." He took a big gulp out of the gallon of water he always brought to class. Football required plenty of hydration, I guessed.

I considered what he said. "That's an interesting point. Do you think we could categorize the stories by the violence of the crime?"

"Definitely," said Kat. She'd had enough time to think about her answer. Plus she enjoyed sparring with John. "And maybe even by the motive. Some are straightforward, and others are ... I don't know ... more complicated. Those are the ones that interest me."

I asked her for an example.

"Like the 'Cretan Bull.' The motive is complex. But in the next story," said Kat, thumbing through her text, "'The Horses of Diomedes,' it's all about drugs. Seems a little clichéd to me."

John shook his head, twisting the cap back on his gallon jug. "It's not. My uncle's a cop in Dallas, and he says most of the murders he's seen have something to do with drugs. It's really kind of forward-thinking of Christie. Even in, what, the 1930s, she knew drugs were a problem. Maybe that's what I'll do my paper on. Drug use as a theme in Christie's work."

"If I wanted to read about drug addicts," said Kat, giving him a look, "I'd open up the newspaper."

I was going to tell John the idea for his final paper was a solid one, but he responded to Kat before I could. The energy between them was palpable, and anyone witnessing the exchange could see they knew how to push each other's buttons. I would definitely be pairing them up for peer review. Once they got over their mutual annoyance, they might make a pretty good team.

"Yeah, I will," said John, not backing down. "I'm telling you, Christie knew what she was talking about. Look at that professor who died Saturday. Miles something-or-other? He was probably on drugs—could have even been a prescription. My uncle says tons of adults are addicted to opioids."

Kat ignored him. She spoke to me instead. "Was it drugs that killed him?"

While the class waited on me, the wind blasted through a crack in the window, sounding like a train whistle. It was a warning, perhaps, telling me to keep my mouth shut. But when it came to my students and their questions, I had a hard time censoring myself. Maybe it was my Detroit upbringing. The city was full of violence and everybody speculated on crimes. Here in this little town, with kids from communities of hundreds instead of thousands, I knew I should consider the listener, but I didn't. "It wasn't drugs. The police have yet to determine the cause of death."

Kat smacked her hand on the desk. "See?"

The class looked at her, and she slunk back into her hoodie. She wanted to prove John wrong but hadn't meant to draw attention to herself.

"Back to the story, though," I said, trying to model classroom control, "Poirot could have easily dismissed Hugh's actions as insane or even drug-related." I directed my next words to John. "What made him doubt the veracity of the story?"

"There were the dreams," said John. "Hugh had nightmares that he turned into a bull, a rabid dog. When he woke up, he was thirsty but couldn't drink."

"There was his locked door, too," added Jackie.

I nodded. Hugh's father locked him in his bedroom at night, yet Hugh supposedly got out somehow and killed animals. Poirot noted the discrepancy.

"It was the hallucination," said Kat. She was so sure of herself when it came to literature. If only she were that sure of her own writing. "Think about it. Hugh imagines seeing someone while he's talking to Poirot. The skeleton behind him? He hallucinates."

"Yes, he hallucinates ..." I repeated. But I was thinking of Miles Jamison now and not Agatha Christie.

Miles had called me Aphrodite. At the time, I'd dismissed it as part of his come-on, but he could have been hallucinating. He could have been seeing Aphrodite, not me. I had taken Greek mythology as an undergrad. I knew she was the goddess of love, and beautiful. But what was she supposed to look like, specifically? I couldn't remember and wouldn't be able to refresh my memory until after class.

When the discussion ended and the last student filed out of the room, Kat approached the podium. She only had a moment, but she wanted to tell me that she'd talked to her friend who went to school in Minneapolis. I stopped packing my bag.

"Don't get excited. I didn't find out anything about Professor Jamison," said Kat. "It was literally a dead end."

"What do you mean?"

"The girl who joined that band? Brittany Keller? She doesn't go to school anymore. She died of a drug overdose." She hoisted her pack on her back. "Just don't tell John. If he says the word 'opioid' one more time, I'm going to explode."

I smiled as I considered the new information. I knew exactly how she felt. If Jane Lemort brought up methamphetamines one more time, I would surely combust.

Chapter Sixteen

———

It was the time of the semester when being in my office became unbearable. Students lined up outside, waiting to tell me their life stories, and more importantly, how those stories had impacted their grades one way or another. Even worse, my desk looked like it had been hit by a hurricane. Stacks of papers, quizzes, journal entries. And then there were books—tabbed, not tabbed, read, unread, halfway read. They were next semester's assignments. Beneath it all lay my shiny MacBook, which I hoped would yield the answer to my latest non-academic question. How much did I resemble Aphrodite?

A quick Google image search told me not much. Of course artists had imagined her in many different ways. When I thought of the Greek goddess, or her Roman counterpart, Venus, I usually thought of red hair, probably because of the painting by Botticelli. I guessed that would be the point of reference for most people, including Miles. Her hair was much longer than mine, less curly—and red. At the time, I thought Miles was making a reference to her as the goddess of love, a cheesy come-on. But now I guessed he'd been hallucinating; he had to be. That's why he'd pulled out my hairclip. He'd expected all that long red hair to come tumbling down.

I tapped my pencil, jotting down the name Kat had given me before I forgot. Then I turned up the volume on my phone, staring at the animated snowflake wallpaper for several minutes before putting the phone back into my pocket. It didn't make sense. Beamer said Miles wasn't on drugs, yet what else could cause hallucinations?

"I love *The Birth of Venus*. I never tire of looking at it," said Claudia, peering over my shoulder.

I jumped. "Claudia, I didn't hear you come in," I said.

She glided into the chair in the corner alcove. "Your mind was obviously elsewhere. Tell me it was the holidays."

I thought for a moment, turning my desk chair to face her. "No, it wasn't, but now that you mention it, I have problems there too. My mom is begging me to come home this weekend because my aunts will be in town. There's no way I can, though."

"Well, you *could*," she said, taking off her gloves. They were leather and expensive-looking. "But you would miss Lenny's performance, and I can't imagine you doing that."

"Besides, I have a lot of grading to do," I said.

"Which has always been your top priority," said Claudia with a smile.

"It has. My system just takes more time than others'. Freshmen make a lot of grammatical errors." And they did. The sentence fragments and comma splices in some students' papers astonished me—and omission of capital letters! I blamed it on technology. A lot of text-speak sneaked into their essays. As their English professor, I felt obligated to correct it, which took an ungodly amount of time. So, while Claudia and Giles could chide me about my grading pile, I knew there was no way around it, except to relax my standards. And as a new professor, I wasn't prepared to do that. Lenny said that in a year or two I would be.

My cellphone rang (or sang, actually) in my blazer pocket, a festive ringtone version of "We Need a Little Christmas." I grabbed it, knowing it had to be Officer Beamer. It was. I tried to be mildly surprised as he asked me to come to the police station to give a DNA sample. He explained it was voluntary but related to the death of Miles Jamison. My cooperation would be most appreciated.

"So, my participation is completely voluntary?" I repeated this for Claudia's benefit. She was listening carefully.

Officer Beamer said that was correct. He didn't have a search warrant.

I had a little over an hour between classes. Would that be enough time? He said it would take less than thirty minutes, so I told him I would be right down. He thanked me and ended the call. Claudia waited for an explanation.

"So, funny thing." I attempted to be casual. "Beamer wants me to come down to give a DNA sample. I think I'll do it right now to get it out of the way."

She studied me for a moment. "I'm going with you," she said, rising from the chair. "I know you think highly of Officer Beamer, and maybe you even consider him a friend, but this is serious. He's trying to tie you to Miles's death."

"Or untie me—however you want to look at it." I grabbed my coat from the chair. "We don't know if the DNA will match mine."

"I'm pretty certain it will. You were the last one to see him alive. And you struggled."

I locked my office door after Claudia exited behind me. "I wouldn't call it a 'struggle.' He pretty much fell right down."

Thomas Cook, the only faculty member with less experience than I had, was just coming out of Giles's office. He was new to the campus last fall, and I had a year on him. I always reminded myself of this when he was around. He had that sophisticated look about him that said *serious and smart*. Plus, he wore expensive shoes.

"I hear you were involved in the death of Miles Jamison." He didn't bother to pretend he hadn't overheard—or say hello. "What happened?"

"Hi, Thomas," I said, pausing long enough to emphasize

the greeting. "I was there, I wasn't involved, and I don't have time to explain right now. We're on our way out."

He walked down the hallway with us. "You know I'm conducting research about violence on college campuses, Emmeline. If you could help me out, I could quote you in my latest paper."

Thomas Cook's degree was in composition and rhetoric. His new project involved studying the way language incited violence at universities. I couldn't see how my experience would directly relate.

"*Quote* her?" Claudia said. "Really, she would need a byline."

He hustled to keep up before we reached the door to the stairs. "That would mean helping me write the article."

"Perfect. Emmeline's teaching a class this semester on Crimes and Passion."

"Which has nothing to do with language or rhetoric." I stopped. Thomas Cook had been researching violence on college campuses for some time. And he was smart. Maybe *he* could help *me*.

I turned to Thomas. "However, I'd be happy to assist you. I understand the importance of research and publication, especially for tenure. Can you meet me in the library tomorrow?"

Thomas nodded. "Of course. What time?"

I didn't teach on Thursdays. "One o'clock."

"Wonderful," said Claudia. She got excited every time I used the word *tenure*. "Alyssa's teaching a workshop on nutrition over the lunch hour. I'm going. You can meet me before you meet Thomas."

Knowing Claudia, I guessed this was her way of making sure I showed up at the meeting—and on time—even though learning healthy eating habits was the last thing I wanted to do before the holidays. The topic would've been better saved for January.

"I'll see you at one o'clock then." Thomas stuck his hand

out. "Thank you, Emmeline."

I shook his hand and left, puzzling in the stairwell over his request. Maybe he needed more help than I thought. Pointy shoes and camel hair coats did not a professor make.

"I'm glad to see you're finally thinking about your career," said Claudia. She threw a brilliant red scarf over her shoulder. "Thomas Cook would be an excellent resource for you. He's so … trendy. We all love old books, but you can't study them forever. Besides, you and he know a lot about language." She stopped outside the back door that led to the parking lot. "We'll take my car."

I put on my earmuffs. "How can you say that? Of course you can study old books forever. They might be the *only* things you can study forever."

"You're such a romantic, Em." She unlocked her silver SUV. "I just meant there are other avenues you could explore. Good for you that you're open to them."

I climbed into the SUV and buckled up. "I'm interested to learn what he knows about crime. It could prove helpful."

She threw me a look. "Helpful as in getting published, which would be a win-win for both of you. It would give you another credit before your book comes out."

"Comes out"? That was a little premature. I hadn't even finished writing it yet, but I was confident I would. The book was about early creative spaces for women writers. It started with medieval letter writing and ended with twentieth-century mysteries and romances. My Crimes and Passion course was helping me complete what I hoped would be my final chapters. When I was finished, I would submit the book to the scholarly presses I'd been researching, which was more daunting than writing the book itself. Each press had its niche and specifications, and while writing, I was also perusing their previous publications to make certain my book would be a good fit.

Claudia turned up the volume on her car radio to hear a poet being interviewed on NPR over the lunch hour. I was glad I wouldn't have to discuss Lenny, DNA, and now Thomas Cook. We were both silent on the way to the police station, where I assumed Claudia would have a lot to say.

Few cars were in the lot when we arrived, so we were able to park close to the brick building. That was lucky for us. Although the walkway had been scooped and salted, a crusty layer of ice had formed in the parking lot. We stepped out of the car carefully, not completely trusting the grippers on our boots. Jingle bells rang out as I opened the front door; the holidays had not been neglected in the functional building. The local station played Christmas music over the lobby speakers, and the front desk had a swath of twinkling lights tacked to it. Even the stationed officer wore little bow earrings.

"Hello, I'm Emmeline Prather, and I'm here to give a DNA sample. Officer Beamer requested that I come down."

"You're Sophie's professor. I remember you," said the officer, picking up the phone. "Criminology?"

I smiled. "No, English. This is my friend, Claudia Swift. Is it okay if she comes, too?"

"Oh, sure," said the officer. "I don't see why not. It'll just take a minute. Jena? I have a DNA for you," she said into the phone. She returned the phone to its cradle. "She'll be right out."

The officer's phone rang, and Claudia and I took a step back from the desk.

"I don't know if this is a good idea. Gene says the police can keep your DNA in their database indefinitely."

Gene was Claudia's husband and also an attorney. But I wasn't sure how much I trusted his advice. According to her, he had a wandering eye. Plus they fought like cats and dogs— at least they *had* until their couples' cruise to Italy. Now their relationship was better. At least they weren't living on separate levels of their house anymore.

"So what if they do keep it? Why do I care?"

She pulled at my arm, and I moved closer. "Don't you see? Once you're in the database, you're ten times more likely to be linked to a crime—wrongly linked. They can only query the DNA they have on file when it comes to a new crime."

The information gave me pause, but there was nothing I could do about it now. Jena was walking through the door. She wore a black visor that said POLICE—her hair pulled into a ponytail over its band—and a white short-sleeved shirt and dark pants.

"Ms. Prather?"

"Yes," I said. My voice sounded as hesitant as I felt.

"Come with me."

Claudia and I followed her to a small room with a white table and white cabinets. There were also a few plastic chairs, but we didn't sit down. Jena immediately opened a drawer and pulled out a pair of blue, latex gloves. The collection trays were already on the table.

"We've got two tests for you today, Professor. A hair pull and a cheek swab," she said as she stretched the gloves over her hands.

"I haven't failed a test yet," I said, attempting a joke.

"Well, this might be the one you *don't* want to pass," said Jena.

Claudia was skeptical. "Why two tests?"

"Well, we need the root of the hair to get the DNA," she said, approaching me. She was much taller than I and had no trouble yanking out a couple of curly strands.

I winced.

"Sorry. Like I said, we need the root, but it doesn't always cooperate." She put my hair into one container. Then she picked up the long Q-tip. "So we have the cheek swab."

I opened my mouth, and she was done in thirty seconds.

"How soon will you know the results?" I asked.

"We should get them back tomorrow, Friday at the latest," said Jena, sealing the second container. "This is a pretty simple case of identification, and we don't have a backlog." She tossed her gloves in the trash. "You're free to go."

"Thank you," I said. The door was still open, so Claudia and

I left the way we came.

"I don't like it, Em," said Claudia as we got into the SUV. She turned the heat on high. The fan blasted lukewarm air.

"There's nothing to like or dislike as far as I'm concerned," I said. "The police want to know if it was my hair they found on Miles, and I'd like to know, too. I want to get to the bottom of what happened that day."

"This isn't a whodunit; it's your life. If it *is* your hair, what's the next step? An arrest warrant?"

"Why would I kill Miles? What's my motive? It doesn't make sense."

She put the car in reverse. "The police don't need a motive for manslaughter."

"But like I keep telling everyone, I didn't push him hard enough," I protested. "And even then, wouldn't it be self-defense?"

She shrugged. "I don't know. I do know lots of crimes are committed in a fit of passion, and so do you."

"The good news is I know where to find a lawyer if I need one." I laughed, but Claudia didn't join in. She drove us to the campus wearing a concerned frown. I, however, was confident the truth would prevail.

Chapter Seventeen

———

B ack on university grounds, Claudia and I went our separate ways. I had class, and so did she. After a slow-moving fifty minutes with my composition students and two busy office hours, I walked over to the Fine Arts building. One of my students, Hannah Johnson, was having a piano recital, and I wanted to show my support. Plus, I loved the piano. As an educator, my mother had been more into books than music, so the opportunity to take lessons had never presented itself when I was a child. Now, as an adult, I was too busy. I'd have to go on living vicariously through my books—and CDs.

Approaching the building, I was surprised to see Lenny's car. Aqua-blue and quite old, it stood out from the other vehicles. I quickened my pace, wondering what he was doing here. Perhaps he knew Hannah, too, or was finalizing concert details with Tad. The performance was just two days away.

I scanned the hallway for signs. Thank god for yellow copy paper. The university had an abundance of it to point participants in the right direction of an event. Hannah's recital was to the left, in Clayton Recital Hall.

The room had theater-style seating and a stage large

enough to fit a good-sized ensemble. The backdrop was black with a straight, red valance. The focus was on the musician. In the middle of the wooden floor was a gorgeous grand piano in a bright spotlight. How thrilling it must be, I thought, to come to that instrument and make music with your own two hands.

About thirty people were present, dotting the seats of the hall, and I saw Lenny's blond head right away. He sat alone, in the middle of the auditorium, and I quickly scooted into his row, thinking he looked dashing in his dark coat. I shook off the thought, surprised at my attention to Lenny's good looks. *Dashing?* Maybe I needed to take a break from reading romance novels.

"Hey."

"Hey," I said, taking the seat next to him. "I had my DNA test today. I should know the results in a day or so." I indicated to the stage. "You know Hannah?"

He smiled. "You make that sound completely normal, you know that? An average day at the office."

I shrugged and took out a mint, offering one to Lenny.

"I know Hannah from Café Joe," he said, taking the candy. "She sells her CDs there."

"Nice. She's my student." I untied my scarf. "And you know I love the piano."

His eyebrows rose. "I didn't know that. I mean, I knew you had an affinity for singing, but not piano."

I smiled. He was the only one who could have convinced me to sing in public—once. He (and the red wine) had eased my inhibitions. "Well, I can't play. I always wished I could, but I love to listen. It was the only reason I liked going to church when I was young."

"You know I could teach you. I play a little piano."

He played more than a little. I'd overheard him and was convinced he was a natural when it came to all things musical: guitar, piano, voice. There didn't seem to be a note he couldn't hit. "Thanks for the offer, but I'm sure I'd be a klutz."

"No way. You've got a terrific memory. You know every line

of literature that was ever written. I bet you'd be awesome." He reached for my hand. "Your fingers are a little on the small side, though. And cold." He warmed them.

I felt my fingers melting and possibly my heart. Maybe my thoughts had nothing to do with reading romance novels. Maybe Mrs. Gunderson was right: I spent too much time alone.

Lenny let go of my hand, and I looked around the auditorium. I noticed Tad Iverson, the chair of Music, seated in the front row. I assumed he attended most of the senior recitals and pointed him out to Lenny.

"Did you hear? He had one of his compositions accepted for publication. Charles Hammer told me the other night at *A Christmas Carol.*"

Lenny was taken aback by the comment, which surprised me. I could tell him anything, and he always looked as if whatever I said was somewhat expected.

"*Really?*" He shook his head. "I can't believe it. Getting music published is hard. And Tad has a wife and kids. How much time does he have to travel and network?"

I wondered if Lenny had tried to break into the music industry. I could have sworn some of the pieces he played were originals but had never asked him about his compositions. Now I wanted to, but it wasn't the time. Maybe music was what he kept under lock and key in his trunk. I would have to make it the subject of my next investigation.

"I don't know, but I do know Charles Hammer thought it was a pretty big deal. Does that mean Tad's song will be on the radio?" I asked.

"Probably not, but vocal and choir groups are always looking for new music. Schools might pick it up." He glanced at the stage. "It's a huge coup for him."

Tad walked to the microphone. It was minutes before the recital, and they were ready to begin. He did an excellent job of introducing Hannah and her music. She would be graduating at the end of fall semester, and he hated to see her go. He said she was one of their best classical musicians, and as she began to play a sonata by Mozart, I agreed. It was as if she became one with the piano, moving close to the keys, then far away, playing from memory. It was incredible. The first song went on for about ten minutes, and I was astonished she could hold all those notes in her head. No wonder she needed an intermission after forty minutes had passed.

I leaned over to Lenny. "I've been thinking about what you said, about Tad and his publication. Remember when we met him over in Pender?"

Lenny nodded.

"He said Miles was a prolific songwriter. Do you think there's any chance Miles co-wrote the song with him? He'd have a better chance of getting it published because of Miles's gigantic network."

"Plus, Miles ran a successful studio," said Lenny, rubbing his five o'clock shadow. Like his eyebrows, his whiskers were dark and contrasted with his light hair. "It would make sense. Did Tad mention Miles?"

"Not when we were with Charles." I leaned in closer. "Do you think he could have killed Miles to avoid giving him credit? Or stolen the song altogether?"

"Tad a thief *and* a murderer?" He shook his head. But his gaze followed mine as we looked at Tad in a new way. It was easy to see how any performer or artist might want to be center stage, and for a professor at a small college like ours, the spotlight might normally escape him. Having friends like Miles who traveled, networked, and won shiny awards would be difficult. Even our university placed value on those, value that might be very appealing to Tad. Appealing enough to kill for? I pondered that question as Hannah finished her recital.

Afterwards, we congratulated Hannah on her fine performance. With family and friends surrounding her, some with flowers or cards, she thanked us for coming, and we scooted away. Outside the Fine Arts building, tiny snowflakes were beginning to form.

"Are you hungry? Let's grab something," said Lenny.

I nodded. "I only had a candy bar and bag of chips for lunch."

"They gotta start stocking that vending machine with healthier snacks," Lenny said. "How about Harry's?"

"Perfect," I said. The Main Street Grill, known informally as "Harry's," offered better-than-average bar food—nightly specials, good sandwiches, and the best crinkly fries in town. It was a general gathering place for college students, professors, and local farmers. The owner, Harry, was a gossip, and townspeople came as much for the talk as for the food.

I didn't see Harry when we walked in, but I did see the bar was roped in silver garlands, colored holiday bulbs hanging all in a row. Ho! Ho! Ho! signs dangled from the ceiling vents, twisting about when the heater turned on or a customer entered. Lenny and I chose a booth that faced Main Street. Outside, the old-fashioned street lamps, decorated with wreaths and wrapped in garlands, were just beginning to glow.

Lenny pointed to the nightly specials on the menu. "I'm having the pot roast. They only offer that at Christmas."

"Me too," I said. "I'm starving."

The waitress came to take our drink and food orders, then returned within minutes with the local craft beers she'd recommended. Lenny took a healthy swig of his. I waited for my foam to disperse.

"So, about Tad …" I began.

"I knew this was coming."

"What's that supposed to mean?" I asked.

"It means why can't we talk about normal things." He looked out the window. "Like Christmas. Like your mom and aunts. Where does that stand?"

"Oh, she's fine. She's still upset I can't come this weekend, but she's better. My dad helped smooth things over." I took a drink of my beer and followed his glance out the window.

Shoppers walked past with Christmas packages. It was crazy days downtown, and the stores were open late. After people-watching for a few minutes, I turned again to Lenny.

"So, with the pleasantries out of the way, can we talk about Tad?"

He let out a breath. "Yes, I think he could have murdered Miles. He argued with him, was jealous of him, and he might have been the man out on the back porch that night. In fact, I hope it was Tad. That would mean it wasn't someone else."

"Like me," I said.

"Or me."

I laughed. I hadn't considered Lenny a suspect, but of course he was. All of us at the inn were. "True. But do you *really* think he did it? And how? My Crimes and Passion course this morning got me thinking. This guy in the Agatha Christie story we're reading hallucinates. Maybe Miles was hallucinating, too. Maybe that's why he called me Aphrodite. I googled her after class, and really, I look nothing like the Botticelli version of her."

"It's just a saying," said Lenny. "It doesn't mean you look like her. She's mythical, and artists have depicted her in different ways. This is a classic case of you confusing characters and people. Your only-child syndrome is starting to show again."

I took another sip of my beer. Lenny claimed if I'd had a brother or sister, I wouldn't have relied so heavily on my books when I was a child. Because I substituted stories for siblings, he said, I expected things to turn out as they did in novels. It was true: I lived in a world of my own making. Maybe it prevented me from seeing things as others did, but I liked to think it proved nothing was impossible.

The waitress returned with two heaping dishes of meat, potatoes, and carrots, yet I hardly noticed. I was distracted by a noise outside—jingle bells. They grew louder and louder until I could see where they were coming from: two enormous Clydesdale horses and a carriage.

"What? Are those—is that—a sleigh?" I asked the waitress.

The waitress nodded. "Yep. The Lindgrens are offering sleigh rides every night until Christmas. The dad says he's caught the holiday spirit, but the mom says he charged up his credit cards at the Black Friday sales on Amazon."

"How much for a ride?"

She pulled our order ticket from her apron pocket. "Ten bucks, I think. Enjoy your dinner."

As she walked away, I looked at Lenny, who read my mind. He was good at that.

"Yeah, we're going. I wouldn't want to be the one to stand between you and your good deed. Interest rates are deplorable this time of year."

WE WERE THE LAST SLEIGH ride of the night. Mr. Lindgren helped us into the back, and we buried ourselves beneath the wool blankets. The chestnut horses gave their manes a toss, clopped their feet, and just that fast, we were off, heading down Copper Bluff's Main Street.

The air was cold but my body wasn't. Snuggled in next to Lenny, I felt warm and happy. The lighted windows from the stores shone on the sidewalks, and little puffs of smoke brightened the star-lit sky. It felt as if I had disappeared into a greeting card, the kind I liked to buy long after the holidays were over.

"You're such a city girl, you know that?" Lenny said with a nudge. "You're eating this up. I bet you would've paid twenty dollars for a ride."

I started to deny it and then stopped. He was right. Something like this would never happen in Detroit. But here it was different: small, intimate, old-fashioned. To me, this was the dream that was Copper Bluff. Maybe it was corny to say so, but I didn't care. To be part of this world was all I wanted, even as an outsider looking in.

"It's okay," he said. "I would've too."

He grabbed my hand under the blanket, and we rode for five or six blocks in silence, looking down the lanes decorated with holiday lights. Only the jingle, jingle, jingle from the bells on the horses rang out in the night. Then, at the edge of the city, where rows of houses gave way to farmland, the sleigh circled and returned downtown. Mr. Lindgren pulled up next to the post office, a block away from the pub, and retrieved his stepstool. After tipping him, Lenny held out his hand to help me down from the carriage. For a moment, we paused, transfixed. His hands slid down my waist, and we just stood there, locking eyes as if we didn't see each other every day. He bent his head and kissed me, and for that one moment, I thought I loved him. Possibly I had always loved him, and it had taken a Hallmark experience for me to realize it. But then that moment was gone. It was spoiled by the sound of Jane Lemort's teasing voice.

"Well, isn't this cozy."

I wanted to die. I really did. If I could have bludgeoned myself to death, I would have.

Lenny had no similar discomfiture. He sized her and her packages up with a quick glance. "I didn't know you had family, Jane. Those must be for them."

"Well, of course I have family," Jane said. "Do you think I was dropped out of the sky via stork?"

Lenny's forehead creased. "Did they have storks in medieval times?"

It didn't take long for Jane to recover. "I don't know. I know they had *love birds*." She looked at me. "Aren't you going to say something, Emmeline?"

I couldn't think of one thing I wanted to say to her. "I know they had cuckoo birds. That's where we get the word 'cuckold.' They lay their eggs in other birds' nests so they don't have to raise their own young."

Lenny chuckled and grabbed my hand, pulling me toward his car. "Goodbye, Jane. Happy Hanukkah."

Lenny was still laughing when we got into the car, but a little black cloud hung over me, left there by Jane Lemort. It's not that professors couldn't date each other; they could. Plenty of them got married. But with our shoddy dating records, I didn't want us to be the focus of departmental gossip. I knew Jane would find a way to tell Giles, working it into one of her oh-so-informative side conversations. She would tell half the faculty if she got the chance. I looked over at Lenny. It obviously didn't matter to him. Did it really matter to me?

Chapter Eighteen

———

The next day, the weather was so sunny and mild that for a time I forgot all about Jane Lemort. I sat on my three-season porch, which was almost warm, and drank my coffee. Since it was Thursday, I didn't have to teach but did have that appointment with Thomas Cook in the library. I'd also promised Claudia I would meet her early at Alyssa's workshop. And then there were those final portfolios to grade and library quizzes to tabulate. I took another sip of coffee. I couldn't wait for semester break. Obligations would disappear, and I would be left with several days that didn't require mental checklists a mile long.

My phone rang, and I knew before looking at the caller ID that it was my mom. She was the only one who called this early in the morning. I just hoped this wasn't her last-ditch effort to talk me into coming home for the weekend. I had enough going on right now with the murder of Miles Jamison and my feelings for Lenny. The holiday season didn't need one more stressor.

"Good morning, Emmeline!"

She was in a good mood, which wasn't unusual. I never saw

my mom go to work grumpy. Each day was a new possibility to reach out to a student. I think she looked at art that way.

"Hi, Mom. How's it going?"

"I have wonderful news."

I really hoped it didn't involve me catching a last-minute flight to Detroit.

"My sisters are staying until Christmas. You'll be able to see them after all!"

I was elated for my mom but worried for my dad. Two weeks in the house with four women might be the end of the holidays as he knew them. For myself, I was happy to be off the hook. Besides, I loved spending time with my aunts. They were as colorful as any characters in a book—and twice as unpredictable.

"That *is* wonderful news," I said. "How did they swing two weeks off?"

"Only Charity still works, and she had three weeks of PTO saved," she said. "Joy and Grace are retired."

I smiled. I loved hearing their names said out loud. My mom's name was Hope. "What does Dad think of it?"

"Oh, you know him. He's pretty accommodating, and he knows how important the holidays are to us. Also, next year, Joy's taking a cruise to Belize. She's trying to talk us into going with her. You, too, of course."

I had one holiday tangle undone; I didn't want to get snagged in another one. I knew how important the holidays were to them. Many years ago, they'd lost their parents in a car accident on Christmas night. I was only two years old and had no recollection of the incident. Ever since, they'd spent Christmas together. In-laws, children, jobs—it didn't matter. They *would* get together. Thankfully, this year would be no exception.

We said our goodbyes, and I walked into the house to pour myself one last cup of coffee. I glanced at the stack of folders on my bow window. If only I could get rid of them with a phone call. I gathered up my colored markers and red pen and turned on my record player for atmosphere. With "I'm Dreaming of a White Christmas," tinkling in the background, everything was more tolerable, even highlighting comma splices.

AT NOON, I WALKED TO campus. I was excited to meet Claudia but wasn't excited about the discussion topic: "Healthy Food and You." I felt heavier just reading the word "healthy" this time of year. Alyssa was an excellent cook, though. If anyone could make healthy cooking delicious, it was she.

The Student Center was crowded, and I said, "excuse me" a dozen times before reaching Claudia. Half the seating had been roped off for Alyssa's presentation, so the commons area was more congested than usual. Claudia was sitting in the front row, and I joined her. We exchanged quick hellos, but she was engaged with a student behind her who was asking for an extension on an assignment. Glad I didn't recognize any of my students, I focused on the arrangement of food. As part of her presentation, Alyssa had an eight-foot table jam-packed with vegetables—at least I thought they were vegetables. They were green, anyway, and very leafy. It looked as if they'd been pulled fresh from a garden. That was impossible, though. Midwestern winters made fresh fruit or vegetables a long truck ride away.

Alyssa smiled as I took my seat, and I gave her a wave. In an elegant tunic and leggings, she beamed with good health. Her hair was twisted into a sleek chignon, revealing her high cheekbones and slender neck. She glanced at the gold watch circling her wrist. It was time to begin. She made everything look effortless, and I knew despite my dearth of healthy eating habits, I would enjoy hearing her speak.

The green stuff was kale, she said, and completely organic. She taught a health and wellness course every spring, and if students enrolled next year, they would be able to grow their own GMO-free food, too. Wasn't that exciting? It actually was. She was so sincere about healthy food that even I, a candy fiend and chipster, became interested.

She continued with the rest of the produce on the table,

discussing what each vegetable was and how it benefited young people. Some produce was loaded with vitamins C, A, or B and could boost immunity, improve eyesight, and help mood swings. They were super foods with super powers. They could help during this critical development period, when students formed habits that would impact the rest of their lives. She was concerned about what they were putting into their bodies and wanted them to make smarter choices.

"Your body is your temple," Alyssa said. "Please don't destroy it with drugs or alcohol. Feed it with love and good food." Her passion was palpable—and personal. I wondered if she'd ever struggled with ill health. "Now, come up here and try all this good-for-you food!" She gestured toward the produce and sample cups of fruit smoothies.

The students started to circulate, and Claudia and I gathered our purses. I was eager to try Alyssa's samples and wasn't the only one. We were tenth in line.

"Amazing," Claudia said. "That woman is simply amazing. If she can get *you* excited about healthy recipes, she must be a demigoddess."

"I've been thinking about changing my eating habits." I didn't admit the thought had occurred to me in the last half-hour.

She smiled. "Good for you. Alyssa's printed recipe cards," she said, pointing to the table. "You can take some with you. I'm always trying to find ways to sneak vegetables into my kids' meals. I'm going to try that smoothie. It'd be perfect for hectic school mornings. They could drink it in the car."

I nodded, watching Alyssa make her case for healthy eating to a student. She was really into this.

"And Gene has never been much of a cook," Claudia continued. "He'd feed the kids fast food every night of the week if he could get away with it."

We reached the table, and I grabbed the last miniature cup of coleslaw.

"This is delicious," I said to Alyssa. "You must use only the freshest ingredients."

"Really, it's the dressing. Take a card. You'll be surprised to learn I use fat-free mayonnaise."

I was surprised. Fat-free mayonnaise wasn't even mayonnaise to me.

Unfortunately I didn't have time to stay and hear more. I had to meet Thomas Cook in five minutes and had a long walk through the Tech lab to take. I thanked Alyssa and scooted away. Claudia picked up where I'd left off. I heard the words "Magic Bullet" and "Christmas" in the same sentence and knew what I would be getting her and the family this year.

Walking through the corridor, I admitted to myself that Thomas Cook was the kind of academic I longed to be. He was young, he was smart, and he was hip. I was young and smart, but the differences between us were vast and myriad. I was infatuated with the past, and he was … not. He lived in that hazy place called *future*, discussing trends I might hear about in six months. *Might*. And he wasn't shy about sharing them. While the majority of the English Department was content with dialogue taking place inside their heads—a respectable place for the introverted—he voiced all his ideas out loud. This meeting, for instance. It was his suggestion, and maybe I could learn something from him. He'd been studying the language of crime for almost a year. He might bring a unique perspective to Miles's murder, an angle I hadn't considered.

Thomas was waiting at one of the long wooden tables on the first floor of the library. He was reading something on his laptop, his head bent and long bangs disguising his face. As I approached, he glanced up, and his thick hair fell back in place. *His highlights are better than Claudia's*, I thought as I took the seat across from him.

"Emmeline," he said with a smile. "You're right on time."

"Don't believe the rumors," I said, scooting in my chair.

"Your habitual tardiness isn't the only buzz. Rumor has it you're fast becoming an expert on campus crime, a *known* entity. So I ask myself, who is this lady of mystery? And why is crime dogging her like an evil hound?"

I laced my fingers together in front of me, preparing for a challenging conversation. "Technically, the crime didn't happen on campus; it happened at a bed and breakfast. And having been present doesn't make me an expert."

He leaned in across the table. His jaw was outlined with just the right amount of stubble. "Yes, but you were in the room with the man when he died. Quite remarkable."

I frowned. "How do you know that?"

"Barb. She said the police interviewed you in your office, and it wasn't the first time they'd been there."

The only one who knew I was in the room with Miles was Lenny, and he wouldn't have told Barb. She must have overheard Officer Beamer, though she had various ways of finding out information. She managed our paychecks, evaluations, and classroom locations. I wouldn't be surprised if she knew my favorite food and drink. (Coffee or wine? It was a tie as far as I was concerned.)

"Anyway," he continued, "you know my research is in composition and rhetoric."

I nodded. Who didn't? If anyone was a known entity, it was Thomas.

"My latest project concerns language and how it incites violence on campuses. Most of my research is on students' digital world, cyber stalking and bullying, but perhaps you could add something concrete, explicit. Words Miles used, or words used against him."

I forgot about the latter part of his statement. An idea had come to me. It had to do with the girl who'd stopped by unexpectedly the night of the open house. "So you're familiar with social media. Facebook, Twitter, YouTube?"

"Of course."

Thank god everybody wasn't a Luddite like me. "If students get harassed online, isn't it possible a professor could be, too?"

He considered the idea. "It's an interesting theory. Being the leader of a popular band, Miles certainly could be subject to harassment, especially from other bands or fans. And you know that most teachers don't publish their phone numbers for the same reason."

"Is there any way you could examine his online accounts to see if he was being hassled?"

"Luckily for you we're in a library," Thomas said, "and I'm a professional lurker."

I walked over to his side of the table. "May I?"

"Of course." He slid his laptop into the space between us. "Take a seat."

He opened the Internet application. Going to Twitter, he found Miles's handle right away, but nothing suspicious, just tweets and retweets about upcoming events. He opened Facebook, and after a few failed attempts, found a page for Jazz Underground. It had over ten thousand "likes."

"Popular band," said Thomas. "I'd never heard of them."

"Me neither," I said, looking over his shoulder.

Thomas scrolled through some old posts. "Look at this. The same person keeps commenting: JazzGirl763."

JazzGirl didn't have a photo, only an avatar. On the group's posts, she said Jazz Underground gave "awesome" live performances. She also said they were well worth the high admission price when another attendee complained. Although the comments were complimentary and even defensive, they'd stopped last year. Someone had commented about Miles being a playboy as recently as last month, yet there was no response from JazzGirl or anyone else.

"Couldn't he or the page administrator delete that?" I asked, pointing to the offensive remark.

"The page allows comments. It doesn't guarantee they're all going to be pleasant."

"With comments like those, why allow them at all?" I asked.

"Facebook's a beast," Thomas said, continuing to scroll. He explained that Facebook uses an algorithm to spread popular posts to more people. The more likes and comments a post gets, the farther the post travels into cyberspace. It behooved the group to leave the comments feature active, no matter how negative. And most of the comments were positive.

"What about JazzGirl? How can we find out more about her?" I asked.

Thomas clicked a few times. "We can't see her profile without friending her, but you can see she's a music fan. Look at all these public events she's shared. And she lives in Minneapolis." He pointed to the left side of the screen. "Or at least she used to. She hasn't shared an event for quite some time."

"That picture program on social media ... what about that? Can we find her picture there?"

"Instagram?" he said with a smile.

I nodded. "Yes, that's it."

He opened Instagram and searched for JazzGirl. She had hundreds of pictures, most of them taken at concerts, bars, and nightclubs. I spotted a picture of Jazz Underground on stage; I would recognize Belle's Barbie doll locks anywhere. I touched the screen and the caption read, "Live with the amazing Jazz Underground." Thomas continued to scroll, but the girl took lots of photos of bands and her guitar. Finally we hit pay dirt. Dressed in black, JazzGirl was in a selfie with Miles. She was young, maybe nineteen, and despite her gothic attire, quite innocent-looking. Wide and gray, her eyes were hauntingly familiar. I studied the picture more closely but couldn't place her. I'd met so many young people over the course of my teaching career, I was starting to forget faces and names. I turned to the caption, thinking it might help. It read, "A+ performance!" The picture was taken last year.

I glanced at Thomas. "You're a genius."

"I can't argue with that, but just because she's in a picture with Miles doesn't mean she was stalking him." He turned thoughtful. "She's just another grain of sand in the vast hourglass of cyberspace."

He was no poet, but he had a point. The picture didn't prove this girl wanted to harm Miles. The piece to the puzzle

Thomas didn't have, however, was the party crasher the night of the open house. Fortunately, I knew someone who had that piece: Pen, the employee at the Candlelight Inn. Now that I had a physical description, she could confirm whether the person was JazzGirl.

He rubbed his eyes. They, like mine, must have hurt from staring at the screen.

"Could you email me this picture?" I asked.

He laced his fingers. "For a small price."

"You know what our salaries pay. It had better be reasonable."

"You'll write this paper with me." His eyes narrowed.

I decided he was not only smart but shrewd. "First, tell me why. What could I possibly bring to the paper that you don't have already?"

"Involvement in three death investigations."

I nodded in agreement. I couldn't argue with that.

Chapter Nineteen

———

After I left the library, I called Lenny on his cellphone. First, I wanted to tell him about JazzGirl, and second, about Barb. She was spreading the news that I was in the room with Miles when he died. All thoughts floated out of my head, however, when he answered; they were replaced by reminders of last night's sleigh ride and kiss. Luckily he was used to my distractedness and seemed to think nothing of it. He was in his office, conferencing with literature students, and had a short break. I told him I was on my way.

Passing students as they rushed in and out of buildings, I refocused on Friday night and my suspicions. The unannounced girl didn't have a car; if she did, she would have left when Alyssa told her the gathering was faculty-only. If that person was JazzGirl, how could she have driven from Minneapolis without a car? Maybe she'd made the trip with a friend or knew better than to drive under the influence. Maybe she'd taken a cab or had her friend drop her off. These were all possibilities.

I entered Harriman Hall and ascended the stairs. Lenny's office door was open, with a folding chair placed outside of it for students awaiting their appointment. I took a seat, removing my gloves. It sounded as if the current student had missed his conference and was trying to get it rescheduled.

"Sorry, Dan. I'm booked. Just get the paper in before the end of the week, and you'll be fine, as long as it's decent."

Lenny and the student appeared at the door. The student looked relieved. "Thank you so much, Professor Jenkins. I'll get to work on it right away."

Lenny nodded. "Ms. Prather. You're next."

"Thank you for squeezing me in, Professor," I joked.

Lenny shut the door behind me.

"Do you think you should do that?" I said, unwrapping my scarf and nodding toward the door. My mind had returned to last night's kiss.

He sat down in his wooden office chair, leaning back. "What? Shut the door? Why not?"

I didn't want to admit that I was worried about gossip, about Jane Lemort. But he had only a short break between conferences. I would just keep him a minute. I shook off my concern. "Never mind. I wanted to ask you something. I was in the library with Thomas Cook, and he said—"

"That's the most unlikely thing I've ever heard you say," said Lenny, opening a bag of chips. "You guys are like water and oil."

"I know. Claudia talked me into it. Well, not really." I paused. "Thomas is writing a paper—when isn't he writing a paper?—and Claudia thought it would be a good idea for us to collaborate. But I met with him out of curiosity. I wondered if he could help with Miles's death, since he's an expert on violent language."

"And did he?"

"He did." I told Lenny about the uninvited guest and her connection to JazzGirl.

"So you're basically saying that Miles had a stalker, a super-fan?" He munched on a chip. "I guess I could see that. He was a good-looking guy, according to every woman with eyeballs, and pretty damn talented."

"I'm glad you agree." Being a musician, Lenny would know better than I about the likelihood of attracting a crazed fan.

"I didn't say I agreed. I just said I could see it. The girl from Friday night could have been anyone. Students are always looking for a party."

"A few miles from Copper Bluff? I don't think so," I said.

He held out his bag of chips. I took one, despite my earlier declaration to change my eating habits.

"It's worth asking about. The band members and I are meeting at the B&B Friday night after the performance. I can ask then."

"I'm sure the Beautiful Belle has had stalkers aplenty," I said, pointing with my chip. "Start with her."

"Em Prather, are you jealous?" asked Lenny. "Because that hint of snark in your voice tells me you are."

I rolled my eyes and took another chip.

"You know what this means, right?" He leaned forward in his chair. His jacket fell open, revealing a button-down shirt. His broad chest pulled at the material. "This means you have feelings for me. Otherwise you wouldn't be jealous."

I opened my mouth but couldn't deny it, especially with him so close. He smelled of sandalwood and soap.

"Careful what you say, Em. You're an open book." His long eyelashes blinked lazily as he waited for an answer. He reached out and touched my hand. My mouth went dry. Was he going to kiss me again? I couldn't even say who kissed whom last night; the moment passed so quickly. But now everything moved in slow motion, except the beating of my heart.

Three raps on the door answered the question. Giles poked in his head, glancing between Lenny and me. "Excuse me. I have a lost student looking for your office."

Lenny dropped my hand. "Thanks, Giles. Let him in."

A tall boy ducked through the doorway, and I stood. My cheeks felt warm. Thankfully, Giles had left. Maybe he hadn't noticed me flush, but Lenny did. His look was apologetic.

"Call me later."

I started toward the door.

"Prather."

I turned around.

"Is everything okay?"

"Of course."

I stumbled out of Lenny's office, only to meet with another difficulty. I wondered if I was being tested, and if so, how I was scoring. Officer Beamer and Giles were shaking hands outside Barb's office door, and Jane Lemort was walking in our direction. It was a trifecta of bad omens. If I could have ducked back into Lenny's office, I would have. Anything was better than facing Giles's expression or Jane's inquisition about last night's encounter. Thankfully, Beamer guessed at the complications.

"There you are, Ms. Prather. I was just asking Jim Giles where you were," said Beamer. "Let's walk."

I turned toward the stairs, and Beamer followed. I waited until we were in the deserted stairwell before thanking him for remaining silent in front of Barb. She had overheard one conversation. I didn't want to make it two. "Is this about the DNA results? Are they in?"

"They are."

"And …?" I asked, stopping by the vending machine on the first floor.

"They are a positive match for your hair."

I let the information sink in. This time my involvement in a crime was fundamental. I was fighting for my own freedom. Somehow, that made it no more important than the other cases I'd been involved in. The difference was my absolute certainty that the police had the wrong person.

I grabbed a dollar bill from my pocket. Only a king-sized Bing candy bar could bring me solace right now. "It doesn't mean anything, Officer Beamer. Miles grabbed for me before I pushed him away; you already knew that. He pulled out some hair, obviously."

Beamer adjusted his hat. "Uh-huh, except there's something else."

It figured. The candy bar dropped with a plunk, and I reached for it.

"Are you teaching a mystery book in one of your classes?" he continued.

What did my class have to do with Miles's murder? "Yes, in my Crimes and Passion course. Why?"

"Can you recall the name of that book?"

"Of course. *The Labours of Hercules*. Why?" I repeated, unwrapping the chocolate and cherry confection.

"Hercule Poirot. I bet he's one of your favorite sleuths. Being French and all."

"He's Belgian." I met Beamer's eyes for the first time and stopped unwrapping my candy bar. His look was grave. "Officer Beamer, why are you asking these questions? What do they have to do with Miles?"

"We found that book in Miles's belongings. We think it's one of the books from your class."

Instantly, I turned defensive. Taking a class on crimes did not make anyone a criminal. "My students wouldn't do anything like this," I said. "None of them were there. None of them knew Miles."

"Maybe not, but you were."

Beamer stood with his hands on his hips, legs just apart. He looked a lot less friendly than I knew him to be.

"You can't really believe *I'd* do something like this, can you?"

"It's crazy what I see in this business, Professor. I don't *want* to believe it, but I *can*. I have to. It's my job." He pulled down the earflaps on his hat. "You know the old baseball saying? Three strikes and you're out?"

I nodded.

"This is strike two."

I RAN FOR THE SAFETY of my books, not just because I was

worried, but because I thought they might help. I made a pot of coffee and started rereading *The Labours of Hercules*. This wasn't the first time the book had prompted investigation. In class, Kat had recalled Hugh's hallucinations in "The Cretan Bull," which made me wonder if Miles was hallucinating when he called me Aphrodite. It was possible, even probable, and maybe rereading could prompt more revelations. I started at the beginning, scanning stories, poisons, murders. These were Poirot's dead-end cases. Maybe they would prove dead ends for me, too. But why would Miles have the book in his possession? He wasn't from our campus, and he didn't even like books. If he'd had an interest in mysteries, wouldn't he have asked me?

I tossed the book on the floor. Maybe Lenny was right. Maybe books were my problem. The thing to do was to put away the book for now and focus on tomorrow. I had twenty-two papers to grade and one class to prep. Although rereading the Grande Dame of Mystery was a fun way to spend a late afternoon, it was doing Miles—or my career—no favors. And considering my recent indiscretions involving Lenny, a sleigh, and his office, I needed to focus harder than ever on my work. Giles needed to know I was serious about tenure. With murder and now love on my mind, I had to prove to him, and perhaps myself, that I still cared about academics.

For the rest of the night, I graded papers and entered percentages into the database. I didn't even break for supper. I had a turkey sandwich and chips, eating them at the kitchen table while I worked. Once in a while, I would glance at my Christmas tree and wonder if I shouldn't move a bulb or add a piece of tinsel but stopped myself each time, remembering to stay serious. Plus, I had the bad habit of rearranging the decorations on my Christmas tree the entire holiday season. Once I started, it was hard to tear myself away. Tinkering could occupy the rest of the night.

It was only after I'd graded the papers, planned my lesson, and taken a bath that I picked up the book I'd left lying on the floor. Padding into my bedroom in my Eiffel Tower pajamas and Paris slippers, I turned on my nightstand lamp. I might as well finish up where I'd left off. There was no harm in that.

I leaned back onto the bed pillows with the book in hand, listening to the wind whistle through the house. Nature had a way of reminding me of my own insufficiencies. No matter how hard I tried, someone tried harder—in this case, Miles's murderer. He or she had been able to commit homicide without leaving a trace of evidence at autopsy. Except for my hair (and now book), nothing linked the death to another person. But as I shut off the lamp and snuggled into my down comforter, I was more convinced than ever someone had killed him, someone who wasn't me.

Chapter Twenty

I arrived on campus early Friday morning, my tote stuffed with folders. I felt like Santa Claus with packages to deliver, albeit some were akin to lumps of coal. After making copies of a worksheet, I went to my office and reviewed my lesson plan. Although no one was around to witness my ambitious start, my diligence paid off. I knocked out ten more quizzes before I rushed off to my Crimes and Passion course, nearly bumping into Giles as I turned toward the passageway.

"Good morning, Emmeline," he said. He looked serious, but that wasn't unusual. He had three deep horizontal grooves in his forehead that made him look perpetually concerned. Sometimes his sweep of brown hair covered them up, but not until later in the day, when the wind had taken its toll.

"Good morning," I said. "I'm off to deliver good tidings." I gestured toward my sack.

He smiled. "When you have a moment, could you stop by my office? I want to talk to you about something."

My chest tightened. *Something?* Giles was never ambiguous. What could be the trouble? "Of course. No problem."

"Have a good class," he said, and I continued down the

hall, wondering what he wanted to discuss. Was it about Lenny and me? An archaic rule probably existed that said untenured colleagues couldn't date. It was buried somewhere in chapter sixteen, line twenty-seven of the handbook, or something like that. I had a handbook. I'm sure it was in my desk or closet or file cabinet. *I should have been thumbing through that in the middle of the night instead of my Agatha Christie novel*, I thought. Yet maybe my actions would benefit my class somehow. Maybe someone would be writing a paper on the stories I had reread.

The room in Winsor was no warmer than it had been on Wednesday, but sunlight cascaded through the dormer windows today, making it seem cozier. I shrugged off my coat, taking a chance that my long purple sweater and gray leggings would be enough to keep me warm. I wrote the day's lesson on the chalkboard and dusted off my hands. The class chatted in their circles until I walked to the podium and smiled. Unlike my freshmen students, they knew enough to stop talking when I approached the lectern.

"Here we are again, in the middle of a murder. And speaking of murder, I finished grading your papers."

The class laughed as I returned their second essays. The final essay was due soon, and today we were reviewing their first drafts. I asked them if they had any questions about their grades or the grading rubric. They remained silent, which didn't mean they didn't have questions. It just meant they would ask me privately or in an email.

"So, last class period, we talked about the hallucinations. How they tipped off Poirot to Hugh's problem. We also talked about final papers and topics. Do you have questions about your final essay? It's due a week from today."

One student asked how many sources to include, and another asked a question about MLA (Modern Language Association) format. After answering, I sorted them into groups for peer review. They would be reading their rough drafts to their group members. Kat asked me to read hers because she hated reading aloud, as many students did. The fact was, though, lots of students found errors or omissions by reading their essays aloud, and none of them read aloud outside of the classroom. So I kept it on as an activity despite their objections.

I settled into Kat's group, which included John and Jackie, and began to read. Kat was a good writer, and her paper was easy to deliver. Although she hadn't included research, which wasn't required in this draft, she had quoted several passages from our last short story, "The Cretan Bull." I stopped midsentence on one of the quotations, rescanning the text. During one of Hugh's hallucinations, he sees a skeleton. But that's not what gave me pause. What surprised me were his eyes: they were "widely dilated."

"What's wrong?" asked Kat. "I'm supposed to include the page number, not the year, right? I knew it."

I nodded. MLA required the page number, not the year. But I wasn't thinking of formatting rules. I was thinking of Miles Jamison. His eyes were dilated, abnormally so. *That's* what had given him the wild look I mistook for a drug overdose. I continued reading Kat's paper, but all the while, my mind stayed on Miles. They say eyes are the windows to the soul. I hoped they could also be clues to cause of death. With more evidence mounting against me, I needed a new direction to follow. Maybe this was it.

AFTER CLASS, I PRACTICALLY RAN back to the English Department. Only when I hit the rickety passageway between Winsor and Harriman Hall did I slow down. I had an idea and needed to call Sophie Barnes. In the story Kat quoted, "The Cretan Bull," Hugh's aftershave is tainted, which makes him hallucinate. Could someone have poisoned Miles's possessions? If evidence couldn't be found in his system, maybe it could be found in his belongings. Obviously the police had his things, because Beamer made the connection between the Agatha Christie compilation and me. What else had been collected as evidence at the time of his death and what, if anything, could be tested?

I was glad to see Giles had Allen Dunsbar in his office as I walked past. He couldn't talk to me if he was already talking to Dunsbar, who was famous for his habitual laziness. I overheard the word "participation" as I unlocked my door and closed it behind me. I shook my head. That was one word not in Dunsbar's toolbox.

I picked up my office phone, a relic pushbutton with a coiled black cord. I had Sophie's number in my cellphone's address book, which I referenced as I dialed. I wanted to keep my cellphone available in case I needed to search the Internet. With all my papers graded, I'd left my laptop home.

Sophie answered on the second ring. "Detective Barnes."

"Sophie, it's me, Em."

"Professor Prather? Is everything okay? You sound ... different."

I twirled the phone cord around my finger. "Yes, fine. I'm in my office and don't want my colleagues to overhear our conversation."

"Sure, I get it. Nosy neighbors. So, what's up?"

"I had an idea. I wanted to run it past you." Then, more quietly I said, "It's about Miles Jamison."

"Go ahead. Shoot."

"Beamer said nothing was found in his system, as far as drugs go. But what about his belongings? Could you take another look at them? Maybe he had ... I don't know ... aftershave with him. It could have been tainted."

Sophie readjusted her phone. "That sounds really specific for an idea. Do you have cause to believe someone tainted his aftershave?"

I looked down at my Agatha Christie book. "No, not technically. But you keep the victim's belongings as evidence, right?"

"Sure, in cases like this we do. But I can't go searching through them without a reason."

She was starting to sound an awful lot like Officer Beamer. I leaned back in my chair, staring out the frost-covered window. I didn't want to bring up the book, especially since it linked me to the crime, but I had to tell her where the idea came from if I wanted her to investigate.

"Professor?"

I cleared my throat. "You know I read a lot of literature."

"Of course. You teach it."

"I read a lot of mysteries, too, and I recently read one where the victim's eyes are dilated, and it reminded me that Miles's eyes were incredibly dilated Saturday morning. It was his eyes that gave me the idea he was on drugs."

"Drugs can cause the eyes to dilate. That's true," said Sophie. "Crack, cocaine, methamphetamines. They all cause extreme dilation of the eyes."

"So, what if something like that was put into his aftershave or cologne or body wash? Maybe he took it unknowingly, like this guy in the story."

"But if he absorbed enough to kill him, it should have shown up in his urine or blood," said Sophie.

She sounded pragmatic, but I was convincing her to take a second look. It made sense that the killer used something that had gone undetected by police. "True, but since nothing was found during autopsy, why not check his belongings? It might not be one of those common drugs that killed him. It could be anything. It could be," I looked again at the Christie novel, "a poison or chemical. Remember Austin Oliver?"

She didn't respond right away, and I knew she was thinking about last fall. Austin Oliver was a student of mine who had died in the theater, and it had taken the police an awfully long time to figure out how.

"I'll see what I can find," said Sophie.

"Thank you, Sophie. Will you tell me if—" A loud knock at my door interrupted our conversation. Lenny stuck in his head, and I almost dropped the phone. I waved him in. Surprisingly, Belle followed, her hair arranged in an elegant fishtail braid over her shoulder.

"Professor? Are you there?"

"Yes. Would you please just let me know what you find? Thank you." We said goodbye and hung up. I didn't want Belle to know I was talking to the police, and with my office being as small as it was, privacy was impossible. I had one other chair in the room, but they both remained standing. Lenny had on his coat.

"Did we interrupt?" said Lenny.

He had a way of knowing when something was on my mind, so I reassured him everything was fine. "No, not at all. I was just finishing up a call. It's good to see you again, Belle. I hear congratulations are in order. You're going to judge the Cliburn."

"Thank you, Emmeline. I appreciate that," said Belle.

"We were wondering if you wanted to go to lunch," said Lenny. "I know you have an afternoon class, but so do I. Belle has the van outside."

Lunch would give me more time to talk to Belle about how the college was handling Miles's death. Besides, I was hungry. "Sure, just let me grab my coat. Where are you going?"

Lenny shrugged his shoulders. "Something quick. Roca de Taco?"

"Oh, good idea. It's Fajita Friday." Roca de Taco was a terrific Mexican restaurant downtown, and on Fridays, two fajitas cost just five dollars. Locals mispronounced it "Rock-o day Taco," but the food was authentic. The fajitas were hot, spicy, and fast.

I donned my coat and turned the office key, which was still hanging in the lock. I hurried Lenny and Belle down the stairs before Giles, who was walking Dunsbar to his office, could stop us. I didn't want him to see this as his chance to talk to Lenny and me together.

"Where are Kim and Josh?" I asked on the stairwell.

"At the inn. They ate on the way down, but I deplore fast food. They're unpacking."

Unpacking. I wondered if that wasn't all they were doing.

"Who were you talking to on the phone?" Lenny asked me

as he held open the outside door. It was almost warm outside. "It looked serious."

"My mother." I couldn't think of anyone else. He quirked an eyebrow as I walked past him, and I mouthed, "Sophie." He nodded in understanding and said nothing more.

"This is us, the big brown van," said Belle.

Getting into the vehicle, I noticed it was used to transport instruments. A few black music stands were propped up in the back.

"Sorry about the mess. Things have been in disarray since Miles's death. After this performance, we're going to have to have a serious talk about Jazz Underground."

"Do you think you'll stop performing?" I asked as I buckled my seatbelt. Belle let out a chuckle. Despite being only a few years older, she had a knowledgeable air not found in many young professors. If she weren't so talented, I would have called it conceit.

"God no. Jazz Underground is incredibly popular. And although Miles will be desperately missed, he won't be hard to replace. Lenny, for instance, could take his place in a heartbeat. Not just for this performance."

For the second time that morning, I was speechless. Did Belle want to replace Miles permanently with Lenny? She was, after all, the link between the quartet and Lenny's invitation to play. If she hadn't known him, the invite might not have been extended.

"Right. I could never keep up with your schedule," said Lenny. "Besides, I'm an English teacher."

"Haven't you heard?" said Belle as she accelerated out of the parking lot. "We have a big university up in Minneapolis."

"Big. That's the key word. I like keeping things small."

"Your parents would be thrilled," said Belle. "And there are so many more opportunities up there—musically."

"I like Copper Bluff. It's a cool town. Take a right. Roca de Taco is there, on the corner."

"No offense, but not much is happening here. I can't see

how it can be good for your career."

Lenny and I exchanged glances. Neither of us had a retort. Copper Bluff probably wasn't the best place to launch a star-studded career such as Belle's. We wouldn't be asked to be jurors on panels or fly across the world to judge competitions. We wouldn't publish best-selling work or meet esteemed academics. But maybe our careers weren't the most important aspect of our lives either. We were still figuring that out.

Belle pulled into an open parking spot in front of Roca de Taco. The restaurant was busy, and the walk-up line to place an order was five deep. Yet the room was stuffed with little orange tables and could accommodate lots of customers. Belle glanced at the mural as we waited in line. Spanning the opposite wall, it showcased a Mexican landscape with a large rock shaped like a taco. At the bottom of the rock, people wearing colorful sombreros rested or ate.

The line moved quickly, and soon we ordered our food and filled our drink glasses. Then we found a clean table and waited. We had all ordered the fajitas, so the wait wouldn't be long.

I emptied two sugar packets into my iced tea and stirred. "So how is the college dealing with Miles's death?"

"Fine," said Belle. "You know universities. They have lists of people a mile long waiting for open positions."

No, I didn't know that. Our college rarely had openings, but when it did, they took a good deal of legwork to fill. The pay wasn't the most persuasive and neither was the rural location. But those of us who'd relocated had found something, or escaped something, that others hadn't. I wouldn't have traded it for a plummy appointment at Oxford University.

"The real loss will be felt with his recording studio. He worked with so many artists." She let out a sigh. "I still can't believe it."

"I heard he was a songwriter," I said.

She nodded as she sipped her diet soda. "He was. He was a *published* songwriter. I've never had the desire myself, but

Lenny, he's dabbled in writing songs since we were kids." She laughed and gave him a nudge. "Remember that one? About the cat?"

He nodded. " 'Calico Socks.' How could I forget?"

"I didn't know you write songs," I said.

"I don't."

"Oh, he does," said Belle with a sly smile.

There was that nudge again, the one that felt like a kiss. It made sense that Belle knew things about Lenny that I didn't. She was his childhood friend. That didn't mean I had to like it.

"It doesn't surprise me," I said. "Lenny can be quite poetic."

Lenny smiled. "Thanks, Em."

Three steaming pans of fajitas were delivered to our table. I waited for the crackling to die down before I continued, "So, what will happen to Miles's studio?"

Belle heaped guacamole and sour cream onto her fajitas. I didn't know where she put all the extra food, certainly not on her hips. "I don't know. I suppose Josh will have sole proprietorship. He gives private lessons, you know. That's how he makes his living—though really, I don't know how he does it. I can't think of anything worse. Can you? Giving drum lessons to preteen boys? No thanks."

"Hey, preteen boys aren't all that bad," said Lenny.

"Sorry, no offense," said Belle. "I forgot you were once a preteen boy yourself, and a cute one at that."

We finished our lunch and chatted about the concert for the next twenty minutes. I asked them both about stage fright, but Belle said she never got it. Lenny professed to some anxiety, especially since this was his first time playing at the university. He didn't want to make a fool of himself.

"I can't believe it," I said as we returned to the van. I resumed my seat in the back. "You're never afraid to perform. I love that about you."

Belle glanced at me in the rearview mirror.

"In the sense that I love that quality about you. Because I don't have it myself, which I wish I did." My stuttering only made my embarrassment worse. I opened my mouth to try again, but Lenny stopped me.

"You're wrong, Em. You're incredibly brave. Sneaking around a theater after dark, stopping an award ceremony mid-agenda. What about that?"

I laughed. In those cases I hadn't considered my actions brave; I considered them my duty. "That's different."

Belle pulled into a handicapped spot in the parking lot of Harriman Hall. "So, I will see you later. Warm up one hour before?"

"I'm planning on it," said Lenny. "I'll call you after class. You need to see our new venue."

"Good luck," I said as I unbuckled my seatbelt. "Or is it 'break a leg'? I can never remember."

"Goodbye, Emmeline," Belle said. "I'm sure I'll see you later."

Lenny gave the van door a shove behind us. My class was in Stanton, but I needed to grab my textbook first. He was going directly to class, meeting a student early. We paused for a moment before heading in different directions.

"So I'll see you at the concert, I guess. You're going to be great, by the way. I can't wait."

He smiled, showing his perfect dimple. "You'll come with us to the Candlelight afterwards, right?"

"Of course. I wouldn't miss it."

He walked toward campus, slinging his messenger bag over one broad shoulder. I turned toward Harriman Hall, still thinking about Lenny and tonight's concert. The suspects would be assembled again in one place. All of them had motives, all of them were musical, and all of them were competitive. Suddenly a chill came over me that had nothing to do with December, and I worried about more than someone playing off key.

Chapter Twenty-One

———

Giles was outside the English office; there was no dodging him this time. He smiled and asked if we could talk. I told him I was on my way to class, but he promised what he had to say was important and would take only a minute. He followed me to my office, chatting about the English Department holiday party. He hoped I would be able to join the festivities at his house. He and his wife, Katherine, hosted a potluck twice a year in their gorgeous Queen Anne-style home, and at Christmas, red wine flowed copiously. Everyone brought a bottle or two, though one had to be careful to avoid the grad students' cheap stuff. Whenever they asked me what to bring, I always answered "chips."

"So, I mentioned earlier I wanted to talk to you," Giles said, as I gathered my text and handbook off my desk. "I have to ask you something, and I want you to be honest in your answer."

I nodded curtly, steeling myself for what was coming. Really, it was none of Giles's business whom I dated. In fact, Lenny and I weren't even dating. I could feel confident saying that because it was true. Jane seeing us kiss meant nothing. Well, it meant one thing: she needed to get a life outside of the campus.

"I need someone to write an article on Shakespeare's Garden for the alumni newsletter, and I think you're just the person."

I stopped zipping my backpack. Maybe this wasn't about Lenny and me.

"I know it's an incredibly hectic time of year, but hear me out." He swept his brown hair off his forehead, preparing for battle. He knew nobody had time to spare during the last few weeks of the semester. "You like to investigate … and, well, this situation requires a bit of investigation. You would need to visit the campus conservatory, take some pictures, and write about one thousand words to update the alumni on the garden restoration taking place this spring. What would you say to that?"

I almost laughed. Despite the extra work required, I felt as light as a butterfly. "Of course. I'd be happy to. But what about Reed Williams? Shouldn't he be the one to write the piece?"

Reed Williams was the Shakespeare scholar. He was considered the expert on anything that began with Thee or Thou.

"Perhaps, but he's knee deep in procuring Shakespeare's first folio for display next spring. He wants to coordinate it with the reopening of the garden."

"I understand. I'll get started right away."

He let out a small cough. "And Emmeline, there's one more thing …."

I hoisted my sack on my back. "Yes?"

"I need it by next week."

"I will get started on it after class, then."

"Thank you, Emmeline. You can't imagine what relief this brings me."

Nor could he imagine what relief it brought me. I thought he was going to corner me about Lenny. A thousand words were a drop in the bucket compared to being sanctioned by one's boss about a relationship. Not that it still couldn't happen,

I reminded myself. He might be timing his questions wisely, as in, after I completed my assignment.

Finished gathering my materials, I crossed the quad to Stanton Hall. The day was unseasonably warm, and the campus couldn't have been lovelier. Above, the sun glinted off the towering peaks of Stanton, the snow-crested steeples dazzling white. Belle's university might be bigger, I thought as I pulled open the heavy door, but it certainly wasn't better. She could keep her opportunities; I would keep Copper Bluff.

Ignoring the clumps of students pushing past me to get to class, I stood inside Stanton. I had a full three minutes before the top of the hour. They weren't going to rush me. Taking a breath, I ascended the stairs. André was filling his water bottle on the second floor, and I inquired about his class.

"The best thing about it is it's almost over."

I shrugged. "Some semesters feel that way."

"Tonight, you will be at the concert?"

"Yes, I'll save you a seat, or vice versa. Take your phone with you. I'll send a text."

He laughed. "*You* take *your* phone. You are the one who never answers."

I pointed to the faucet, but it was too late. The water was spilling over. "See you tonight," I said with a wave.

I walked into my classroom and looked around at the filled seats, smiling. My freshmen had redeemed themselves. Despite the fact that it was Friday, the day was decently warm, and we were on the downside of the semester, every student was in attendance. Their participation made my job easy, and before I knew it, fifty minutes had passed. My day was officially over. I had the greenhouse to explore and a few pictures to snap for the Shakespeare's Garden alumni article, but that wouldn't take long.

On my way to the conservatory, I walked by Shakespeare's Garden, stopping to take a quick picture. Maybe it would serve as a "before." It reminded me a little of André's class: the best thing about it was it would soon be replaced with something else. I opened the creaky black gate under the arched, wrought-iron sign that read "Shakespeare's Garden, dedicated by the class of 1923." It looked as if it hadn't been tended to since 1923. Little stubbles poked out here and there from beneath the snow, and the one bench in the garden had become encrusted in rust. But the area was good-sized, and with a little planning and care, it could be beautiful. As I shut the gate, I was interested to see what the new garden would look like.

I continued walking toward the conservatory, which was connected to the science building by a long breezeway. I tried the door, but it was locked. I needed a key to get in. It was Friday afternoon, and although this normally meant fewer personnel, I knew most faculty were clocking extra hours right now to meet upcoming grading deadlines. I turned back to the Thompson-Carter Science Center and walked to the second floor, which housed the Biology Department.

A friendly, middle-aged woman greeted me as I entered the main office. "Hi! How can I help you?"

They had a much perkier professional assistant than we did. "Hello, I'm Emmeline Prather, and I teach for the English Department. I'm in the process of writing an article for the alumni newsletter and hoped I could take a peek in the greenhouse. We're growing some plants for Shakespeare's Garden, and my chair thought we should update our alumni on the progress of the renovation, especially since lots of them are donors."

She grabbed a large key ring from a hook beside her desk. "Well, let's just get you in there so you can take some pictures!"

Her energy was infectious, and I smiled. "Thank you. That would be wonderful."

She stood, and I followed her down the stairs and through the hallway. She gave the impression of being busy and moved quickly and with purpose, her dark bob swishing back and forth. "I'm Tanya, by the way. It seems unfair that I know your name and you don't know mine."

I was going to ask her name as soon as she slowed down. She didn't bother to turn around as she spoke, which made conversation difficult. "I'm glad to meet you," I called out. "I'll probably be back sometime in the future, so it's great to have a contact."

Tanya stopped at the door and shoved in her key. "Well, I don't know a darn thing about these plants, but I sure can tell you about all the biology professors' weird quirks." She glanced over her shoulder. "Just kidding. Not about the plants, though. Here we are."

The greenhouse wasn't as muggy as I thought it would be. It was a comfortable seventy-two degrees inside—and green. Everywhere I looked, ornamental plants and flowers along with vegetables and herbs were organized by rows or purpose. A miniature cornfield took up the entire corner, and a crop of leafy greens stretched over the walkway on our right. If color was any indication, Shakespeare's Garden was the array of flowers to our left. I squinted at the sign: "Property of the English Department." The garden had its own walking path, and I turned down it.

"You don't mind, do you?" Tanya asked. She stood at the door. "I have to get the mail out by three thirty."

"No, of course not, but how do I lock up?"

"It will lock itself when you leave. Have a great weekend."

She was gone before I could wish her the same.

I knew nothing about flowers. I was a terrible gardener. Sometimes just my presence could make plants wilt. I tiptoed down the path, trying not to touch anything. The last thing I needed was to inadvertently kill something.

I was surprised by the flowers' size. Full grown, many plants had buds, flowers, or berries on them. This project must have been going for some time. I circled the corner, noting that the flowers were arranged by plays, first the comedies then the tragedies: *A Midsummer Night's Dream*, *Love's Labour's Lost*, *The Taming of the Shrew*, *Hamlet*, *Macbeth*, *Romeo and Juliet*. Restoring Shakespeare's Garden to its original splendor was a great idea, and I was glad someone in the department implemented it. Its history and connection to literature was too important to let it go. *These are ideas I should be having,* I thought to myself as I snapped several pictures. Like André's French movie night—why hadn't I thought of something like that? Giles was right, as usual. I needed to put my investigative skills to better use. As soon as this semester was over, I was going to ask him what else I might get involved in, besides murder.

The door locked behind me as I left the conservatory. Walking through the breezeway, I looked through some of the pictures on my phone. They were bright spots of color in an otherwise white winter. Anyone would love to see these pictures pop up in their inbox. I almost bumped into Pen, the employee from the Candlelight, as I crossed into the science building.

"Oh I'm sorry … Pen!" I exclaimed. This was an opportunity to ask her about last Friday's party crasher. "I was walking and looking down at my phone, just like one of my students."

"No worries. Everyone has that bad habit," said Pen. She wore a long wool coat that tied around her waist and a tight stocking cap that revealed only the pixie ends of her black hair. She could have passed for a grad student; she had a trendy look that made her fit in easily.

"What are you doing on campus? I thought you'd be helping Alyssa with tonight's reception."

"We have everything made. I'll be back to help serve, though. I'm here to see my dad," Pen said, glancing up the stairs. "He's a professor in the Biology Department."

"Oh, I didn't realize. What's your last name?" I reached for my gloves.

"Dobbs."

I stopped putting on my gloves. "Dobbs? Cornelius Dobbs?" Professor Dobbs was a major philanthropist in Copper Bluff and probably the richest man in town. I couldn't believe Pen was his daughter, but now her name made sense. Academics loved naming their children after famous people, events, and laws. Penelope was the faithful wife of Odysseus during the Trojan War. Perhaps she was Professor Dobbs' inspiration. Plus, Cornelius? Maybe unique names ran in the family.

She laughed. "Everyone has that reaction. They don't get why a millionaire's daughter is working as hired help at the Candlelight Inn."

"I didn't think that at all," I lied.

"That's okay. He's a good dad, sent me to one of the best culinary schools in the U.S., and now he's going to loan me the money for my new business. He believes in hard work, and so do I. It was great working under Alyssa, but I'm ready to do something on my own. Besides, with the death at the inn, Dad thinks now is the perfect time. He doesn't want our good name 'sullied.' "

"It has been in the papers a lot lately." I finished putting on my gloves. "Poor Alyssa. She's worked so hard to maintain a beautiful place for visitors. I hope it doesn't affect her business."

Pen shrugged. "She'll be fine. She's sitting on a gold mine out there. Look around." She gestured with her hand. "There aren't a lot of other options for people to stay."

"True," I said with a nod. "Have you told her yet?"

"Alyssa? No. I want to make sure my dad is ready with the loan. In fact, I'd better get moving. I don't want to keep him waiting. He'll accuse me of being *irresponsible*."

"Of course. If I could ask you one thing, really quickly …. That girl who tried to attend the party last Friday, at the Candlelight?"

Pen nodded.

"Where did you bring her? Is she a student here?"

"Nice, right? I'm even Alyssa's errand girl when I need to be."

I waited.

"Anyway, yeah, she's a student here. She heard one of her professors talking about it. He said it was an open house, so that's why she came. She thought he meant 'open' to everyone."

"Who was the professor? Did she say?"

"Johnson? No. Jenkins." She fanned her face. "Oh, that girl was hot for him. I can see why, too. He *is* hot. But I like blonds."

She turned to walk up the stairs.

"Wait! Do you remember her name?"

She thought for a moment. "Her friends called her Karen. I dropped her off at the pub."

"Thank you. See you later," I said. Maybe her dad was right. Pen's actions were irresponsible at best. She shouldn't have taken a young girl who had been drinking to a bar. She should've taken her back to a dorm or to a trusted friend's house.

Pen took the stairs two at a time to her dad's office while I stood below, digesting the information. So the party crasher wasn't Miles's stalker JazzGirl; it was Lenny's student. And to be fair, she didn't really crash the party. She simply tried to attend. I would ask Lenny if he had a Karen in his class and get a description. It was possible Karen *was* JazzGirl, if she'd relocated. Maybe that's why she looked so familiar. Maybe I'd seen her on campus. Although the idea was a long shot, I wasn't ruling it out.

Bracing myself for the outdoors, I realized something else I'd gleaned from my conversation with Pen. Miles's death had benefited her. It had prompted her dad to loan her the money for her new patisserie. Without this gift, who knows how long she would have had to work for Alyssa before he thought she was "ready," which was a myth anyway. Yet I'd seen many parents make the same error. They had a hard time believing their sons or daughters were ready for anything, especially the working world.

I quickened my step as I approached Oxford Street. The conservatory had been a short hiatus from winter, but now the late hour reminded me of the season. What I needed was a hot cup of coffee and one of Mrs. Gunderson's cookies. Sitting down at my computer with refreshments, I would begin the article for the alumni news right away. My enthusiasm for

Shakespeare's Garden was still with me, and I wanted that to come through in my words. Once it was time for the concert, I knew I would think of nothing but Lenny and the quartet. Well, not quartet anymore, I corrected, approaching my house. Trio.

My bungalow shone happy yellow beneath the white snowcapped roof, and with Dickinson waiting for me in the front window, I was glad to be *home*. I smiled. Copper Bluff surprised me like that, revealing little ways I was beginning to fit in. A city transplant, I sometimes doubted whether I belonged. The town was like a great book and I, the reader who hoped it would never end. But sometimes, like today, Copper Bluff promised other volumes, and I was content to turn the page.

Chapter Twenty-Two

Two hours later, I had seven-hundred-and-fifty words, not bad for someone who hadn't read Shakespeare in years and knew nothing about plants. Giles had forwarded me the minutes from the planning committee meeting, which gave me the context I needed to write the article. I would finish it this weekend and hand it in on Monday. But now it was time to get ready for the concert, and I was eager to try on my crimson dress, a festive favorite. I just hoped the roads were clear enough for my '69 Mustang because there was no way I was walking to campus in heels. It might have been the best car in the world, but it was not so good on snow, and the town of Copper Bluff was slow with snow removal.

I rose from my desk, stretched, and walked into the kitchen to grab a snack before changing. The Candlelight Inn was hosting a reception after the concert, so I only needed something to tide me over for a couple of hours. I cut a few slices of cheese to go with my apple and brought them to the table, thinking of Lenny. I hoped the rescheduled concert was well attended. The university would want a good showing to entice other performers to come to Copper Bluff. I had done my part, I thought as I took my last bite of apple. I'd offered ten points of extra credit to any student who attended the concert and wrote their response to it. Knowing the low scores my freshmen had received on their recent grammar quizzes, I expected to see quite a few of them at the concert.

After putting away my plate and washing my hands, I started to get ready. The concert was an hour away, and I wanted to arrive in time to secure a good seat. I took my crimson dress out of the closet and laid it on my bed. Dickinson took the opportunity to jump on it and examine it up close. I shooed her away, deciding the material was perfect. It was long-sleeved, with just a sprinkle of gold beading at the cuffs, and the hem hit just above the knee. The fabric was silky and flowing. Plus, I had a pair of dangly gold earrings that would look fabulous with it. After finding them in my armoire, I put on my dress and shoes and took the earrings into the bathroom with me. I stacked my curls in a high ponytail, leaving a few around my face. Then I put in the earrings with the hint of sparkle.

Grabbing a black clutch that matched my heels, I slipped my cellphone, lip gloss, and cash inside and walked out the door. It seemed silly to drive the two blocks to campus, especially considering what a nightmare it was to find parking, but it was early enough that a few spots remained open near Pender Hall. The tires on my Mustang spun as I put it in reverse, easing into an open spot. The mild weather earlier had warmed the ground, and the cold evening air created a heavy fog, covering the roads with frost. I would need to drive carefully after the concert.

I noted several people approaching Pender and decided the foot traffic boded well for the event. From the front, Pender looked like a plain, three-story brick building. Only from the other direction would a visitor realize it housed a large auditorium. Tonight I took the elevator to the third floor; there was no way I'd dare to mount stairs in high-heels. I could be klutzy enough in tennis shoes.

An usher handed me a program, and I walked down the

middle aisle, scanning the room for André. I didn't see him but did see Giles and his lovely wife, Katherine. I smiled and waved as I approached his row. My smile faded when I saw who sat next to him: Jane Lemort. Although I wanted to avoid her, I didn't see how. Claudia and Gene were also in the row, which meant it was the general seating area for English faculty. It would be rude not to join them.

"I knew you'd be here, Emmeline; I just didn't know you'd be so dressed up," said Jane as I scooted into my seat. Not surprisingly, she sported gothic black.

"What a lovely outfit," said Claudia. "You look gorgeous." She stood, leaving her purse on her chair and providing a buffer between Jane and me. Claudia wore an emerald-green dress with fur around the cuffs and hem, and her hair was tied up in a gold scarf. Had I attempted the outfit, I would have looked like an elf, but on Claudia, the effect was artistic and chic.

"How did the meeting go with Thomas?" asked Claudia. Then to Giles, "I don't know if you've heard, but Em is collaborating with Thomas Cook on his latest article."

"Glad to hear it," said Giles. "It's gratifying to know faculty members can work together as a team."

"Especially when it involves a sleigh ride," Jane added.

Giles gave Jane a quizzical glance and continued, "When will you submit it for publication?"

"We're still in the … research phase," I said. It wasn't a lie. Not a word had been written, at least not by me.

"That's where you excel," said Claudia. "Research. You're never afraid to get below the surface. Some people prefer to stay on the shallow end of things." Although she didn't so much as look in Jane's direction, the criticism was meant for her.

Katherine asked Giles a question, drawing his attention.

Jane's lips formed a thin line. Maybe she was mad at Claudia or maybe she was mad that I was writing an article with Thomas. Or maybe she was just a contentious person. I was starting to believe the latter, which she confirmed by saying, "I'm dying to know. How long have you and Lenny been seeing each other? I assume Claudia knows."

Had she asked me the question somewhere else—anywhere else—I might have handled it differently. But with my boss one seat away, I felt vulnerable and exposed. *I* didn't even know where our relationship stood. How could I describe it to Jane, or worse, Giles? Nothing had been the same since Belle arrived in Copper Bluff. Excluding our cherished moment in the sleigh, things had been different. And as I looked back, the kiss was so fleeting that I could've almost dreamed it—except that Jane had witnessed it and now wanted to discuss it. She waited for an answer.

My phone buzzed, and I took it out of my clutch, happy to leave Jane hanging. André was here, and I texted him our location. I stood to watch for his entrance, glad for the interruption. The main floor of the auditorium was filling, and very few seats remained near the stage.

Dressed in a purple Oxford shirt and black blazer, André was hard to miss. Every woman's head turned as he walked down the aisle, but he was looking at me. I waved and smiled, then sat back down in my seat, pleased with the stupefied look on Jane's face. If anything could silence a woman, it was a hunky Frenchman.

The row had filled, so Claudia returned to her seat next to Gene, and André took her place. It made me happy that Jane would be close enough to André to smell his expensive cologne and hear his dashing accent. I doubted she would ask anything more about Lenny. She was distracted enough by André's *bonjour*. All she could say was "Hi."

"You look *très belle* tonight," said André. "The holidays are my favorite time for this reason. People are at their best. Wouldn't you agree?"

Had it not been for Jane Lemort, I would have agreed. I nodded anyway. "You look very nice. Purple is your color."

He dismissed my compliment. "You're just being kind, but thank you." He glanced around the room. "A wonderful turnout. Good news for our dear friend. Truthfully, I was worried for him, so I told my on-campus class I would allow them to take home their final if they attended." He indicated to his right. "They did not disappoint."

I smiled at him. "How kind of you."

"He's our good friend, no?"

"Yes, he's our good *friend*," I said, repeating it loud enough for Jane to hear.

The lights dimmed, and the band appeared. Tad Iverson approached the center microphone. He thanked everyone for attending, especially during this busy time of the year. After reading off the long list of awards, distinctions, and honors showered on Jazz Underground members, he introduced Lenny as their guest performer. Although his list of accolades was minimal, the applause was heavy as Lenny joined the trio on stage. He gave the audience a brief wave before taking his place.

They began with a song I didn't recognize, or thought I didn't recognize until Belle started her solo riff. Then I identified it as "Carol of the Bells." The way she hammered the keys made the music familiar, like bells at midnight Mass. Her playing mesmerized the crowd, and I wished I wasn't just a bystander, wished I had an ounce of talent. But we were outsiders looking in. Jazz Underground had a special bond that had formed over many songs, sessions, and performances. An intimacy existed among them that excluded outsiders. Other than Lenny. He tapped into it when he joined in on his guitar. He had been invited. The rest of us would have to settle for being inspired.

The concert lasted for ninety minutes and featured a mix of holiday, jazz, and blues favorites. When the lights came on, I had forgotten all about Jane. The holiday spirit had whisked away any ill will. Our row clapped loudly as the band took a bow and disappeared behind the curtain.

André gave me a little nudge as he shrugged on his overcoat. "*C'est magnifique*! I enjoyed myself very much. Who knew Lenny could play such music? I did not."

He helped me with the sleeve of my short, faux-fur coat. "They did a fantastic job. I'm so happy with the turnout. After the rescheduling, I was worried."

"I think Tad made sure every student in the Music Department attended," said Giles, moving toward the aisle with the rest of us in the row. "And I suspect a large percentage of our English students are present, too," he added with a smile.

"I'm up for a celebratory cocktail. Anybody else?" said Gene, Claudia's husband. Giles and Katherine agreed, and André said a glass of wine would be the perfect ending to the evening. Vinny's had a delectable French wine featured in December, and he wondered if they might go there. The group nodded.

"How about you, Em?" asked Claudia. "Do you want to drive with us?"

"I would love to, but I already have plans," I said. "Lenny invited me to the Candlelight Inn. They're having a little reception for the musicians and their guests. I'm sure he wouldn't mind if you came along, though."

Jane laughed. "That's okay. It's probably for *dates* only."

"You require a date? I could accompany you," said André.

Jane's face turned a lovely shade of purple as she tried to explain what she meant but couldn't. Lucky for her, Claudia intervened.

"You go congratulate Lenny for us, Em, and we'll go to Vinny's. Gene and I only have the babysitter until ten o'clock."

The group nodded in agreement.

I wished them a good evening and walked to my car. The night had turned chilly, and attendees' shoes had made dozens of footprints on the frosty sidewalk. I opened my car door and started the engine, watching people cross the street as I waited for it to warm up. Students had turned out in droves. They rushed out of Pender—laughing, pushing, yelling. The cold didn't seem to affect them. Some of the male students didn't even wear coats. The thought chilled me as I put my car in drive and turned toward Main Street. The temperature was in the twenties, at most, and with the fog cloaking the Midwestern sky, the night was that much murkier. I hoped they didn't attempt anything foolish such as bar-hopping or walking home from a frat party. A cloud passed over the moon as I reached the end of town. I shivered again. A night such as this could be dangerous.

Chapter Twenty-Three

———

The Candlelight Inn was the center of warmth and merriment, and as I approached, I forgot all about the chill in the foggy air. Although I didn't see Jazz Underground's van, I did notice a few more cars in the drive than usual. Some guests were already here. I parked my car and climbed the steps, the railings of which were draped in fir and holly, and was greeted by the smells of hot apple cider. Pulling open the door, I knew Alyssa had outdone herself, which was saying something, considering everything she did was lovely and fine. She met me wearing a short, flared skirt that accentuated her small waist and a fitted red sweater. All her healthy eating had paid off.

"Lenny's not here yet," she said as she took my coat. "But some of the people from the college are in there." She motioned to her left, to the parlor. "What can I get you to drink?"

We entered the room together. "Did I smell apple cider when I walked in?"

She smiled and nodded. "Yes, it has just a hint of cloves and cinnamon. That's probably what you smelled." She walked to the sideboard and poured the steamy caramel-colored liquid into a clear mug, garnishing it with a cinnamon stick. She returned with the mug. "I need to refill the carafe. Please help yourself to a snack."

A "snack" didn't begin to describe the spread Alyssa and Pen had prepared. Meat and cheese, fresh fruit, cookies and cakes—the fare was elegantly arranged on a sideboard beneath the window. Red, green, and gold tablecloths were draped across the antique piece, and drawing nearer to gather a plate, I noticed the cloths were sprinkled with glitter snow. Gorgeous.

"Emmeline, I'm glad you came."

I turned around. It was Tad Iverson, looking just as jovial as he sounded. He wore a black suit with a red bowtie, and his shoes were shiny new. The entire outfit might have been fresh off the sales-floor. It looked that nice. "Hi Tad. I'm glad Lenny invited me. This food looks amazing," I said, taking a slice of fruitcake.

"Let me introduce you to my wife."

His wife, Lexy, was a shrewd banking officer. Even after a few minutes of introduction, I had a feeling she knew everyone's monetary business. Copper Bluff had one bank and one bank only, and I silently recalled my last overdraft fee.

"If this is fruitcake, I've been missing out all these years," I said after I swallowed a bite of the moist dessert. I wanted to change the conversation from banking.

Tad nodded. "The food is incredible. I'm hosting as many of our musical guests as possible out here. Alyssa's hospitality—and Steinway—are stellar. It's the perfect venue for artists."

"She might need more business, after the incident with Miles," I said, dabbing my lips with my napkin.

"Maybe, but I doubt it," said Tad. "It's just a case of wrong place, wrong time. Anybody can see that."

"No, Emmeline might be right. Alyssa will need the business when Pen Dobbs opens up her new patisserie," said Lexy. She took a sip of her whiskey cocktail. "She's one heck of a baker."

"Who knows when old Dobbs will be ready?" said Tad.

"Everyone knows she's waiting on him for the money. And that man makes molasses seem fast."

She raised her eyebrows. "It might be sooner than you think."

Tad leaned in closer. "Do you know something?"

She laughed. "If I did, I couldn't tell you."

Tad turned to me. "That's my wife for you. A big tease."

I smiled at his joke.

"I'm all business. He's all music. We're like fire and ice, but we make it work."

Tad laughed. "Someone has to support the starving artists, right?"

"Not *starving* anymore," I said. "Now that your song has sold. Music has to pay better than teaching."

Lexy looped her arm through Tad's. "An early Christmas present, for sure. I don't know when he finds the time to write songs. Between work and the kids—and events like these—I think it's a Christmas miracle."

I liked Lexy's no-nonsense style, but I had the feeling Tad would rather talk about something else. Maybe he was embarrassed by the attention. Or maybe he didn't want to get into how the song got published, especially if it involved Miles Jamison or his connections.

The door opened, and the members of Jazz Underground filed in. Lenny closed the door behind the group, carrying his guitar, and those of us in the front sitting room clapped. They dismissed the attention but were pleased and perhaps a little bit relieved that the night had gone so well. I was, anyway. I had a dreadful feeling that something else might happen to one of them, that murder might repeat itself. Seeing Lenny safe and red-cheeked was reassuring. Seeing him walking toward Tad, Lexy, and me was even more so.

Alyssa and her husband, Eric, approached the group. He took their coats, and Alyssa asked Lenny what he'd like to drink. He pointed to Lexy's whiskey. "I'll have what she's having." After taking everyone's requests, Alyssa flitted away to the kitchen. Belle walked in the direction of the bathroom.

"Congratulations, Lenny!" I said, giving his shoulder a little squeeze. "You were amazing."

"We did all right, didn't we?" he said. "I thought it might have been weird, with Miles gone, but it came out okay."

Kim and Josh joined us, and I was struck by how close they were. Maybe Kim was leaning on Josh for support after Miles's death, and Josh decided to make his move. With her crush out of the picture, nothing stood in his way.

"You were more than okay. You were excellent," said Tad. "No one would have known you were one guitar short."

Kim's face froze, and I could see she was thinking about Miles. So could everyone else. Josh changed the subject.

"Just a few weeks left of the year for you guys. Then you're off till, what, January?" said Josh. The way he said it made teaching sound easy. Business owners didn't get much time off.

Tad answered, "Yes, we're on the downhill stretch. One more concert to go tomorrow, and then my musical duties will be officially over for the semester. Well, I have a few more recitals to attend, but *then* my duties will be officially over."

"It's ridiculous, if you ask me," said Lexy. "All the extra work teachers put in, and yet they're supposed to find time to publish and perform their own work. It's insane."

"At least you guys get a break," said Josh. "I give lessons out of the studio six days a week—to fourth graders. It's gotta be better working with adults."

Tad, Lenny, and I didn't say anything. Some days working with fourth graders would be preferable to freshmen. At least their youth would be an excuse for not completing homework.

Alyssa returned with Lenny's cocktail and a glass of wine for Kim. "I hope you found the mouthpiece for your trumpet," she said as she handed her the glass. "I scoured the inn and didn't find a thing."

Kim scrunched up her nose. It looked like a little button. "What mouthpiece?"

"The one Emmeline and Lenny came looking for?" said

Alyssa, glancing at us for confirmation. "The one you left behind?"

"Oh that's a funny story," I burst in. "Lenny didn't want to admit it at the time, but he had forgotten his collectible … guitar pick." I smiled at Lenny.

"Right. I, uh, bought it on eBay," said Lenny. "It's one of Paul McCartney's, and to be honest, it was kind of expensive. I felt pretty stupid about mislaying it."

Alyssa laughed politely, but Kim frowned. I guess she didn't like being used as an excuse.

"All's well that ends well," said Alyssa and left to insert a CD. Christmas music began tinkling from the antique-looking player.

"I'd like to see that," said Tad.

"What?" said Lenny.

"The pick. From Paul McCartney," Tad said.

"Oh sure. I'll stop by the office sometime." Lenny took a sip of his whiskey. "I wanted to talk to you anyway, about how you got your song published."

I gave Lenny a silent cheer. He hadn't forgotten to ask.

"Do you write?" Tad asked.

Lenny nodded. "Some."

"It's not for the faint of heart. It takes a lot of wherewithal."

"And the right circle of friends," added Lexy. Tad shot her a look.

Lenny chuckled. "Well, no one's ever accused me of having a faint heart, but my only friend in the business is Brett from karaoke night at Harry's. Who put you in touch with a publisher?" Lenny paused. "Or was it sheer luck?"

"Miles," said Tad. "He was kind enough to introduce me."

Josh began recounting stories of all the aspiring songwriters Miles had helped make demo CDs in the studio. "He worked with you on that one song, Tad. Remember? We recorded it in the studio."

Tad's face reddened, making his beard go from auburn to russet. It was confirmation enough for me that he and Miles had worked on the song together, a song for which Tad would now be receiving all the credit.

"He was a heck of a guy, that's for sure. What are you guys going to do now, about the quartet?" Tad asked Belle, who had finished in the restroom and just joined the group.

It was a change of subject to be sure, but if Belle realized it, she didn't say. She was now in charge of the group's destiny, a role that came to her naturally. She was the obvious choice to lead the quartet.

"Lenny did wonderfully tonight, don't you think?" she said, batting her long lashes in his direction. "Maybe we can convince him to fill in for a while."

I wish Belle wouldn't have made her request so publically. Replacing Miles would give Lenny a motive for murder, and I was already a suspect. But Belle was a pro. She needed a substitute, and here was Lenny, a great performer.

We all waited on Lenny's answer, but I was the most anxious to hear his response. He finished his drink, the ice cubes clinking as he set down his glass. "Maybe, on a temporary basis. I'd have to think about it."

Belle, Kim, and Josh were relieved, but if someone had thrown me a brick, I wouldn't have felt as low as I did just then. What was he thinking? How could he possibly fill in for Miles? Jazz Underground was a popular group and played all the time. It would mean trips to Minneapolis every other weekend. It would mean less time for teaching. It would mean less time for me.

I excused myself from the group and approached the sideboard under the window, where Alyssa had placed two wine decanters: one Malbec, one Pinot Noir. I poured a large glass of Pinot Noir and took a drink. The fog had settled over the evening, coming in on a cloud of darkness. It hung in the bushes and trees like gossamer, rising a few feet from the ground. The effect was haunting, even under the brightness of the outdoor holiday lights.

"Hey, don't worry about Belle. She's like that with everyone."

I was surprised to see Kim. She had never been particularly chatty with me, and I suspected she still believed I had something to do with Miles's death. But now her brown eyes were sympathetic.

"She's gorgeous and she knows it," she said, placing a few pieces of cheese on her plate. "She can get a guy to do just about anything by batting her eyelashes."

Her words made me feel better. "She *is* gorgeous. I guess you can't blame them."

"And she's so talented. You heard her tonight. She's amazing."

Kim sounded more like a graduate student now than a band member. She obviously admired Belle as a teacher and performer. "Very gifted," I agreed. "I heard she'll be judging the Van Cliburn Piano Competition. I guess that's quite the coup."

She reached for the crackers. "And quite the second chance."

"What do you mean?"

"Miles said she was accused once of showing preference for her own student during a competition." She gave me a questioning glance and then spread her cracker with hummus.

"I don't see how one could help it," I said. "Any teacher would give preference to her own student."

She nodded. "I totally agree. But they are supposed to recuse themselves and invite an impartial judge to intervene. She didn't *disclose* he was her student, and that's a big no-no. Miles knew she left out that piece of information. She should have disclosed it."

I nodded, beginning to understand. Belle felt guilty. "Otherwise, why tell Miles?"

"Yep." She took a bite of her cracker and chewed thoughtfully. "With all the talk about student preference in big competitions, though, I can't say as I really blame her. It might have disqualified her."

"And made her ineligible to judge other competitions, like the Cliburn." I reached for an appetizer. "Lenny said there's a lot at stake in those larger competitions."

She arched an eyebrow. "Fifty thousand dollars and a shot at a three-year concert tour."

I was stunned. I had no idea music competitions meant such big business for the winners. The most I'd ever won was fifty dollars for a poem I entered as an undergraduate. No wonder they wanted top-notch judges. With that kind of money on the line, only the best teachers and musicians would do.

Kim laughed as she finished stacking her plate. "I didn't have a clue either until a few years ago. Most people don't."

I joined her, sharing a laugh at my expense. Walking back to the group, I thought about the secret Belle had divulged to Miles. Maybe since he was a colleague, she felt comfortable confiding in him, especially since he himself was a rule-breaker. But I had a feeling Belle's indiscretion was the kind of thing Miles hated about academia: the favoritism. He wanted talented musicians, even those outside of academia, to have an equal chance, and maybe his recording studio provided them that opportunity. But would he have gone so far as to inform the organizers of the Cliburn? I couldn't say. I did know, though, that secrets could be dangerous. They relied on mutual trust. If that trust was broken, trouble followed. Relationships were destroyed, reputations were tarnished, lives were changed. I took a sip of my wine. This was one secret, perhaps, that had changed Miles's life forever.

Chapter Twenty-Four

After finishing our appetizers, we moved into the library. Alyssa, who had missed the concert, asked if Belle would play. She loved music and played the flute, but with the inn so busy on the weekends, she was rarely able to attend performances. Belle graciously accepted the invitation, asking if Alyssa might join in. For a moment, I thought she would, but then she quietly declined, saying it had been too long since she'd practiced. Kim and Lenny accompanied Belle at the piano. Josh, whose heavy drum set remained back at the theater, sat off to the side with me.

As they began to play "I'll Be Home for Christmas," the spirit of the season settled over the room. I thought about my parents and aunts and longed for winter break. Looking around the library, I could see that I wasn't the only one reminiscing. Tad and Lexy smiled at each other, perhaps thinking of their children and the late hour, while Alyssa looked on from the doorway, her face touched with melancholy. After they finished, we clapped politely, but the trio could see the effect their selection had on the party. As they considered something more upbeat, Josh and I fell into a side conversation.

"Do you leave tomorrow?" I asked.

Josh nodded, his heavy bangs falling into his eyes. He swept them to the side. "I've got to get back. We all do. There's a lot to be done at the studio."

"Will you put it up for sale?" I wondered how he would manage it alone, especially with his full-time lessons.

Belle fingered a few keys on the piano, and Josh shook his head. "No way. Miles and I were required to take out insurance on each other. We were each other's sole beneficiary. Now I'll be able to pay off the loan at the bank and quit teaching six days a week. I'll make the studio bigger than ever—for Miles. It was important to him."

The trio was beginning to play "Rockin' Around the Christmas Tree," and although I wanted to continue the conversation, I didn't want to be rude, so I wondered to myself about Josh's good fortune. With Miles gone, Josh's life would change for the better. For a person who'd been working six days a week while performing, the outcome had to be a relief. Publishing contacts and recording artists would certainly extend the olive branch to Josh now that Miles was gone; the studio's reputation was already established. All Josh had to do was continue what Miles had started. It sounded easy enough, but hard work alone didn't make a music career; you needed charisma too. Of the first you had full control, the second none at all. And charisma was what made a musician stand out from their equally talented, hard-working competition.

Pen walked into the library, pushing a drink cart stacked with an elegant silver coffee service. After leaving it near a shelf of books in the corner, she turned to go. Alyssa stopped her at the doorway. From where I stood, it looked as if Alyssa was reprimanding her for forgetting something. Pen left in a huff, returning with a tray of petits fours. She placed them on the second shelf of the cart before walking away. Tad and Lexy pounced on the sweets, and I intended to do the same, but my phone buzzed in my pocket. The trio was playing in full force, so I stepped outside the library, not wanting to interrupt.

The call was from Sophie Barnes. I needed to know what she'd found out about Miles's belongings.

"Sophie! Do you have information about Miles?"

"Is that you, Professor? Where are you?"

The band had begun the raucous refrain, and I realized I would have to step outside to hear what she had to say. I grabbed my coat from the hall closet and slipped it on haphazardly. "Just a minute. Let me get somewhere quiet."

I walked outside. I could still hear the dulcet sounds of the piano, trumpet, and guitar, but they were softer, relegated to pleasant background music in the chilly night. I kept walking toward the back of the house, where it met with the bluff. Fog hung in the air as thick as caramel. The prairie was gorgeous, but on nights such as these, also terribly desolate. Even with the lighted house behind me, I might have been standing at the edge of the world.

"Is that better?" I said. "Have you found out what killed Miles?"

"Yes, and yes," said Sophie. "Well, yes and no. The noise is better, but I haven't found out anything, specifically, about what killed him. He had shaving cream but no lotion, and no medications. Nothing had been tampered with."

I let out an exasperated breath.

"There's something else."

"What is it?" I took another step, as if someone might hear what she was about to say.

"I know about the book, *The Labours of Hercules*." Her voice was serious, perhaps even accusatory. Beamer had obviously relayed his concerns, and now she'd examined the evidence for herself.

"It's not mine." I sounded desperate even to my own ears.

"It has passages highlighted," said Sophie. "It looks like something a professor would do—or a student." Sophie was my former student, after all, and knew what an annotated text looked like.

"I need to look at that book," I said. All along, I'd had a feeling the solution to the mystery of Miles's death could be found in fiction, and now I was certain. The text was highlighted. Was it possible that one of my students was involved with Miles's murder? As I gazed over the bluff, searching my mind for answers, my head spun as I ticked off the names on the roster in my Crimes and Passion course. It was unlikely, yet conceivable. People had used Christie's mysteries to plan real crimes; I had read about it in my research. But one of my students? Never!

Realizing how close I was to the ledge, I stepped backwards, looking for a rock to sit on, but I met with a hand, which gave me a shove. The last thing I recalled before falling was remembering to scream.

WHEN I AWOKE, I REALIZED that one, I hadn't plunged to the bottom of the bluff, and two, I had a fairly large bump on my head that hurt like hell. I was grateful for the gnarly tree branches that had prevented my fall, and I clung to the dead wood like a life-preserver. My head rested on the icy rock it must have collided with, and moving proved impossible. But I knew I wasn't so far away from the top that I couldn't climb back up. The trouble was the fog. It had made everything slick.

I pointed my toe, just to test my footing. All I felt were branches, no solid ground. It was ironic, really, being saved by a tree on the prairie. Though the land became hillier and rockier at the bluff, and trees more abundant near the river, the landscape was still sparse. Had I not landed on this grassy knoll, I'd be dead. At least one person thought I was.

I looked up at the edge of the bluff and instantly regretted it. I saw stars, or perhaps Christmas lights, but not a person. Someone had pushed me. If only I could get back to the ledge, I might discover whom. But I still couldn't move. I would have to wait a few minutes until my head cleared. I shivered. I'd lost all sense of time and felt very cold. I wondered how long I'd been out. It couldn't have been long. If so, people would have realized I was missing, wouldn't they? I could scream, I *had* screamed, but now I kept quiet. If the murderer was outside, I wanted him or her to think I was dead.

I heard something in the distance, and at first I thought it was the band. Then I realized it was a siren, coming closer and closer. Sophie! Of course. She'd been on the phone with me when I fell, the phone that was now somewhere at the bottom of the bluff. She would have heard my scream.

The cold wouldn't kill me after all. Sophie would rescue me, and I would solve Miles's murder and my attempted murder. Obviously I was a danger, a threat to be removed. What had I stumbled on that raised the stakes, that made the murderer strike again? I tried to recall the night, but pain ripped through my head like a bullet, and I clung harder to the branch. Now wasn't the time for thinking. Now was a time for action.

I stretched out a leg. The wet air made the dead grass moist. With help, I could make it back up to the edge of the bluff. I silently said a Hail Mary as the siren grew louder and louder. I heard two car doors shut and knew my prayer had been answered. I waited for a rope, a ladder, anything I might climb up. But nothing came. Instead I heard voices, lots of them, and then nothing at all.

I chided myself for neglecting weekly Masses. When this was over, I was going to Father McGinnis straightaway to make a confession. I dug my foot into the coldness of the cliff. When it was secure, I swung over my other foot and hit a rock. I was able to balance most of my weight on it as I tried to figure out a way up. The hill was not as steep as I first thought. I could do this, with a little athleticism. The question was: could I muster a little athleticism?

Luckily I didn't have to put my rusty skills to the test. A burst of noise came from the inn, as well as the sound of Lenny calling my name.

"Here! I'm over here," I yelled. Never had my voice sounded so weak. I swallowed, and tried again. It was like one of those bad dreams where you scream but nothing comes out. Still, I kept trying.

"Stand back from the edge, sir. You're compromising the area," said Sophie. "Everybody, please. Get back."

It sounded like hundreds of footsteps moving above my head. No one was listening to Sophie. They were scouring the bluff, but how would they ever see me in all this fog?

"Professor? Professor Prather?" yelled Sophie.

"Sophie!" I yelled. This time my voice carried. I was desperate.

"Thank god. She's alive," Sophie said to the group. "Stay where you are. Don't move."

I heard shuffling, then zippers, then the clang of a chain or chains. Someone was pounding something into the ground. A chain ladder with rope was swung over the cliff and hit the knoll with a plunk. I was never so glad to see one of my students as when I saw Sophie Barnes. I wanted to hug her. But all I could do was smile.

"Professor!" said Sophie, still on the ladder. "Are you hurt?"

"My head is, but my arms and legs are fine."

"We're going to get you out of here, I promise," she said. "Are you okay to climb with assistance? Or do you need to be carried?"

"I can climb, with your help." I could see Sophie contemplating whether or not to believe me. If my strength waned, falling was still a possibility.

I must have convinced her, for she latched a harness around my chest and connected it to hers within minutes. Then we started the difficult climb. Sophie used her body, pushing me upwards, and I was surprised how close I was to the top of the bluff. Within minutes, another officer was pulling me to safety, bringing the entire ladder with him. He and a fellow officer hoisted me onto a stretcher, which I thought completely unnecessary. But I was so happy to have Lenny standing beside me that I didn't resist. I couldn't wait to talk to him alone. He wasn't going to believe what had happened.

"Emmeline," said Lenny, reaching for my hand. His voice was husky. "I didn't know what happened to you."

The emotion in his voice moved me, as did his use of my full name. I hadn't heard him call me Emmeline since the day we first met. I squeezed his hand before the officer instructed him to step aside. The entire group at the inn was looking on. Huddled together and not wearing coats, they must have been freezing. I waved with my fingertips then stopped. I was waving at a murderer. One of them had to have pushed me off the cliff. As impossible as it seemed, it was true.

An EMT rolled me to the ambulance, and I heard Lenny asking her about my condition. "I'm fine, Lenny," I assured him. "A few bumps and bruises maybe. I did hurt my head. I think I hit it on a rock. Where's Sophie?"

"I'm here," I heard her say, a little out of breath. She was catching up with us. "I'm riding with you to the hospital. I want to know exactly what happened."

"I am, too," said Lenny. His voice brooked no argument.

The EMT, a tall woman with long arms, looked impatient at the idea.

"Please?" I asked.

She and another medic lifted me into the ambulance in one fluid motion. "Get in, but don't get in my way," she said to Lenny.

I was surprised at how small the ambulance was, especially when Lenny joined us. It was as if the van shrunk two sizes when he squeezed in beside me. But the medic must have been used to working in tight quarters, as she efficiently went about the business of checking my vitals. I cringed as she examined the bump on my head, and she told me not to move.

"That must hurt," said Sophie. "I'm so sorry."

"That's okay, Sophie. Did you bring the book?"

"What book?" she asked.

"The book we were talking about on the phone."

"Heck no. You screamed, and I threw it down and got into my squad car. I knew you were in trouble."

"Thank you for reacting so quickly. You probably saved my life." With those words, I remembered why my life was in peril and hastened to tell her what had happened on the bluff. "Somebody pushed me."

"I knew it," said Lenny. "I knew something like this was going to happen someday."

"Who?" said Sophie.

I thought as hard as I could about the moment before the fall. Nothing. Not a sight, not a smell, not a clue. I automatically shook my head and winced. "I don't know."

"Don't move your head," the EMT commanded.

The EMT was right: I shouldn't have moved my head. The ambulance began to spin, and my stomach did a flip-flop. I closed my eyes, willing away the dizziness.

"That'll be enough questions for now," said the EMT. We rode the rest of the way to the hospital in silence.

Chapter Twenty-Five

I was released from the hospital several hours later on the promise that I would return if I felt ill or developed any of the symptoms on the concussion checklist. My CT scan was fine, so all I needed was rest—and an icepack. I suggested to Sophie that we stop by the station on the way to my house so that I could examine the marked-up copy of the book, but both she and Lenny said absolutely not. If that was my idea of rest, they would make certain I was admitted to the hospital. Sophie assured me that everything possible was being done to solve the crime, or crimes, if one counted my attempted murder. Beamer was already talking to people at the inn. He'd sent over an officer to escort us home since none of us had a car. I could talk with him tomorrow about the book. Although I'd recounted everything I remembered to Sophie, he wanted to speak to me personally.

When Lenny and I walked to my front door, I realized how weak I still was. My head pounded, and my skin felt scratchy from the bushes. Had I been less tired, I would have gone straight for the bath. As it was, I decided on the couch, since it was closer.

Lenny, who promised Sophie he'd stay with me for a while longer, worked swiftly, Dickinson padding behind him. He put some ice in a Ziploc bag. Then he found a blanket and pillow in my bedroom, lifted my head, and gently placed the pillow behind it.

"Do you think it could have belonged to one of my students?"

"The book you and Sophie were talking about?" He placed the makeshift icepack on my head.

"Yes," I said with a cringe. The ice felt cold, and a shiver ran through my body.

He pulled the blanket up to my shoulders. "Why would one of your students want to kill Miles? It doesn't make sense."

"I don't know. Maybe they had him as a teacher—maybe one of them transferred from Minnesota."

Dickinson jumped on my stomach, and Lenny scratched her ears. "I suppose it's possible. But none of your students were at the Candlelight Inn."

"True," I agreed, "but one of your students was." I filled Lenny in on JazzGirl and the uninvited guest. I told him Pen said she'd dropped off the girl, and her name was Karen. He recognized the name instantly.

"Karen Rogers? She's in my American lit class; she's a music major. She must've been confused about the event. I suppose I mentioned it in class. Poor kid."

I asked what she looked like, but he was vague in his answer, so I told him to pull up his class roster on his cellphone. Karen's student ID picture would tell me unequivocally if she was JazzGirl. He was irritated but ultimately acquiesced. He knew I wouldn't be able to rest until I knew for certain.

One look at Karen, though, told me she wasn't JazzGirl. Karen had dark-brown eyes and eyebrows. They were nothing like JazzGirl's wide gray eyes. So why did JazzGirl look so familiar? Where had I seen her before?

Lenny tucked away his phone, switched off the lamp, and turned on the tree lights. He stood back to admire the decorations. "This turned out pretty good."

"It did, didn't it?" I said. The tree was crowded with red, green, and gold ornaments. Despite my earlier proclamation to keep decorations minimal, I'd added more tinsel, bulbs, and twinkle lights.

He took the afghan off the corner chair and sat down. Dickinson joined him. We sat for several minutes in silence before I realized he, too, was thinking about Miles's death.

"Is anybody missing their book, in your class I mean?"

"That's a good question," I said, trying to remember the last few sessions of class. I didn't recall a missing book. I usually noticed when someone wasn't following along. "I don't think so. Not that I remember. We've been working on papers."

"It's not *your* book, is it?" said Lenny.

"Of course it's not my book …." I sat up. The icepack dropped. "Lenny, do you think someone is trying to frame me, to make it look like I killed him? First the DNA, now this. It has to be a *setup*."

He stood and picked up the icepack from the floor. "Hey, settle down, Sherlock. You've already been injured twice. You don't know if the third time will be a charm."

"But Lenny—"

"Especially if you're being framed, which, yes, does make sense." He swept a stray curl from my forehead and repositioned the icepack. "The hair, the book. You're right. The evidence is stacking up against you. But for now, just focus on getting some rest, okay? Like you promised. Otherwise, I'm going to haul your ass back to the hospital."

I smiled. "You don't have a vehicle."

He smiled back. "I have a feeling I could get a squad car out here pretty quickly."

I sighed. Despite my conclusion, I was getting sleepy. My limbs felt numb. I tried to blink off my tiredness. "How are you going to get home?" I said, stifling a yawn.

"Don't worry about it. I'll walk."

I started to say something about the cold or the mile

between our houses, but his fingers were on my lips, shushing them. As he regarded me, I noticed the concern in his deep-blue eyes. I decided to close my lids and give in to sleep. If it made him feel better, I would feel better. We were becoming linked like that in small, uncertain ways. And it made me feel good just knowing he was around.

THE SURPRISE CAME THE NEXT morning when he was still there. I opened my eyes briefly as I rolled to my side. I turned back with a wide-eyed stare. Lenny had stayed overnight. His blond-streaked head was crooked into the chair; he would be the one in need of an icepack when he awoke.

Dickinson made a noise as she jumped from Lenny's chair to the couch. The motion was enough to rouse him. "Hey," he said, blinking.

"Hey." I couldn't put anything into words yet, but physically, I felt much better. I'd slept soundly with Lenny watching over me.

He sat up and winced, rubbing his neck. "Well, this isn't how I imagined an overnight stay."

I stood to keep him from seeing me blush. I was determined not to call attention to my embarrassment. "I'll make coffee."

I stopped at the bathroom and brushed my teeth. *Thank god I wore waterproof mascara*, I thought as I looked into the mirror. With the scabbed bruise on my temple, makeup should have been the last thing on my mind. Still, it was nice to know that some of those products that promised twelve-hour wear really did hold up their end of the bargain. Unfortunately, my smoothing hair-care product had worn off hours ago, so my only option was a hasty ponytail.

Finished, I opened the door and walked into the kitchen. I'd laid out one of my unused toothbrushes from the dentist, which I knew Lenny would appreciate. I heard the water running as I made coffee, and when he joined me, it appeared as if he had showered. It was completely unfair. He could run some water over his face and hair and look great, and I had to look like … I glanced down at the fuzzy yellow robe I had thrown over my dress … *this*.

"How are you feeling?" he said from the kitchen doorway.

"Much better," I said, reaching for the coffee cups. "My head doesn't hurt nearly as bad as it did last night."

"I guess I fell asleep, crappy nurse that I am. Sorry."

"There's nothing to be sorry about." I handed him a cup, and we walked to the living room. He'd folded his afghan and my blanket; the Christmas tree lights were still on. I glanced out the window. The fog was gone, and the sun glinted off the tree lights. Other than the knot on my head, it was a perfect December morning.

"So what's the rest of your weekend look like?" He gave me a smile and took a sip of his coffee.

I looked at the new stack of reading responses on my coffee table. "Grading has a low probability."

"I would say surviving an attempted murder is a good excuse not to grade."

"Hey, the Winter Festival is today," I remembered.

"That's right. I promised Mrs. G we'd go … if you feel up to it."

I took a long sip of my coffee. "I do. But I have to go to the station first, to talk to Officer Beamer. I need to look at that book Sophie mentioned."

"I don't think you have to go anywhere," Lenny said.

"I feel fine, I promise."

"That's not what I meant," he said with a nod toward the door.

I set down my coffee. Officer Beamer was walking up the front path. Dressed in a wool coat and hat with earflaps, he was knocking on my screen-porch door. "Ms. Prather? You in there?"

I looked at Lenny. I wanted to tell him to hide but couldn't. I tried to compose myself as I opened the door. It was ridiculous. I was almost thirty years old. If I had a man spend the night, it was nobody's business. Besides, he'd stayed as a concerned friend, nothing more.

"Officer Beamer, I'm glad to see you," I said as I opened the door. "I was going to stop down at the station today."

"I figured you might." He wiped his boots on the mat. "That's why I'm here. I thought I'd save you the trouble—and the headache. You have quite a bruise, there."

"It looks worse than it is," I said.

He stopped and stared at Lenny. "Oh. I didn't realize you had company."

"It's okay. Sit down. It's just Lenny Jenkins, my colleague."

"Mr. Jenkins," he said, taking off his hat and smoothing his hair.

"Hey, Officer Beamer. How's it going?"

"Interesting, I must say that. I never know what to expect anymore when academics are involved. Maybe it's like the townsfolk say: you have too much time on your hands."

"That's completely false," I said. "Look at that stack of papers. And I just got through a stack twice that size last week."

"Don't get excited, Professor. I'm only joking." He pointed toward the tree. "Nice tree."

"Thank you," I said. "Would you like some coffee?"

"Wouldn't mind a cup, actually," said Beamer, sitting down on the couch.

I poured the coffee and returned to the living room.

Beamer took the cup. "This is cozy."

I'm certain he meant my house, with the tree and the lights, but I immediately thought of Jane and her "cozy" comment. The implication was that Lenny and I were close and comfortable.

"Actually, I'm glad you're both here, you know that?" he said after he took a sip of coffee. "It cuts my time in half because I needed to talk to you anyway, about last night." He said this to Lenny, who nodded.

"Sophie Barnes asked me some questions last night," said Lenny, "but we were both pretty worried about Em at the time."

"Of course. I understand." Beamer gave me a glance. "I was pretty worried about her myself, truth be told."

"Thank you, Detective Beamer. That means a lot," I said.

"That's another reason I'm here. Officer Barnes said you reported somebody pushed you off the bluff last night."

I nodded. "I did. Luckily, I landed on a grassy knoll."

"Ah," he said with understanding. "A grassy knoll. Sounds familiar. Tell me exactly what happened."

I retold my story to Beamer, leaving out no detail. Even as I said the words aloud, they sounded like fiction, too fantastic to be true. But he had to believe my account. All that stood between me and more suspicion was my word. I just hoped it was enough.

"So, if everyone was in the house, who could have pushed you?" he asked.

I shook my head. "I don't know. Somebody followed me out. I don't know who."

"Were the hands large or small? Could you say?" asked Beamer.

I thought about the question. It was a good one. The trouble was I couldn't answer it. "I'm sorry. I just don't remember."

"Someone said they saw you with a glass of wine. Is there any chance you had one too many and misgauged your proximity to the bluff? Or sometimes people get that … what's it called? Vertigo."

"No way," Lenny said before I could answer. "She had one glass and didn't even finish it. I saw it sitting there, half full. That's why I went looking for her."

"You went looking for me?" I said. It warmed my heart to know Lenny had noticed my absence.

He smiled. "Of course I did."

I cleared my throat. "Anyway, I think it's … suspicious that someone said I was drinking. Who was it?"

"I'm not at liberty to say. But it sounds as if we had at least one person—Lenny—surveying the grounds, so not everyone was accounted for in the house, like you first thought."

He was right about that. How could I possibly know everyone's whereabouts while I was distracted with Sophie's phone call? Still, he couldn't possibly think Lenny would do me any harm.

He reached into his side coat pocket. "I brought that book found with Miles's belongings. The same book you're teaching this semester."

As he took it out of the evidence bag, I hoped it wasn't mine or one of my student's. I sucked in a breath; it was the same edition. I swallowed the knot in my throat, trying to remain calm. "Does it have a name in it?"

"Funny you should ask." He flipped to the inside of the front cover. The initials E.P. were scratched in red ink.

"That's not mine!" I said.

"That's not Em's!" said Lenny at the same time.

"Oh good. For a minute there I worried it might stand for Emmeline Prather."

"I'm serious, Officer Beamer," I said. "My handwriting is much better than that."

"You know those people who take ten minutes to write a check in the grocery store?" Lenny asked Beamer. "She's one of them."

I gave Lenny a glare. "Penmanship is an important skill."

"They send the check through a machine and give it back," he said, throwing up his hands. "It's not the time for your Zaner-Bloser."

Ignoring Lenny, I turned to Beamer. "May I look at it?"

"Knock yourself out," said Beamer. "It's already been dusted for prints. We're waiting on the results."

I thumbed through it. It wasn't mine, and it wasn't one of my student's. The underlining was all wrong. Sure, some passages stuck out, but others we'd spent a full class period on weren't marked at all. I told Beamer as much.

"So how do you think our victim got ahold of this book, if it's not yours?" asked Beamer.

I shook my head. "It could have come from the Candlelight Inn," I explained. "Alyssa has a sizeable collection. Let me ask her."

"It hardly looks like library material, Ms. Prather. It's not even a hardcover." He looked at Lenny. "What do you say? You were there last night. Is Ms. Prather in any danger if she goes back to the inn?"

Lenny gave me a smirk. I bet he loved holding the cards to my next move. "I think she's in danger of going crazy if she doesn't solve this mystery. If I were you, I'd let her go, for the sake of her mental wellbeing."

Chapter Twenty-Six

Officer Beamer agreed to let me take the book to the Candlelight Inn on two conditions: one, that I not go alone, and two, that I return the book to him when I was finished. I agreed to both of them, promising to take Lenny with me. I needed to pick up my car, still parked at the inn, and he needed to say goodbye to the trio. Beamer nodded as I told him my plan. He would give Lenny a lift back to his house; it was chilly this morning, not even twenty degrees. It would be a cold walk.

Lenny put on his coat and gave me an awkward shoulder pat. I guessed he didn't want to show too much affection in front of Officer Beamer. He promised he would be back to pick me up this afternoon, and I said that would be fine. I needed to clean up (I still had my evening dress on under my robe) and finish my article for Giles. I believed completing assignments under duress was better than not completing them at all. If only my students followed the same creed, their semester grades would be much higher.

After Beamer and Lenny left, I headed straight for the shower. I reviewed last night's events as the hot water poured over my head. Someone had pushed me, but who? Though there had been a break in the music, Lenny, Belle, and Kim were occupied, and all eyes were on them. That left Tad and his wife, Josh, and the staff at the inn. It seemed impossible that any one of them wanted me dead; I hardly knew them. And although I had my suspicions about who killed Miles, I didn't have proof. Kim was the only one who blamed me for Miles's death. She could have sought retribution by following me out of the house and pushing me off the bluff. And she saw me pour my wine at the table. Still, she had been kind to me then, and her initial suspicions seemed a normal reaction to Miles's death.

I got out of the shower and slipped into a red and green sweatshirt and jeans, pulling on fuzzy jingle socks that rang out as I walked back into the bathroom to put on my makeup and dry my hair. Though I didn't have the energy to fuss with my appearance, I wanted to look decent at the Winter Festival, which meant diffusing my curls with a hair dryer.

After pouring a second cup of coffee, I went into my office and turned on my laptop. It felt good to sit down and put last night out of my mind. Reading and writing proved to be a solid escape. I added two more paragraphs, which completed the thousand words, and decided to insert the pictures. Since my iPhone and MacBook were both linked to iCloud, the photos showed up immediately in my Photos app. I scrolled through them, noting the names carefully as I toggled back and forth, typing captions. One of the plants (a gorgeous thing with droopy flowers and dark berries) wasn't labeled, or if it was, I hadn't taken a photo of that label. I went to the next photo. Nothing. I let out an audible sigh. I didn't want to go to campus on a Saturday, especially with so many other things going on. Besides, how would I get into the conservatory with no key or secretary?

I dug through my notes from the meeting, scanning the names of the flowers. I'd listed them all in my article: primrose, love-in-idleness, gooseberry. I had no idea what this unidentified flower could be.

I pushed away from my desk. Pen's dad, Professor Dobbs, taught in the Biology Department. He would not only have a key, he could also tell me what the flower was. But would he really be available on a weekend? There was only one way to find out.

It was Saturday morning, and Pen should be helping with brunch. I called the Candlelight Inn, congratulating myself for maintaining my landline despite everyone telling me to get rid of it. Luckily I had an old cellphone I could hook up to my number when I finished.

"Good morning, Alyssa. It's Emmeline. Is Pen there? I'll just keep her a minute."

"Oh, Emmeline! We've been so worried. Are you okay? Are you in the hospital?"

"I'm fine, thank you. Just a few scrapes and bruises. How is everyone there?" I heard her walk away from the noise of the room she was in.

"As good as they can be, I suppose. To tell you the truth, Emmeline, after last night, I'll be glad when this group is gone. Every time they get together, something goes wrong. At *my* inn."

I sympathized with her situation. The incidents reflected poorly on her establishment. "I'm sorry, Alyssa. Rest assured I won't tell a soul about last night."

"*You're sorry*? Oh my gosh, please no. I'm the one who should be apologizing. Please accept my sincere regret for what happened."

I mumbled my thanks and switched topics. The poor woman had enough to deal with. A murderer was staying at her inn. "Pen. Is she working today? I need to get ahold of her dad."

"Of course. Just a minute." She put the phone down and Pen picked up a minute later.

"Hey. What's up?" said Pen.

I was a little surprised she didn't ask about my welfare.

Maybe she was really busy. I'd better keep it brief. "Hi, Pen. I need to get back into the conservatory for an article I'm writing. I was hoping I could call your dad and ask him for assistance. Do you know if he's busy today or where I might reach him?"

"What time is it?" she asked.

I thought it was a strange question. "Almost eleven o'clock."

"He's at his office. He's there every Saturday morning until noon."

"Wonderful. Thank you, Pen."

"Yeah, sure."

She clicked off the line, and I found my old cellphone, charging it as I dialed the customer support number. Thirty minutes later, I grabbed my coat, hoping Professor Dobbs hadn't skipped out early.

The air was cool, despite the sun, but the wind was mild. Walking to campus on days such as this was easy, enjoyable, and probably the only thing keeping off the extra pounds from Mrs. Gunderson's cookies. I glanced at her house as I walked by, and she waved from the window with her crochet hook. I wondered if I would be getting new mittens this year. I also wondered if she had seen Lenny or Officer Beamer, or Lenny *and* Officer Beamer. I rolled my eyes. No need to wonder. Of course she had. She knew everything that went on in the town, let alone the neighborhood. I'm sure she would expect a full explanation later, at the festival. It would require a good story to connect Beamer and Lenny plus the early hour of day, one that would put my skills to the test.

As I approached campus, I quickened my step, looking forward to the warmth of the conservatory. The wind had picked up, stinging my cheeks, and tears pooled in my eyes. I ducked into the brick building and shook off the cold. The stairwell was silent. The entire building was silent. Ascending the steps, I decided weekends were the best time to get things done on the campus. Unfortunately, they were also the best time to get nothing done.

The second floor was dark, except for a light halfway down the hall. I walked to the closed door; it was Dobbs's office. "Professor Dobbs? Are you in?"

"Yes, come in," he said.

Mr. Dobbs was the classic old-school professor. He had wavy gray hair, a silver beard, and wore a plaid corduroy jacket. He nodded thoughtfully as I told him my reason for being there. He was distinguished and incredibly polite, especially considering my intrusion. When I was finished, he smiled for a long moment then responded unhurriedly.

"Jim Giles is one of the best people we have on campus. I'm glad to hear he's restoring Shakespeare's Garden. It was meant to be a gift from the class of 1923. Did you know that?"

I nodded. "Yes, I found that out when I was writing my article on the garden."

"Outstanding," he said. "You are a Shakespearean scholar."

"No," I said, sorry to disappoint him.

"Ah! Even better, a volunteer."

I smiled. I loved this guy.

"Let us go," he said. He opened up the deep wooden drawer of his desk and pulled out a box of keys. "I keep extras, for grad students. Maybe you'd like one, just until you're finished with the article?"

"Sure," I said. It couldn't hurt. I might have to write another article for the spring newsletter.

"The thing about having a key," he said as he locked his office door, "is that it gives you some authority. I have a key; thus I belong."

I laughed. "You're right."

"Of course I'm right. Don't let the plants intimidate you. Are you from here?"

"Not originally, no."

He paused on the steps. "Where are you from?"

"Detroit," I said.

He kept walking toward the greenhouse. "Okay, well … then you have a right to be intimidated." He smiled when he got to the door. "I'm just kidding, of course. People say the stupidest things about places they've never visited, don't they?"

He was five steps ahead of me, looking for Shakespeare's Garden.

"It's over here," I said, indicating to my left. I was surprised he didn't know its location. I assumed he knew everything that went on in the greenhouse. But that would have been impossible. First of all, the area was huge, and second, some sections were maintained by other departments.

"See? You already know more than I do," he said, joining me by the flowers. "Excellent," he repeated several times as he walked the path, viewing the flowers. I remembered one of the flowers from my photos and moved toward it. The purple plant was near it somewhere. I looked to the left and right. I kept walking. There on the corner, by itself, was the plant I had snapped a photo of. No wonder I couldn't identify it; it didn't have a tag. Maybe it didn't even belong in the garden. I hoped I hadn't wasted Professor Dobbs's time. I reached toward the flower.

"I wouldn't touch that if I were you," said Dobbs, joining me.

My arm froze. "Why not?"

"Because it's one of the most toxic species in North America: deadly nightshade."

I didn't know much about plants, but anything with the word *deadly* in it sounded suspect. I dropped my arm.

Professor Dobbs examined the plant more closely, craning his neck to inspect the berries. He looked at it from all sides before straightening. Then he walked away, leaving me to stare at the flower. Really, it was a pretty plant. Only the berries, which were blackish purple, gave one pause.

Dobbs rejoined me with a piece of paper and a Sharpie. He scribbled the name and a warning on the paper and tacked it to the shelf. *Atropa belladonna*. Now I recognized the name, or at least the belladonna portion of it. It meant "beautiful lady" and was used by women in ancient times to dilate their pupils and thus increase their physical attractiveness. At that time, women thought it increased their sexual allure, perhaps because pupils dilate during arousal.

"Is the entire plant poisonous or just those berries?" I asked.

"The entire plant: the leaves, root, and fruit. The fruit is especially troublesome because of its sweet taste. As few as two berries could kill a child, and you can see why a child would pick one."

I could. The berries were shiny and plump and looked delicious.

"The genus name, atropa, comes from the Greek goddess Atropos, one of the three Fates."

I nodded. "She's the one with the scissors. She used it to cut the thread of life."

"That tells you just how deadly it is," he said, sticking the marker into his jacket pocket. "I'm not sure why they would want to include it in Shakespeare's Garden. Do you?"

"I don't, but I'm going to find out. It's been a long time since I read Shakespeare, but I don't see any justification for including something so hazardous in a public place. Even with the fence, an animal might get in, a rabbit."

"Funny you should mention that. People have been known to die eating rabbits that have ingested the berries." He shrugged. "Other animals, like some birds, are completely immune."

I shook my head. "Why would anyone grow it?"

"It grows wild in Europe, Iran—even in the U.S. The dump grounds are full of it. But in controlled environments, it's grown for its medicinal properties. Its compounds can be used to treat all sorts of things, even Parkinson's disease. You recognized the name, 'belladonna'? Not only women in ancient times had a use for it. Doctors use the compound atropine to dilate pupils before surgery."

Pupils again. I studied the plant, the ripe fruit sprouting from the spent purple flowers. Could I be looking at the murder weapon used to kill Miles? It made sense: his pupils were dilated, noticeably so.

"Would the poison show up in a tox screen?" I asked Dobbs.

"No, it's very unlikely. The doctor would have to test the liver, an organ where it's secreted. In other words, they'd have to be looking for the plant alkaloid. Why? You're not looking to do away with a delinquent student, are you?" He laughed. Then his face became serious. "This has to do with that music professor, the one who died at the inn where Penelope works, doesn't it?"

"I'm afraid it might," I said.

Chapter Twenty-Seven

After thanking Professor Dobbs, I hurried to the English Department, placing a call to Detective Beamer on the way. I explained what I'd found in the conservatory and asked if Miles could be tested for atropine. Of course he *could* call in the pathologist on a Saturday, he said, but *should* he? After I told him what Dobbs said and reminded him about the dilated pupils, he agreed. He ended our brief call, but not before warning me to be careful. With this new information, our murderer might be tempted to act again.

Our Shakespeare expert, Reed Williams, probably wasn't in his office, but I checked anyway. His office was near the Writing Center, on the opposite end of the hallway from mine. His door was shut. I knocked and waited a moment before walking toward my office, my jingle socks ringing all the way down the hall. Each year Barb printed out a faculty list with addresses and phone numbers. I'd tacked it to the side of my desk.

I unlocked my door and spied the list. Leaving my coat on, I plopped down in my chair. There on a small piece of paper was another name I'd written: Brittany Keller. I blinked. I'd forgotten all about it. I shook off my distraction and dialed Reed's number. It wouldn't be long before Lenny picked me up.

After a few rings, Reed answered, and I explained the reason for my call.

"Are you sure it's belladonna?" he asked.

"Quite sure," I said. "Professor Dobbs from Biology confirmed it."

"It certainly had its uses in Shakespeare's time. It's been said—but not proven—that it might have been the draught Juliet drank to induce her death-like coma. But I didn't order it for the garden. Had I wanted to include a nightshade, it would have been mandrake. It has much more relevance to his literature."

That was true. The myth and folklore that surrounded the mandrake were centuries deep. From Shakespeare to J.K. Rowling, authors had included the plant, the roots of which are said to resemble the shape of a man, in their creative works. Medieval illustrators often drew the plant with a head and alluded to the "scream" the puller would hear if he or she disturbed the plant. The sound could induce madness, they said.

"So, if it wasn't you, who planted it?" I needed to know how the belladonna ended up on our campus. Whoever planted this flower had put our entire student body and faculty in danger. And probably killed Miles.

Reed was silent for a moment. "No one in the English Department. I can guarantee that. Although I didn't physically plant any of the flowers, I signed off on the order, and there wasn't one mention of belladonna. I would remember."

Reluctantly, I ended the call. It was lunchtime, and I must be hungry. At least I hoped that was why I felt dizzy and lightheaded. I touched the bump on my head. The swelling hadn't gone down. I stood to leave, and my knees wobbled. Sitting back down, I dug for coins to feed the vending machine. The day Miles died I'd felt the same way. Hovering over his dead body, doing chest compressions, I grew dizzier and dizzier until I grew faint. I shuddered. The memory of his lips came to me, and I tried to forget. No matter how hard I tried, I could still feel the touch of his cool mouth.

The touch of his cool mouth. I reached for my lips, and the quarters scattered. I'd had my lips on his when performing mouth-to-mouth resuscitation. I hadn't felt faint because I was traumatized; I'd felt faint because I was poisoned. Of course! That's why my eyes were dilated. The medic had said so herself when she examined me. Miles must have had enough poison on his lips to pass it on to me, which meant he'd ingested the belladonna that morning.

I grabbed my change and hurried out of the office, only stopping to purchase a Snickers. I might have been playing the reality version of Clue. I knew the weapon: poison; I knew the location: the inn. Now all I needed was the murderer, and I would be able to solve the mystery.

WHEN LENNY DROVE UP TO my house that afternoon, I didn't wait for him to come to the door. I'd found the final clue in Miles's murder and wanted to get to the inn as soon as possible. I bounded out of the house and into his car, tucking the Christie text into my jacket. His raised eyebrow told me he realized I'd had a break in the case.

"I guess you're feeling better," he said as I buckled my seatbelt. He was wearing a tight-knit red sweater with white snowflakes, which brought out the blond streaks in his hair. He hadn't shaven, and the stubble of whiskers accentuated his chiseled jaw.

I nodded. "Much. I've been to campus."

"And that made you feel better how?"

I explained the article, the missing label on the flower, and how I went in search of it. "When Professor Dobbs told me what plant it was, I connected the dots right away. It had to have been the poison used to kill Miles."

He turned onto Main Street. "Think about it, though. Who at the inn had access to the greenhouse? Nobody."

"That's not true. Any faculty member could access it without much trouble." I pulled the key Professor Dobbs had given me out of my coat pocket. "See?"

"Great," said Lenny. "That's all you need. Another piece of evidence proving you could be a murderer. First your proximity to the dead man, then your hair, your class textbook, and now the key to the room with the poisonous plant …. You're going to have a lot to explain to Beamer."

What Lenny said was true. The belladonna was stashed among the plants intended for Shakespeare's Garden, a space managed by the English Department, for whom I was writing an article. It was another strike against me. "The murderer is always a step ahead of me. It's as if he or she knows my movements. It's not you, is it?" I smiled.

"I like you too much to frame you, though you would probably be safer in jail right now," he said. "Have you talked to anyone else this morning besides Beamer and me?"

I shook my head. "Just Professor Dobbs and Reed Williams." I put the key back in my pocket next to the Christie book. An idea gave me pause. "Wait. I also talked to Pen. I asked her where I might find her dad."

"She definitely has access to the greenhouse, with her dad being a biology professor. She probably knows more about the department than any of us."

I nodded. "I saw her there one day. Her dad was signing on a loan for her startup business."

"It fits," he said, accelerating onto the highway. "It's stirred up just enough trouble at the inn to force her dad's hand. Maybe she didn't even mean to kill Miles. Maybe she just wanted a good case of poisoning to get in the papers. No one wants to eat where someone has been poisoned. It would be better for her business."

I rethought an idea. "Plus, she kissed him that morning." This should've proved she was close enough to kill him, but for some reason, it didn't. I couldn't say why.

"Just be careful when we get there, okay? Don't go

wandering outside without me. If she is the murderer, I don't want her taking another jab at you."

"I will," I promised. "You be careful, too. My phone call might have put her on edge this morning. She might be desperate."

We drove for a few minutes in silence, watching the stubble of grass disappear deeper and deeper into the snow. The winter buried the land and life itself, keeping secrets still. But one secret had come to the surface, and I was more determined than ever to make it known.

THE CANDLELIGHT INN SMELLED OF brunch when we walked in: bacon, sausage, and freshly baked bread. I decided the delicious scents were what made the bed and breakfast so homey. Although great care was put into the house and the decorations, it wouldn't have been nearly as comfortable without the food. Just stepping inside made one think of home.

I noted a suitcase near the entry closet and assumed it belonged to Josh. He was in the library talking to Tad Iverson. Alyssa appeared from the kitchen and asked us if we would like any of the leftovers, but we declined. We were both saving ourselves for the Winter Festival, I said. If we filled up now, we'd never be able to enjoy Mrs. Gunderson's fudge.

"I'm pretty sure I could eat her fudge any time, morning or night, even if I was full," said Lenny. "That woman can bake."

Alyssa smiled. "If you change your mind, I'll be in the kitchen. And Emmeline? You might want to check your bandage. I have some athletic tape in the first-aid kit in the upstairs bathroom."

I touched the wound, covered in gauze. It was peeling at the corner. I excused myself, telling Lenny I would rejoin him in the library. But I only got to the top of the stairs, stopping short of the bathroom. There on the landing, among the family pictures, was a photo of JazzGirl. Of course I'd seen her. I just didn't know where. Her hair wasn't dyed and her clothes weren't black, but her eyes were the same, wide and gray. I'd recognize them anywhere.

I stepped into the bathroom and locked the door but didn't bother with the first-aid kit. Instead I retrieved my cellphone out of my purse. The girl was also called something else, and I had a feeling it was her legal name: Brittany Keller.

When I returned to the library, Josh noted the wound on my head. It was only then that I remembered I'd forgotten the athletic tape. I touched the skin. A droplet of blood seeped through the bandage.

"Man, that looks awful. Are you okay?"

I repeated the phrase I kept on hand. "It looks worse than it is."

"What happened anyway? Too much of the vino, I heard."

There was that rumor again. It angered me that someone had put the wrong idea in the guests' minds, and I was about to right it with a healthy dose of the truth. Lenny realized my frustration and embarrassment and grabbed my hand, giving it a reassuring squeeze.

"Let's not talk about last night. I'm sure Em doesn't want to rehash it. I know I don't. Let's talk about something else, how about … the studio."

"Let's," said Kim as she joined us in the library. For the first time in a week, she looked like the young, peppy grad student she was. Maybe Josh was right. Maybe Miles's death had been the best thing for her. "I've decided to work at the studio after I graduate. It's what Miles wanted, and it's what I want, too."

Josh was pleased. "I knew you'd make the right decision. It's going to be great. I promise."

Kim shrugged her shoulders. "I can always go back to school, right? Those old professors aren't going anywhere."

"Did I just hear you call me old?" asked Belle.

Belle had entered unnoticed and looked anything but old. She was a rising star, an emerging professional. With her looks, talent, and determination, she would get whatever she wanted. She didn't need Kim, Josh, or anyone else to succeed.

She smiled, her red lips parting to show off perfectly

straight teeth. "I'm only joking. That's wonderful news, Kim. I know you'll do well wherever you go, and like you said, you can always come back. Emmeline, *you're* here!"

It certainly wasn't the warm welcome I was expecting. "It's better than not being here, which I almost wasn't, after—"

Lenny squeezed my hand tighter. "Hey, Belle. You guys taking off?"

"I'd like to stay, but we just can't. We've so much to do." She looked at Josh. "And a business to run. But we'll be seeing you soon, now that you've agreed to play in the quartet."

"I thought about that a lot last night, Belle, and the thing is, I have a life, right here. I don't want to leave it." He glanced at me. "You'll have to find another replacement."

I wanted to hug him. I really did. I imagined one of those movie scenes where the girl's knees bend as she jumps into her guy's arms. *My guy.* That's how I was starting to think of Lenny.

Belle was dumbfounded, and I wondered if any man had ever told her no. By her silence, I'd have said not a one. Josh came to her rescue, which wasn't surprising. If there was anything a man liked doing it was saving a damsel in a moment of awkward distress.

"No worries, Lenny," said Josh. "I know a couple of guitarists that would kill for a spot in the quartet."

The group fell silent.

"God, I'm sorry. That's not what I meant to say."

Everyone started talking at once, mostly about the quartet, and my eyes drifted to the bookshelves. I studied the titles of the novels: *Hallowe'en Party*, *Hickory Dickory Death*, *The Hollow*, *The Man in the Brown Suit*. I excused myself, assuring Lenny I would be right back. Scanning the shelves reminded me of my reason for coming: the Christie book.

Alone in the entryway, with only the dull noise of the library and the tinkling of dishes, I retrieved my coat and flipped through the book pages. They were stories I knew well; everything looked familiar, every line a clue. I stopped at the front of the book. A page was missing, an important one.

I thumbed through a few more stories until I reached "The Cretan Bull." We'd just discussed the murder in class, a young man being driven crazy by his father who wasn't his father after all. The fake dad had used his prescription eye drops to poison the young man's aftershave. Prescription eye drops … *eyes*, I thought, skipping to the end of the story. Of course it was why I kept coming back to the story, why it had led me straight to Miles's killer. I wasn't letting my fictional life seep into my real life. The dad, like Miles's murderer, had used belladonna as the murder weapon. The murderer had meant to frame me by putting the book in Miles's belongings, but that had only helped me solve the mystery. I called Beamer to tell him what I'd discovered, but he was already on his way. Miles had tested positive for atropine.

Chapter Twenty-Eight

I asked Alyssa and her husband, Eric, to join us in the library. Detective Beamer was on his way, I said, and wanted to talk to the group before they departed. She asked if she should put out cookies, but I said, no. This was one occasion that didn't require a dessert to end sweetly.

If the group was irritated by the delay, no one let on. They chatted as they did before Alyssa's pronouncement. Only Pen let out a groan. She was obviously ready to call it a day. Lenny looked grateful. He felt safer with Beamer and the Copper Bluff Police Force in the vicinity.

I peered around the room one last time: the beautiful brocade curtains, the leather-bound books, the silver coffee service, the gilded fireplace, the shiny black piano. I would miss coming here. I would miss the music.

When the police car pulled up, Eric met Beamer at the door, offering to take his coat. Beamer declared he wouldn't be staying long. A sense of relief washed over the room, but it didn't affect me. I knew he'd be taking someone with him, and I was about to reveal whom.

Beamer took off his hat, smoothed his hair, and replaced it

again. "Thanks for staying put, folks. I had some information on your friend Miles that I knew you'd want to hear."

"Of course," said Belle. "We would greatly appreciate hearing anything you've found."

"On a tip I got from the campus, we tested Miles for atropine." He looked at me. "Am I saying that right?"

I nodded.

"Well, it turns out, the tip was right. It was used to kill him."

Kim gasped. "As in *murder*?"

"Uh-huh. As in murder," Beamer repeated.

Josh shook his head. "But how—and why?"

"Since I was pretty hard on Ms. Prather, I'm going to let her tell you. She kind of likes doing this, and it's the least I can do after suspecting her of homicide. Consider it my Christmas present," he said to me.

I advanced from the bookshelves. "Thank you, Officer Beamer. You and your wife are getting a plate of cookies, to be sure." I turned to the group. "It's a happy time of year, isn't it? Christmas. Even if you're not religious, there are the lights, the food, the wine, get-togethers. It's not a time you spend alone."

Everyone nodded in agreement.

"One of you, though, feels very alone, and bitter. Murderous, even."

"What do you mean?" asked Pen. "Who?"

"Who is it? Such a simple question yet one that's perplexed me for a week. All of us could have killed Miles, even me." Lenny shook his head as if to say, don't go there, but I did anyway. "I was the one in the room when he died. I was the one who'd pushed him away. My DNA was found on him, and so was the textbook I was teaching. I was a solid suspect."

Tad took a step away from me.

"But I didn't have a motive. Sure I might have murdered Miles out of anger or by accident. It was possible." I shrugged. "It was also possible that my good friend Lenny was involved. Maybe he would have killed for a spot in the quartet, but you heard him no more than a half hour ago. Even with the group down a guitar player, he declined the invitation. With work and other obligations, the commute would've been too difficult. So that left the rest of you, who had the motives most *extraordinaire* … as that detective with the egg-shaped head might say."

Lenny rolled his eyes. Beamer let out a chuckle.

"You'll have to excuse my dramatics. I can't help but think of the little man with the famous mustache. And you'll soon see why. Although one of you thought the Christie book would implicate me, it actually helped me solve the murder. It's like I always say: most answers can be found in a book."

Tad stood closest to the door, so I began with him before he could disappear. "I don't know how musicians feel about plagiarism, but in the English Department, we frown on it—strongly. It's the most egregious error a student can make, to try to pass someone else's work off as their own."

"I agree," said Tad.

"Do you?" I said.

Tad cocked his head. "I don't know what you're talking about."

I smiled. "I'm talking about the song you and Miles co-wrote, the one you recently had accepted for publication under your own name."

His face reddened and so did his beard. "*I* did the work. *I* wrote the song. He used his publishing history like a carrot, dangling it in front of me. He said using his name would guarantee publication, and I admit, I did use his name." He huffed. "But I never added it to the title page of the song. He didn't deserve it."

"You're a jerk," said Kim. "Of course he deserved it. His name meant everything in the music industry. He was a pillar of the community! You'd know that if you didn't live in South Dakota."

Beamer crossed his arms. I felt like doing the same. Instead I narrowed my eyes in her direction. "You talk like a woman in love, or at least one who's infatuated with your professor. He admired your talent, Kim, but he didn't admire you."

"Lay off, Emmeline," said Josh.

But I didn't lay off. "In fact, he had a small harem of admirers, from which you were singularly excluded. It must have driven you crazy to see other women throw themselves at him, and his enthusiastic response. But did it drive you to murder? That was the question."

"Whatever," said Kim. She stepped toward Josh. "I'm so regretting being nice to her."

"And how lucky for you, Josh, that Miles left you financially secure. With his life insurance policy, you could pay off the loan on the studio and quit giving lessons six days a week, a hindrance to anyone trying to advance his own musical career."

Josh turned to Belle. "Miles and I were business partners, friends. I wouldn't do that."

"You should tell your friend to be quiet," Belle said to Lenny. "She's making everyone uncomfortable."

"It's about to get more uncomfortable," Lenny said. "Trust me."

"Lenny's right, you know," I said. "I thought for quite a while that you were the one who killed Miles. Secrets can be deadly, and I knew Miles was holding a big one against you. You'd failed to disclose a teacher/student relationship during a competition, a failure that could cost you at the Cliburn."

Belle glared at Kim and Josh. "Which one of you did he tell?"

Kim looked away, and Josh dug his toe into the carpet.

"That's all right," I said. "It's not important, because although the group is troubled, it isn't homicidal. You see, no one in the group had access to the greenhouse, where the poison was found."

The room grew quiet. Ironically, I could hear "Silent Night" playing from the CD player in the front parlor. I listened for a moment before continuing, "Only two of you—yes, two—had access to the campus conservatory.

Everyone knows Professor Dobbs. He's a stalwart of

the community and a first-rate scientist. His daughter, Pen, of course had access. She also had a motive, though it was different from everyone else's. A case of poisoning at the inn would mean a direct route to getting her dad to co-sign on a loan for her new patisserie. He wouldn't want the good name of Dobbs sullied, especially after he'd paid for her to go to the best culinary school in the nation."

"Pen, how could you? After all I've done for you," said Alyssa. "It could have ruined my reputation."

I ignored Alyssa's intrusion. "A trip to the conservatory confirmed my suspicions. Of course she could claim ignorance of biology, but she had to know something about belladonna, the plant used to kill Miles. Her dad was a scientist. Then I remembered her kiss with Miles before breakfast."

"Disgusting," Kim said.

"It was just meant to irritate Alyssa; there was nothing between them," I explained. "When I thought about the kiss, though, it contradicted my theory, not supported it."

"Please explain," said Officer Beamer. "You lost me."

"Me, too," said Lenny.

"When I gave Miles mouth-to-mouth, I became ill. My eyes, like his, became dilated from contact with the poison. Remember the medic saying so, Officer Beamer? If the poison caused the side effect, Pen, too, should have fallen ill from kissing him, but she didn't. This told me, in no uncertain terms, that Miles had been poisoned at breakfast, not before. Otherwise, Pen would have showed signs of being poisoned."

I turned to Alyssa. Her husband put his arm around her.

"Not only did you have access to the conservatory, you had a reason for poisoning Miles, and you did it that morning. You had the berry smoothies labeled on the sideboard, the names in cursive writing on the tumblers. You disguised the belladonna berries in his smoothie and washed the evidence down the drain with the dishes."

Kim, Josh, and Belle recalled that morning, whispering among themselves. Belle spoke up. "That's right; we had smoothies before breakfast. But Alyssa didn't know Miles, did she?"

"She didn't, but her sister did." I looked at Alyssa, and she covered her eyes with her hands.

"Her little sister was Brittany Keller. Brittany had Miles as a professor, and he'd convinced her, as he had other students, that she had enough talent to star in a band. She took that advice to heart. Unfortunately, she got involved with the wrong band. She died of a drug overdose a few months later."

I turned to Alyssa, who let out a moan of sorrow. "Lenny found her guitar award upstairs, and I found her picture. One of my students said a freshman girl from Copper Bluff died of a drug overdose, and when I recognized the face, I googled the name to confirm. At first I didn't see the connection, because your names didn't match. But then I realized Keller was your maiden name. AKA stands for Alyssa Keller Anderson. Your sister was JazzGirl."

"I recognize that name," said Belle. "I had no idea she was your sister. I'm so sorry for your loss."

I turned to Officer Beamer and the rest of the group. What I was about to say would prove the murder was premeditated, planned as carefully as one of Alyssa's parties. Part of me sympathized with Alyssa; part of me wondered if I might have sought revenge if I'd had a sister who died the same way. Then again, Alyssa had tried to set me up and even attempted to kill me. Thankfully her fate wasn't for me to decide. I continued, "When the university announced the holiday concert series last spring, a mere month after her sister's death, she set her plan in motion, deliberately laying a trap for Miles. It would be easy to sneak a poisonous plant, something she knew all about from her work as a dietitian and teacher, into the conservatory. Her health class used the greenhouse for growing organic produce."

"You're right. I forgot about that," said Pen.

The tone of her voice betrayed surprise, and I had the feeling no one believed Alyssa could really be the murderer. I would need to prove it. "Being a planner, she orchestrated not only the perfect murder, but the perfect fall guy—or fall girl, in this case. Friday night, we talked about books and my Crimes and Passion course this semester; she knew I was teaching the Christie text. Imagine her delight when she realized the same English professor who'd been involved in two previous murders was teaching a mystery book, the one she'd recently purchased from the campus bookstore for her library."

I took the book out of my jacket pocket. "Page one is missing, and I know why. Alyssa had to get rid of the page with the Candlelight Inn stamp. You see, she thought the book would place suspicion on me, would prove I'd been with Miles before the morning of his death. She'd even put my initials in the text. But if there's one thing a murderer shouldn't use to frame an English teacher with, it's a book—especially one with a murder similar to hers. Belladonna, the plant Alyssa used to kill Miles, was also used as the murder weapon in 'The Cretan Bull.' But she wouldn't have known this unless she read the book. She would've known, though, to move the belladonna next to the plants meant for Shakespeare's Garden, another tie to the English Department and thus to me."

I turned to Alyssa and spoke to her directly. "I don't blame you for framing me—at least I didn't at first. If I'd had a sister who had been led to her death by a professor, I'd be angry, too, especially at the university. It wasn't until you pushed me off the cliff I realized your desire for revenge had robbed you of your humanity. You would stop at nothing to protect your reputation, now at risk. When you found out Kim hadn't left her mouthpiece behind, that it was my excuse for snooping, you knew I suspected. Sophie's call confirmed that."

I nodded in Eric's direction. "Your husband already suspected. That night before Miles died, we heard him arguing with another man on the veranda. It was you, wasn't it, Eric? We forgot all about you since you weren't part of the quartet. You tried to warn him. You knew your wife was going to kill him."

He nodded. "I knew about Miles, the professor who had encouraged Brittany to join a grunge band, and I tried to get him to leave that night. I told him it wasn't safe for him to stay here, but I didn't tell him why." He sighed. "Now I know I should have."

Officer Beamer approached Alyssa with handcuffs.

"I don't regret it, you know," she said, her chin held high in defiance. Far from breaking a sweat or dissolving into tears, she remained the elegant hostess. I kind of admired her fortitude. "None of it. Even if I saved one life, one student, Brittany's death wasn't in vain."

No one said anything, not even Officer Beamer. Maybe Alyssa had saved a life, or several lives. We would never know how Miles's death changed the future, but we did know how it changed the past. Miles had paid the ultimate price for Brittany's death. As Shakespeare wrote in *The Tempest*, "He that dies pays all debts."

Epilogue

The Winter Festival was in full swing by the time Lenny and I arrived late that afternoon. Low in the sky, the sun scattered flecks of its golden rays like confetti down blocked-off Main Street. Young adults and children crowded the avenue, playing games such as Frozen Fish Pond, Ring Toss, and my personal favorite, the Cake Walk. Older adults sat behind tables that lined the sidewalk, selling raffle tickets, pulled pork sandwiches, hot dogs, and baked goods. If anyone was cold, they didn't let it show, and they didn't complain. In Copper Bluff, whenever it was sunny and above twenty-five degrees in mid-December, it was a beautiful day. With Lenny by my side and Miles's murder behind me, I was in the mood to party. So was Harry's, the downtown pub. Their twofer special was hot chocolate spiked with Bailey's Irish Cream.

I took a sip of the warm liquid and sighed.

"Ditto," said Lenny. "It's finally starting to feel like the holidays around here."

Listening to the tinny Christmas music playing from the storefront speakers as we walked beneath them, I didn't disagree. It felt magical. "Will you be going home for

Hanukkah?"

"Some of it. What about you and your aunts?"

I nodded, stopping to look at a rack of discounted books outside the Book Barn. "They're staying through Christmas."

"Does this mean your mom will be setting more food on fire?" He was glancing through a slim collection of Longfellow's poems.

"Definitely. We're taking a cooking class together."

He replaced the book, and we kept walking. Mrs. Gunderson's table was just ahead. She and three other church ladies were manning two eight-foot tables crowded with assorted plates of Christmas treats: cherry chocolate bars, coconut dunks, and whoopie pies. At five dollars a plate, the ladies were practically giving away the goodies. No wonder Mrs. Gunderson had a line five deep for her fudge. I worried she would run out before we got to the front.

Two football players turned around with a stack of cookie plates. Lenny and I exchanged a glance. "Score!" they said as they walked past us. I silently glared at them as we continued to wait.

After watching several more plates of goodies walk off, I was thankful when it was our turn.

"Goodness, I'm so glad you came. I was beginning to worry about you, Leonard," said Mrs. Gunderson.

I opened my mouth to ask about me but didn't have a chance.

She looked up and smiled. "And you, too, dear, but I think we can all agree you've had enough sweets this season." She tied a red ribbon around the plastic plate of cookies we had selected. "Here's a special piece of fudge, just for you." She pulled out a large square of chocolate, carefully wrapped in plastic wrap, and handed it to Lenny. "These others are so small—for re-sale purposes," she whispered.

"Thank you, Mrs. G," Lenny said. "That's really nice of you."

He handed her ten dollars, but she brushed away the money, patting his hand. "We're getting richer than Roosevelt over here. You keep your money. Buy Emmeline a Christmas present with it."

He tried to insist, but there was no use insisting with Mrs. Gunderson. She was the authority on, well, just about everything.

We stepped out of the line while Lenny unwrapped his fudge. As the streetlights turned on, I noticed a few flakes dancing under the dim light. Maybe the flakes fell from a rooftop, or maybe the wind carried them in. No matter from whence they came, they mesmerized me with their flurry flight, and I found myself in a daydream. A bell jingled as a woman opened the door of the shop beside us, and Lenny pulled me out of the way. He still held my hand when Mrs. Gunderson said, "Look, you're under the mistletoe."

All three church ladies turned to stare at us, along with their customers, who just happened to include Jane Lemort. She gave me a wave. I faced Lenny, who clasped my other hand. Standing under the green spray of mistletoe hanging from the store awning, we looked at each other. His eyes held mine with a question. This wasn't the library, and it wasn't a deserted street. It was the middle of Winter Festival. Would I kiss him in front of neighbors and friends? Colleagues? Jane Lemort? I didn't even have to think about my answer. I just closed my eyes and let my heart leap.

The Professor Prather Mystery Series

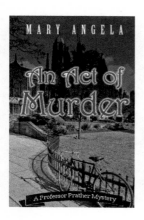

Book One: In the sleepy college town of Copper Bluff, South Dakota, English professor Emmeline Prather is enjoying the start of a new semester. When one of her students dies while working on the fall musical, Em suspects foul play. She teams up with fellow English professor Lenny Jenkins to comb the campus and vicinity for clues, putting their reputations, their jobs, and even their lives at risk.

Book Two: Over spring break, Emmeline Prather and André Duman are to lead a group of students and faculty to Paris. Before she can utter her first bonjour, a professor dies, stranding them in Minneapolis, then sending them back to Copper Bluff, SD. With André as a prime suspect, Em and her friend and colleague Lenny feel compelled to solve the mystery.

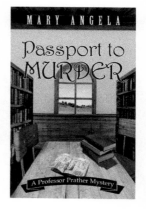

Julie Prairie Photography

Mary Angela is the author of the Professor Prather academic mystery series, which has been called "enjoyable" and "clever" by *Publishers Weekly*. She is also an educator and has taught English and humanities at South Dakota's public and private universities for over ten years. When Mary isn't writing or teaching, she enjoys reading, traveling, and spending time with her family.

For more information about Mary or the series, go to MaryAngelaBooks.com.

CPSIA information can be obtained
at www.ICGtesting.com
Printed in the USA
FSHW010717071218
54226FS